Game of Shadows

Amanda K. Byrne

LYRICAL PRESS
Kensington Publishing Corp.
www.kensingtonbooks.com

Lyrical Press books are published by
Kensington Publishing Corp. 119 West 40th Street New York, NY 10018

First Electronic Edition: July 2016
eISBN-13: 978-1-60183-648-9
eISBN-10: 1-60183-648-1

First Print Edition: July 2016
ISBN-13: 978-1-60183-651-9
ISBN-10: 1-60183-651-1

Printed in the United States of America

The girl next door just got deadly.

On the outside, Cass Turner looks like any other beautiful California college girl. But besides studying at UCLA, she's hiding a shocking secret: she's a highly trained assassin with multiple kills under her belt. After a year spent avoiding the family business, she takes what she hopes will be her final job and winds up saving her target's life and getting way more than she bargained for…

As a lieutenant in LA's largest crime family, Dominic Kosta is determined to find out who wants him dead, and he's convinced Cass can help him. But the longer they search for the truth, the more questions arise…and the deeper their attraction grows. Nick has his own reasons for wanting to resist Cass, but it's a losing battle. And together, they're free of secrets and lies. Still, getting involved with Nick has put a target on Cass' back—and in this game, it's either kill or be killed.

Books by Amanda K. Byrne

Game of Shadows

Published by Kensington Publishing Corporation

Acknowledgements

After I'd finished the first draft of Game of Shadows, I had a moment of panic that no one would want a story about a college student who earns her spending money by killing people. A big, huge thank you to Corinne DeMaagd for loving Cass and Nick enough to want to see it in the hands of readers.

Thank you to Liv Rancourt, CP extraordinaire, for her notes and brainstorming sessions, her ear when I needed to bitch about something (or other), and for cheering me on.

Thanks to Golden Angel for her notes and the gym encouragement – you rock my socks, girl!

And the world's most amazing BF, Aaron, for listening when I needed to come up with more creative ways of killing people. I love you!

Chapter 1

I should have said no.

Even as I walk down the street, hands tucked in the pockets of my hoodie, I'm arguing with myself. So many things about this job are off. The lack of information. The lack of movement. The compressed timeframe. The late deposit on the heels of the rush request. I don't need the money, though it's always welcome. I should be home, trying to finish my essay on sociological theory's roots in Marxism.

I haven't pulled a job in almost a year, which is why I took this one. Practice or a need to prove I can still do this, take your pick. Whoever wants the hit completed took the time to research how I work. I prefer to operate on a "keep me in the dark" basis. I don't need to know whether they're good or evil, whether they're guilty or not. I'm not judge or jury, just the executioner. All I need is a photo and a bare bones schedule, and I can pull it off.

But I didn't have a lot of time to do my recon, and that's the current argument kicking around in my head as I hurry down the darkened street to the site. The e-mail gave me a place and a time along with a picture.

He's why I'm here. I might as well admit it now while I can.

He has this presence that captivates me, even in a photo. Dark hair, dark eyes, a nose, cheekbones, and a jawline that look like they belong on a Greek god.

I'm young and female. Last time I checked, I was alive, and my hormones were functioning on a normal level, thank you very much. I think my reaction was well within the accepted range for someone presented with a visual they found compelling.

It's not so much that he's attractive, though. It's that combined with something else. He looks as dangerous as me. Or the "me" that Turner insists I'm capable of being.

Thoughts like that lead to sloppiness and distraction.

Focus, Cass. Lock it down.

The entrance to the restaurant is on a tiny side street, narrow and cluttered with cars and garbage, clumps of people dotting the sidewalks. The buildings are crowded together, some flush, others with dark cracks barely large enough for a body between them. Those cracks are perfect for my needs. Heading for the alley, I skirt the light pouring from the restaurant entrance onto the sidewalk and slip into a narrow passage beside the restaurant. If there's a back entrance to this place—and there should be—I could very well end up screwed. Just because the entrance is in the front doesn't mean that's the one he'll use.

I poke my head into the alley. Not only is there a back entrance, there's two guys hanging around it, smoking and chattering in Spanish. The alley's so narrow the busier cross street at the end is almost obscured. No wonder the dumpsters are out front. The dark is deeper here, no streetlights or businesses to break it up. Keeping one eye on the two men, I edge into the alley. One building over, on the opposite side of the alley, is another skinny break, much like the one I just left. It empties onto another crowded street. Perfect for disappearing.

The target's supposed to enter the front of the restaurant at nine PM. I pull out my phone, hunching over to block out the glow of the screen. Ten till. Ten minutes to find a decent place to hide, ten minutes to figure out how to pounce.

This is the shittiest job. I should have said no.

I head back to the front of the restaurant and scan the few cars parked along the curb. None of them are large enough to hide behind. I weave through the crowd to the other side of the street, searching for a shadowed nook, an empty doorway, something that will serve as a disguise. Finding none, I pull out my phone again. Almost nine.

Time to walk away. This isn't worth it.

Frustrated, I push my hood from my head and study the street one last time. If I had more time to prepare, I might have been able to make this work. Crowds are actually easy for me—lots of camouflage. Quick jab of the needle and off I go, let the poison do the rest. It's good for knife work, too, though not as reliable. Hanging around to see if the wound I made was fatal could be the difference between walking away and getting caught, so I don't.

The street's too narrow. That's the problem. Not enough room to move, and the shadowed spots are out in the open. A litany of excuses run through my head as I search for a place to hide. Turner would be able to make it work. His voice echoes in my head, a stream of chastising statements, disapproval lending them weight. I glance over at the restaurant one last time. Maybe I missed something.

I did. *Him.*

He's striding toward the entrance of the restaurant, all dominating and alert. He's tall. Built. People stop what they're doing, follow his progress as he walks down the sidewalk. Cars slow.

Cars.

The black SUV rolls along behind him, stopping when he pauses outside the restaurant. I wasn't told there'd be men with him. Newbie mistake, assuming he'd be alone. I can't finish this job. I won't be able to get close enough.

The front passenger side door cracks open, the snub-nosed barrel of a gun barely visible in the light stretching into the street.

Follow your gut, Cass. Your gut will get you out of trouble.

Turner's words have never failed me before, and neither has my gut, as he calls it. My gut says that gun isn't for protection. They wouldn't be tailing him in a car if they were meant to guard him.

I'm not about to let someone else take my payday before I have a chance to decide if I want it. The target's still outside the restaurant, so I dart across the street, shedding my hoodie as I go. Little changes to fool anyone who might have noticed me before. I try not to wince as I think of the syringe I just abandoned, tucked in the pocket of my sweatshirt. "Hey, baby!" I throw my arms around his neck and bounce up, hoping like hell he's a fast thinker.

His hands cradle my ass, his face inches from mine. There's no trace of surprise. Only a slick, sinful smile that ties my tongue into a giant knot. "Who the hell are you?" he murmurs.

I suck in a breath. Mistake. Oh, big, big mistake. He smells incredible. Like cinnamon. He squeezes hard, and I stifle a yelp. Bastard. "I'm assuming you noticed the SUV crawling after you?" He flexes his hands in response, loosening his grip. I widen my grin. "Unless they're yours, I thought you might want some help getting out of here."

His gaze flits down to my mouth and back up, his smile changing to a smirk. It stings, that change, as though he thinks there's no way I could be of any help, and my conviction wavers. Why did I think this was a smart idea? He's a job. The more contact I have with him, the harder it'll be to go through with it. I unwind my legs and slide down his body. He catches my hand in his before I can walk away and leads me into the restaurant.

All the tables are full, the noise level a high hum, punctuated by the clatter of plates and laughter. He slides a hand into the back pocket of my jeans and bends down, his breath tickling my ear. "Help away."

I *really* should have stayed home.

"Back entrance is through the kitchen. We can cut through the alley to the next street." He shifts his hand to my hip and squeezes once. I hope that means he understands.

We're halfway across the dining room when the front door to the restaurant opens. I quicken my pace, pulling free of his hold, winding around the last few tables.

The first shots are loud. It's a spray of them, *crack crack crack*, and I abandon my oh-so-casual stroll to the back door of the restaurant and lunge through the entrance to the kitchen, slipping on the greasy floor. He's right behind me, his hand grasping my elbow before I can go down. The cooks mill around, exclaiming in Spanish and English, getting in the way as we race for the exit.

There's a vise on my lungs. My heart's beating so hard I'm positive I've broken a few ribs. We tumble out into the narrow alley as the next gunshot rips through the chaos of the kitchen.

It's a few hundred yards to the next break between the buildings and the relative safety it represents. Adrenaline churns in my stomach as I sprint for it, banging my elbow on the unforgiving brick as I dart through the opening.

Dark. So very, very dark. The pavement is broken and cracked, and I twist my ankle in my haste to get to the other side. *Fuck*. Pain shoots up my leg as I put weight on my foot.

"You gonna keep going, or you gonna let them find us?"

I ignore him and limp forward, gritting my teeth with every step. He swears, and I swallow a squeak as he grabs me from behind and tosses me over his shoulder in a fireman's carry. "What the hell?" I hiss.

"Moving too slow." He jogs to the next street and sets me on my feet as he pushes out into the open. "You're going to have to walk. We'll draw too much attention if I carry you."

Nodding, I put my foot down, wincing as pain vibrates up my shin. "I'm parked about ten blocks away." He stares down at my feet, and it hits me—we don't have to stick together. "You know what? Never mind." I wave a hand at the street in front of us. "Go. Disappear. Watch out for black SUVs with super tinted windows."

A bullet zips past, leaving behind a burning line of pain along my right thigh. He curses, scoops me up, and runs down the street, dodging people trying to get away from the gunfire. He veers off through the nearest door. It's a bar, and all I can say is it's dimly lit and not even half full. "Back entrance?" he barks. The bartender silently points to the far wall, and my target—for one fleeting second I wish I knew his name—dashes through the bar to the back. He eases the door open, and I stick my head out to scan the alley.

Some of the gunmen are at the far end, facing away from us. Likely searching the street to see if we'll pop up there. I withdraw my head. "Opposite end of the alley. Four of them."

Shouts from the front of the bar push him through the door, catching it before it can slam shut. He keeps close to the building, using the shadows as cover, pausing at the next door to try the knob. It doesn't budge. He moves from doorway to doorway, each second that passes with us out in the open bringing us closer to a date with the wrong end of a gun.

We're running out of doors. He tries another doorknob. It twists easily under his hand. He nudges it open with his foot, and we slip inside as shouts sound in the alley.

When he puts me down, my ankle throbs in protest. Bright spots flash in front of my eyes, pain streaking down my leg. This fucking hurts. Blood seeps through my jeans, soaking the heavy fabric.

He fumbles with the doorknob, muttering under his breath. "See anything we can put in front of the door?"

I shake my head, too distracted by my ankle and the bullet wound to my thigh to notice much of anything. Turner would be telling me right about now to push through it. I swallow hard. "I can walk. I'll find some place to hide out for a little while." The faint wail of sirens sends a wave of relief through me, weakening my knees, and I slide to the floor. Sirens mean cops. Cops mean whoever those bastards with guns are will be clearing out.

Derision's clear on his face as he looks down. "You can walk?" He leans over, grabs my hands, and hauls me to my feet. "Maybe if we're lucky this place has a first aid kit we can use."

The sirens scream closer. It's a comforting sound, which is strange. It's never been a comfort before. I grip his arm as I limp forward. "Looks like some kind of storeroom."

He doesn't respond, just guides me through the dim hallway. We find a small room off to the left, outfitted with a busted couch, a table, and a few chairs, lit by a bare bulb that sputters a couple times before staying on. "Go lie down. On your side. Take your pants off first."

The fog of pain lifts for a minute. Attractive as he is, I'm not letting this guy see me without my pants. "How about not? If there's a first aid kit around, fantastic. I can clean myself up. You can sneak out or whatever."

He levels his gaze at me. "Take off your pants."

The temperature in the room rises about ten degrees. "I can take care of my own injuries, thank you. Your concern is touching but unnecessary."

The button on my jeans is undone in a blink, his fingers lowering the zipper, inch by inch. What the fuck? I swat at his hands, pull them away. "Stop it."

"Pants off, love. You're going to need some help with that bullet graze." He brushes his fingers over the exposed skin above my panties, and the heat of his touch, one simple touch, blanks my mind. He peels them over my hips, working his fingers into my pant leg to pull the fabric from my skin where it's sticking with blood. Embarrassment catches up with me as he kneels to untie my sneakers and free my ankles of their denim bindings. The hottest guy I've ever seen is taking off my pants, and the only reason he's doing it is because I can't bend over and take care of it myself.

The offending clothing item is in a heap at my feet, and he picks me up again. The couch makes an ominous creaking sound as he lays me on my side. "Thought I saw a sink nearby."

I'm half naked. Cold. Cold and getting colder, the adrenaline rush draining from my body. He's prowling the room, probably searching for the elusive first aid kit. Those things are damn hard to catch in the wild. I bite down on my lip to keep the giggles inside and listen for the sirens. They've stopped. Hopefully that means the police are out on the street, rounding people up.

The target holds up a white box. "Found it." He opens the kit and sifts through the contents. A packet of gauze, an Ace bandage, some tape, what looks like a couple of wipes, and a tube of ointment end up on the table next to the box. After washing his hands, he dampens some paper towels from the holder over the sink in the corner and returns to my side, kneeling next to the couch to wipe the blood from my leg.

The first touch stings like hell. I dig my fingers into the couch cushion. What's that phrase? Lie back and think of England? Think of something else. Anything else. The e-mail to send to the client, declining the job. The conversation I've been putting off with Turner. The research paper on nineteenth century poets I haven't started. That stupid sociology paper. "What's your name?" I gasp.

"You can call me Nick." His focus never wavers from my thigh.

Crap. I didn't actually mean for that question to come out. "Nick." Knowing his name will make it harder to kill him. Fantastic. "Thanks for this. You really didn't have to stick around."

"Right. Do I look like a monster? Those men would have eaten you alive. Besides, I owe you."

I don't have an answer for that.

He tosses the used towels on the floor and gathers the stuff he set out. He squeezes the edges of the wound together and reaches for a bandage. Warm. Way too warm, his hand on my leg, the rest of him close enough I can smell him. Cinnamon. Unusual. Intoxicating. "Do you think we'll be able to get past the cops? I mean, if they're still out there? I've got a paper to finish." Maybe if I focus on my assignment I won't notice how good he smells.

"A paper?" He glances over, our eyes locking for a brief moment. "You're a student?"

"Yeah. I'll graduate in the spring."

He smooths the first of the butterfly bandages over the wound. "UCLA? USC?"

"UCLA." I shut my eyes, giving in to the fatigue and pain clouding my mind.

"Thought you looked young," he muttered. "What's your name?"

Ow. Ow ow ow ow *ow*. The wound burns more the longer he pinches the edges together. He can't get those bandages on fast enough. I open my mouth to lie, and the truth falls out. "Cassidy. Cass. I go by Cass."

"Cass." He strokes a hand down my leg, closing it around my swollen ankle. "Shift onto your back for me, and we'll get this wrapped." He lifts his head enough to meet my gaze. "Then you can tell me how a college student gets through a gunfight unfazed."

Chapter 2

I roll onto my back, propping myself up on my elbows. "Pretty easy to do when you grow up in a violent neighborhood." I nod to my ankle. "I can wrap that myself. Thanks for playing nurse."

He ignores me again and reaches for the Ace bandage. My ankle's so hot and swollen I can barely feel his hands.

"Where'd you grow up?"

"East Coast." Always lie, except when it's better to tell the truth. Giving him my name is safe enough. No one would suspect a student is an assassin, and telling Nick about my studies will get him off my back. He doesn't need to know anything more.

Nick. He should have remained nameless. Just the target. Now I'm going to have to return the money. Dammit.

"East Coast covers a lot of territory." He tucks the end of the bandage into place.

"It does." I scoot up and swing my legs over the edge of the sofa, gingerly putting my weight on my injured leg. "Thanks. Again. You didn't need to do any of this." I hobble over to my jeans and sneakers. Getting my pants on might be a bit of a problem. I lean against the table and wiggle them on, wincing in pain as the fabric catches the edge of the gauze covering my wound. I shove my feet into my sneakers and straighten my shirt.

He's still kneeling on the floor, his expression neutral, eyes alert and intense. The urge to sigh is ridiculously strong. I am not a sigher. Or a swooner. Yet he makes me want to do both. I settle for jerking my thumb toward the door. "I'm out. Try not to get yourself shot."

I catch a flash of his smile before I turn and limp for the hallway. Getting back to my car is going to be an adventure. The circuitous route I'd mapped out adds about ten extra blocks. On a banged-up leg, it'll seem even longer.

"Cass."

Sin. Sin itself, the way my name sounds rolling off his tongue. I glance over my shoulder, only to find he's right behind me. "I'll walk you to your car."

Oh, no. I'm not spending any more time than necessary in this man's presence. "I'll be fine. Plenty of people still out. Besides, it might be safer for you if you were alone. If those guys come back, I'll only slow you down."

Apparently, this is the wrong thing to say because his face becomes dangerously blank. "Hold on." He wraps his black canvas jacket around my shoulders, and I slip my arms into the sleeves, breathing in his scent. It goes straight to my head, makes me woozy and want things I can't have. Like him.

He'll never be a job for me.

I've turned down jobs before. Turned down every job in the last year, but I rarely abort one. Shit like that gets around, and people start wondering if you've got the balls to do this sort of thing anymore.

I'm wondering if I've got the balls to do this anymore.

He winds his arm around my waist, shifting some of my weight onto him, and we hobble to the back door.

The alley is quiet and empty, and I point left to the opposite end of the alley. Maybe if we're lucky, there'll be another break we can walk through, dump ourselves back into the busy street. With the bandage around my ankle, I can walk okay, so I focus on the low burn left from the bullet grazing my thigh. It's better than getting distracted by the feel of Nick next to me, his body a warm, hard line, his hold sure.

His hand pressing on my hip. Pressing me closer to him. Scrambling my brain.

I jerk away, trying to put some distance between us. "Stop it," he murmurs. "Fastest way to get out of here is if you let me help you."

"There's no reason for you to help me at all," I grumble. "I'm perfectly capable of walking back to my car." Please, oh please, leave me alone before I do something stupid. Like throw myself at you.

"You don't think they'd recognize you? After the stunt you pulled?"

"No, I don't. They saw me mostly from the back. Here." I stop, and he drops his arm. Plucking the pins from my hair, I tuck them into a pocket and run my hands through the soft blond waves floating over my shoulders. I limp forward a few steps. "Look like the same person to you?"

"Yes," he says.

I shoot him a glare—*I* know the difference is enough to make someone think twice, and if he's anything like me, he does too.

"But the bigger reason is a woman shouldn't be wandering around in the dark by herself."

I stumble into him when he snags me again, and he tightens his hold on my waist to keep me from falling.

"Or don't the boys you play with know better?" The quiet taunt is delivered straight into my ear, and I bite the inside of my cheek to keep the retort inside.

Focus on the pain. I dig my fingers into my thigh. A fresh lance of it races down my leg, the burn rising anew. "All this talk isn't getting me to my car any faster."

"And you still have a paper to finish if I remember." He squeezes my hip.

The walk is slow. Very slow. We don't try to make conversation on the way, and I scan the street, every cell on alert for trouble. Instead of the route I'd planned, we head straight to my car. Circling and winding around would draw unwanted questions. If I'm lucky, Nick won't ask me anything else.

My Honda is where I left it, sitting under a streetlight and in one piece. I poke him in the side to say *See? I know what I'm doing*.

He just grunts.

I fish my keys out of my pocket and unlock the door, unable to hold back the grimace as I lower myself into the driver's seat.

"What's your paper about?"

"Sociological theory's roots in Marxism." Go ahead. Try to trip me up. You'll fail. "Do you want me to wait with you until your cab shows up?"

He braces himself on my open door and leans down, his face inches from mine. "Why would I need to call a cab?"

"Because your car might be recognized. You might be followed." Duh.

His gaze sharpens and, too late, I realize my mistake. Violent neighborhood might explain away my cool under fire, but knowing enough to abandon your car? I shrug. "At least that's what always happens in the movies."

One blink, two, and he chuckles, the sound low and smooth. A shiver snakes its way down my spine.

"Go on. I'm a big boy. I can handle myself."

I snort and reach for the door handle, my arm brushing his legs in the process. "Mind moving?"

He steps back and shuts the door for me, then slips his hands in his pockets. My car starts with its usual growl and sputter, and I ease away from the curb, Nick in my rearview, growing smaller and smaller. What's he doing? Memorizing my license plate number? It won't get him anywhere. I switched out the plates before I left this evening.

The streets are mostly quiet as I take the long way out to Santa Monica. I pull into a drive-thru for a soda, then drive on to my usual spot.

I love the ocean. Not the beach, but the ocean, the wild scent, the crash of waves. There's a stretch that's deserted north of the pier most nights. It gives me a much needed place to pull myself from the blank, cold space I inhabit while I'm working, to regular old Cass, college student. The absolute black of the water is soothing, and I lean against the hood of my car, listening to the water break itself into pieces on the sand, ignoring the faint gleam of bonfires farther down the beach.

Push, pull. Push, pull. The water's rhythm takes a little of the hit away, nudging another part of my other self into place.

Theory. Marxist theory, leading into Hobbes' Leviathan, and—

Dark eyes, warm skin, the smell of cinnamon.

Who am I trying to kid? I couldn't force myself into the game tonight. I was never in it to begin with. Not since his picture sparked my curiosity. Turner always says curiosity has no place in this business, but everything about this job was designed to pique my interest.

"Fuck." After setting my drink on the hood, I rip off the jacket and ball it up, ready to toss it onto the beach for some homeless guy to find. The stiff fabric bunches under my hands, and a gust of wind rushes over me. It might be early October, but it's not warm enough to be sitting by the ocean in a tank top. I put it back on, throw the rest of my soda in the trash, and get into the car. If I'm lucky, Denise will be at Charlie's place tonight, and I won't have to explain the bloody rip in my jeans or why I'm now in possession of a man's jacket.

By the time I pull into the parking garage, I'm exhausted. I want a shower and my bed. Screw the paper. I'll turn it in late. Denise is gone, thank God, which means I don't have to hold back the whimpers as I strip aside my clothes and peel away the gauze covering the bandages.

The wound is angry, red, and almost as swollen as my ankle. He did a good job patching me up, though. I probably won't need stitches. I find some medical tape and a roll of plastic wrap and tear off a piece. I tape it over the wound to keep it dry.

Hot water pounding over my shoulders, I tip my head back and let it run down my face. The fatigue rinses away with the soap, and as I climb out of the shower and dry off, I think I might be able to knock out the rest of my paper.

Three hours later, I crawl into bed, mind fried. That was a bad idea. I'm about to turn in the shittiest paper in my college career, but I can't bring myself to care.

* * * *

"So how do you think you did?" Scott stuffs his notebook in his messenger bag and slings it across his chest.

"Failed, most likely," I admit. Professor Thomas sprung a surprise quiz after we'd turned in our papers. "You?"

"I think I did all right. Better than I did with the paper, anyway." He follows me out into the hall, dodging around a clump of students. "You okay? You're limping."

"Twisted my ankle running yesterday. I don't think I sprained it, though that doesn't make it easier to walk on." His arm sneaks around my waist, and I give him a bland look. "Cute. Real cute."

Scott's a friend, and he's been trying to get me to go out with him since the beginning of the year. He's a nice guy, good looking, smart, fun to talk to. There's just no spark. Before last night, I sort of hoped one might spring up like magic. I mean, if I were to pick a guy to be into, he'd be it. I'm just…not. To be honest, we've been friends too long for me to think of him as anything else.

And after last night? Let's not go there.

"I'm doing a nice thing for you." He grins. It brings out his dimple, makes his eyes light up. I wonder if Nick's eyes do the same when he's happy.

There is a rather awkward conversation in my future. That hopeful glint in his eyes is going to sputter out because of me. I take his hand and move his arm from around my waist. "Thanks for the offer, but I'm okay. Just no excess walking."

The grin drops away, replaced by a crestfallen look. "You're never going to say yes, are you?"

I shake my head. "Wouldn't you rather be with a girl who says yes the first time?"

He manages a half smile. "I guess." His lips push up into a full-fledged smile. "Seriously, though, let me help you, okay? Your next class is halfway across campus, right?"

It is, and it's a walk I'm not looking forward to. So he slips his arm around my waist and takes some of my weight, entertaining me with a story about his roommate's drunken antics from last night as we walk to my next class.

"How is it he hasn't gotten arrested yet for public intoxication or whatever?" I ask. Jeff's an idiot. He thinks any day ending in the letter Y is a good day to get wasted. I've seen him stumbling around campus hung over more than once. I don't know how he's still in school.

"I guess I didn't tell you about the last party Jeff threw. Cops came, broke it up, people wandered back in, cops came again, made a couple of arrests, including Jeff. He told them to wait a minute, then proceeded to do a keg stand. Pretty sure he puked in the back of the patrol car."

Ew. "Who bailed him out?"

"Parents, I think. They've done it before."

We walk the path to Macgowan, Scott supporting most of my weight at this point. I squint up at him as he turns into me.

"You okay from here?" he asks.

Other than my ankle is throbbing, I'm fine. "Go. You'll be late for class." Our parting hug is awkward, and I give him a feeble smile before he walks back the way we came. For a second, I consider calling after him, telling him I've changed my mind. I even get as far as opening my mouth before I snap it shut again. He deserves a girl who says yes the first time. Not one who'll take him as a consolation prize.

I hobble to a nearby bench and sit, roll up my pant leg, and untie my shoe. Rotating my ankle strengthens the throbbing. Definitely swollen. Shit. Looks like there's a night of ice and elevation ahead of me. I tighten the bandage and wiggle my toes, making sure it's not tight enough to cut off the circulation.

Shoe tied, pant leg rolled down, I scan the entrance to the hall. There's a steady stream of people leaving and entering, and through the breaks, I catch glimpses of a man propping himself up on the wall. Tall, built, dark hair, a finely sculpted jaw. My heart stutters. It's not him. Can't be. How the hell did he find me?

I get to my feet and hurry up the sun-dappled walk to the entrance, doing my best to ignore the pain. It can't be him. We don't have any unfinished business, no reason to see each other again.

By the time I reach the front doors, there's no one there.

Chapter 3

I'm awake. Why am I awake?

That. That noise. A noise that basically isn't a noise, a hint of sound, like an invisible mouse scampering across the carpet.

I slip my hand under my pillow and wrap my fingers around the knife handle. I whip my arm out, aiming for flesh and not stopping until the blade bites into the intruder's neck. The intruder rips the knife from me and yanks my hand over my head.

It takes a minute for my eyes to adjust to the fuzzy dark of my bedroom, but I don't need it. His scent gives him away. "You know, you'd do a much better job of sneaking up on people if you didn't wear cologne." The cinnamon is more subtle than cologne, though. Aftershave?

"When it comes to personal safety, most people go with alarms. Baseball bats. Not knives." He releases my wrist and flicks on my bedside lamp. A thick line of red drips along the side of his neck, catching on the collar of his shirt. "Let me guess. Your violent neighborhood taught you to sleep with a knife under your pillow and how to use it in the event you were attacked in your sleep."

"Something like that," I say wryly. I study the wound. The blood flow is sluggish. Missed the carotid. Turner wouldn't be pleased. "How did you get in here?" The building is secure. We don't have a balcony—at my insistence—and there's a heavy-duty deadbolt on the door I installed myself. Any more than that would bring questions from my roommate that I didn't want to answer.

Crap. Denise.

"You better not have woken my roommate." I sit up, push aside the blankets, and hop out of bed, my ankle buckling under my weight. I catch myself before he can and limp to the door.

I stand in the middle of the darkened living room, peering into the shadows. Denise's door is closed, our apartment as still and as silent as it can get in the middle of Los Angeles at God knows what hour of the night. The front door is locked, both the button lock and the deadbolt. We're on the fourth floor. The only way to get through the window is with a ladder.

Nick walks out, and I frown and point at the bathroom. I don't want him dripping blood on the carpet. He clicks on the light, as I shut the door behind us, nudging him to the toilet.

His shirt lands on the floor, and I curl my hands into fists, nails biting into my palms. His chest is so…guh. *There.* Tan and muscled and tempting. Getting shut in a confined space with someone you want to lick all over is difficult. Getting shut in a confined space with someone you want to lick all over who hasn't demonstrated the same urges toward you while wearing nothing but a tank top and panties is several steps beyond difficult. I should have pushed him out the door. Or made certain the knife sliced through his neck.

I get out a washcloth, a towel, and the first aid kit and leave him to it. He's an intruder. He's not entitled to first aid.

I need armor. A force field to shut him out. I settle for a pair of yoga pants and a hoodie, then retrieve my knife from the bedroom floor. Cleaning it takes a bit of the edge off. I ought to sharpen it too. So I don't miss next time.

The knife is safely stowed under my pillow when he returns. He closes the door with a barely discernible click, his mouth curled in a smirk. I've seen that smirk before. It was on his face the night I was supposed to kill him after I'd thrown myself at him in a misguided attempt to keep him from getting killed by someone else.

"No need to cover up," he drawls. "I don't mess around with girls."

The cruel comment has to be deliberate, and the casual delivery buries it right in my chest. To my horror, my nose tingles with the onset of tears. I hold my breath, waiting for it to pass, the struggle to maintain a blank face harder than it should have been.

It must show, somehow, because there's a flash of surprise in his gaze, there and gone. "You never answered my question. How did you get in here?" My voice is steady. My heart is not. It's wobbling all over the place.

He wanders to the bed, the light playing off his bare chest, and I force ice through my veins. "Don't even fucking think of sitting down."

He sprawls on the end of the bed, and I look at the bandage on his neck. Another half an inch, and I would have succeeded.

"Why is that your question? Why aren't you asking how I knew where to find you?"

I stare at him. Waiting.

He doesn't leave me hanging long. "Cassidy Turner. Age twenty-one. Senior at UCLA, majoring in English with a minor in sociology. From Woodland Hills. Mom's an attorney, dad's a computer technician." He sits up, his gaze locked with mine. "Nothing about your background jibes with the Cass who wrapped her legs around my waist the other night. You're a puzzle and a loose end. I hate puzzles, and loose ends get snipped. And the locks were easy to pick. You should talk to your landlord about that."

I imagine his face turning purple from lack of oxygen. It's a strangely soothing picture.

"What are you?" Not who, but what, the question quiet and smooth, almost seductive. He slides over the bed, inching along until he's close enough to touch. Close enough to rub his thumb over my bottom lip, close enough to skim his fingers along my jaw. Close enough connections crackle and spark in my brain, shorting out.

I don't think. Just react. Slam the heel of my palm into his chin, snapping his head back. I follow the movement with another strike to the neck, over the cut. He falls onto his back, and I pin him in place with my forearm pressing on his throat, air wheezing in and out. Anger burns in his eyes, and his face turns red. "I would have thought you'd be smart enough to realize you're not going to get the answers you're looking for from me," I say quietly.

He jerks up and flips us over, the anger spilling from his eyes to his face. "Bad idea. Don't make a threat you can't follow through on, Cass."

He won't kill me. He's had at least four chances to do so in the last ten minutes alone, and he hasn't taken any of them. Even now, he's more concerned with keeping my hands occupied. "Really? Like seducing the answers out of me is any better? There's a special place in hell for men like you." I'm not going to give him the satisfaction of struggling, but that doesn't stop me from glaring at him.

"I came here for you."

What?

His grip is bruising. I imagine the blood pooling under my skin where his fingers clamp onto my wrists. "You know something, and if I found you this fast, you can bet whoever was at the restaurant will be looking for you, too."

"It took you three days to find me," I point out.

His smile is grim. "It took me less than twenty-four hours. You were walking toward Macgowan, draped all over someone. Looked like a douche. Improv 102. Meets at two every Tuesday and Thursday. Three credits."

"The amount of information you have on me is alarmingly stalkerish. All I know is an SUV was crawling along behind you, and then armed men stormed the restaurant you were standing in front of and started shooting." I flex my fingers; they're starting to lose feeling. "You can let go of my hands any time now." He releases me and rolls away. I sit up, rubbing my wrists. I jerk back when he reaches for one of my hands. "Don't."

He snags my hand, holding my wrist up to the light. "Shit." The skin is darkening in spots, shaped like fingers, a bluish red color.

I yank my hand from his. "For someone who doesn't mess with girls, you seem to have no issues invading my personal space." We're getting nowhere. "What do I have to say to get you to leave? Or would you rather get stabbed again?"

The man has the audacity to stand and walk over to my dresser. He opens the drawers, tossing clothes on the bed. "Pack a bag. You're not coming back here until this is over."

Instead, I arrange my legs lotus-style, settling against the pillows. "Because leaving in the middle of the night isn't suspicious at all. Denise will wonder where I am, and when I don't turn up, she'll call the cops."

He stalks over to the closet and sticks his head inside.

"Nick." When he doesn't answer, I unfold myself and get to my feet. I hobble over and slide in between Nick and the closet, punctuating my shoves with words. "Get. Out. Of. My. Apartment."

He's careful not to touch me, his gaze flitting between my face and the bruises he left. But he doesn't head for the door. "Do you think you're safe here? Do you think they won't find you?"

I cross my arms over my chest. "I think I'm safe *for tonight*. They have even less information than you. They know what I look like. Sort of. I'll reevaluate in the morning. Besides, I can't leave Denise here by herself."

His mouth thins and becomes a slash above his chin. "Fine. We'll leave in the morning."

"Why?" The man gives stubborn a whole new meaning. "Why does it matter what happens to me?"

"Because I'm in your debt, and I always repay mine."

I'm so tired I'm delirious. "You owe me? You owe me shit. Whatever debt you think you incurred has been paid off."

"Cassidy." He tips his head back and stares at the ceiling. "You risked your life to help me out. You got shot at. With those type of men, loose ends don't just get snipped, they get cut and buried. Trust me, they're looking for you. Think whatever you want of me, but I owe you. So yeah, you're coming with me until they've been eliminated."

Eliminated. Who is he that he throws that word around with ease? "Gee, your enthusiasm is catching. I don't need a babysitter. If you're so worried, I'll stay with my parents for a while." The commute to campus would be hellacious. I'd deal. And it would get me away from him. But the sliver of softness and honor has wiggled its way through my defenses, and I can't close the gap to kill it.

It's the proximity. The heat of his body radiates off him, his still bare chest temptingly close, and it's scrambling my brain waves. I edge around him and start picking up my clothes, refolding them to put them away. "Go home, Nick," I say. "I'm tired, I've got class tomorrow, and I don't want to have to explain your presence to Denise."

"Too bad. Got an extra pillow?"

* * * *

A hand clamps on my shoulder. "Cass!"

"Mmphrgh."

"Cassidy!" I crack open an eye. Denise is bouncing on her toes, something she does when she's nervous. "Get up."

I roll onto my back. "Coffee."

"The most beautiful man *in the world* is standing at our coffeemaker. Who is he?" she whispers.

I flip back onto my stomach. Somehow I forgot Nick had spent the rest of the night on my bedroom floor, and now I have to lie first thing in the morning. "He's from my mom's law firm," I mumble into the pillow. "Someone's threatened the entire defense team for some inmate. He's taking me to my parents for a few days." Sitting up, I scrub my hands over my face and push my hair behind my ears. "Do you think you could stay with Charlie? I don't want you to stay here until this is over with."

Her mouth trembles open, face paling. "Is it... Is it bad?"

"It's a precaution." Nick walks into the room wearing just his pants and holding a white Bruins mug. The scent of coffee hits my nose, and I stumble out of bed and around Denise, making a beeline for the mug. His mouth curves in a wicked grin as he hands over the coffee. I stifle a moan at the first scalding sip. "It's doubtful anything will come of the threat," he continues. "Your building is secure, but we're trying to cover every angle, and it's possible for someone to get into the building."

Denise squeaks. I swallow more coffee and hand the cup back to him. "We have time for me to shower and stuff?"

"If you're quick about it." He takes the coffee and leaves me alone with my roommate.

Her skin is so pale now it's practically translucent. "Hey. Like he said, it's a precaution. I'll be perfectly fine." Thank God this happened once before. My junior year of high school, Mom got a threat from a recently paroled inmate, and we had a police car in front of the house for weeks. Everyone in my class knew about it within a day. "Nothing happened the last time, and nothing's going to happen this time, right? I'd just feel a hell of a lot better if you'd stay with Charlie."

She bobs her head up and down. "Okay," she squeaks, then clears her throat. "Okay. Um. I'll call him in a little bit." The mattress makes a soft *whoomp* when her ass hits it. "Geez, Cass. Your mom's okay?"

Guilt settles in my stomach as I sit next to her. "She says she is. And Dad's looking after her. No cop car this time, at least not yet. Everything will be fine."

Ten minutes later, she manages to make her way out of my bedroom without falling over. I hurry to the kitchen to grab more coffee, ignoring Nick who's leaning against the counter, all coiled strength and casual elegance. It's kind of not fair how distractingly hot he is, even with the bandage on his neck.

"You have ten minutes."

Ten minutes my ass. I pour a cup of coffee for myself and open the cupboard next to the stove for a clean bowl. I snag the cereal from on top of the fridge. "You want?" I hold up the box.

He plucks the box from my hand. "You wanted a shower."

"First, I want breakfast."

We engage in a game of tug of war, weighted heavily in his favor, since all he has to do is hold the box above his head. When he does, I put the bowl away and open the refrigerator for the bread.

He tries to take that, too, but I'm ready for him. I pull his thumb back and ram my elbow into his stomach, cradling the loaf of bread to me as he hunches over. I pop four slices in the double toaster. "We rush off, it's only going to scare Denise more, and there's no way in hell I'm going to let you do that." I keep my voice low and stare at the toaster, willing it to show me a way out of this situation.

It doesn't. It just dings cheerfully, the toast springing up. I put two slices on a plate and hand it to Nick. "Eat." I take the other two slices for myself and turn back to the fridge for the butter.

He stares at his plate while I doctor my toast with butter and honey. Finally he growls. "Got any jam?"

I find a mostly empty jar of raspberry jelly in the back of the fridge, and he gives it a dubious sniff before spreading it on his toast. We eat our breakfast in silence, and then I jump in the shower, still racking my brain for an answer. A way to lose him.

We're leaving when the light bulb goes off over my head. "Do you want to give me directions, or do you want me to follow you?"

He heads for the door to the stairwell. "You're riding with me."

"What about my car? Leaving it here's a pretty big red flag."

He stops on the stair below me, and I stumble into his back. "Not falling for it, Cass." That fucking smirk is back when he glances over his shoulder. "Besides, car's already taken care of."

"Taken care of?" What the hell does that mean?

He slides my bag off my shoulder and slings it over his own. "I moved it," he says simply.

"You *what*?"

Chapter 4

He stole my car.

The bastard stole my car.

He broke into the underground garage, hotwired my car, and drove away. Left my poor, defenseless, in-demand Honda someplace where it would likely end up trashed.

Naturally, going anywhere with him is out of the question.

The man is nothing if not prepared, and he drags me out onto the street after tackling me on the floor of the garage. Yeah, I ran. He ran faster. I blame my injured ankle. He wrestles me into his BMW and slaps a pair of handcuffs on me—fuzzy ones, bright fuchsia—and chains me to the door so I can't escape.

I've been kidnapped by the guy I was paid to kill. There are so many things wrong with this picture I don't even know where to begin.

Streets roll by, Nick turning left or right without any indication of where we're actually going. "Who *are* you?" It's a question a normal person would have asked a long time ago. Up until the moment he cuffed me, though, I shielded the flame of hope I would still manage to pull this off. Behind schedule, but I could still slip into the headspace necessary to complete the job and prove to Turner, and myself, that I could do this.

"Wondered when you were going to ask. Dominic Kosta." He says it like I'm supposed to know what that means.

I don't. It's a name. Sounds Greek. "And?"

The car jolts to a stop at a light. Nick twists slightly in his seat to face me. His scrutiny is intense, eyes narrowed, taking in every line of my face and long enough the light changes and horns blare. "My family owns most of this city," he says slowly.

I shrug. "Okay."

He puts the car in gear and shoots through the intersection. We careen into an empty lot. He parks, unclips his seatbelt, and shifts around in the seat. Not so easy to do, given how tall he is. "You can drop the act."

What act? "What are you talking about?" I jerk my hands up. "Could you uncuff me?"

"No. And I'm talking about the whole naive thing. You know shit. You knew what, if not who, those men were. You knew how to get out of there. Last night? Another inch, you probably would have sunk that knife into an artery. And you fucking nearly broke my thumb this morning."

"Nick." Maybe if I talk slow and clear, he'll understand me. "I don't know who you are. This"—I jerk my hand up, pointing at my face—"is not an act. Will you please tell me what's going on? You own most of the city? What, you're a real estate mogul?"

He stares, then barks out a laugh, the bitter sound ending on a soft groan. His hair's sticking up where he ran his hands through it, and if my hands were free, I'd be all over that, letting the silky locks play over my skin.

"Stop lying. You stop, I'll uncuff you."

Anger surges, fanning out through my chest, igniting everything in its path. "What? What the fuck do you think I know? What do you think I *am*? I'm a fucking college student. English major, remember? I go to class, I party, I sleep. I happen to kill people for a living. That's pretty much the sum total of me. Would you stop being so obtuse and just fucking *tell me* what I'm supposed to know?" The long chain on the cuffs rattles as my hands move. This is a nightmare. All it needs are spiders. I hate spiders.

Regret splinters the rage, and I slump in the seat. If only I stayed home that night. If only I walked away instead of run to him. If only I did my job. If only I never set eyes on him or his stupid picture. If only, if only, *if only*.

If only I never started on this road in the first place.

The thought threatens to twine itself around my mind, drag it down, and now is not the time for hindsight. I turn away from him, giving him as much of my back as I'm able to. "There's only one person I can think of who might be able to help you." I recite the address, staring out into the overgrown lot.

The weight of his hand on my shoulder is heavy. I try to move away from it, edging as close to the door as I can get. He clasps my shoulder. "You kill people for a living."

Killed. Past tense. Sort of. "Yeah. I kill people for a living. Or spending money, anyway."

His hand presses down, pushing my shoulder into the seatback, and he holds me in place, forcing me to look at him. "You kill people for a living," he repeats.

I stare at him. "Is that so hard to believe?" I ask softly. "After everything that's happened?"

He edges away, slouching down in his seat. "Yes. No." Weariness laces his tone, along with something like disgust. I can't blame him. I'm pretty disgusted with myself, too. "I figured you had to be connected somehow," he says. "Wasn't expecting that, though."

The car fills with the sounds of traffic from the nearby street—window-shaking bass, the occasional horn, a truck rumbling by. The chain on my cuffs clanks as I pull my hands up. "Nick? Please?"

He digs the key out from the pocket of his jeans before dropping it onto my lap rather than handing it over. Or, heaven forbid, actually unlocking the cuffs himself. "My family controls most of the criminal activity in LA. Drugs, weapons. Some of my cousins run escorts, chop shops for high-end cars. If it's illegal, we're in it."

"Like the mafia?" The cuffs make a faint click as they open, and I ease them off my wrists, inspecting the skin. The silly pinky-purple fur protected me from any further marks, though my bruises are throbbing.

"LEOs call it 'organized crime.'" He eyes the cuffs dangling from the door. "Probably shouldn't have done that."

I unclip my seatbelt and reach for the door handle. "No, you shouldn't have."

It won't open. No catch as it engages, nothing. With the car off, the windows won't roll down. Climbing between the seats is out; there's no backseat to speak of. There's nothing lying on the floor I can use to knock him out. "Did you turn the child safety locks on?" I try popping open the glove compartment, but it's locked as well.

He grabs for the cuffs at the same moment I do, the chain rattling as it's pulled free of the handle. I manage to wrap my fingers around one of the cuffs and yank. The problem with this maneuver is Nick's got the other end, and he yanks harder, dragging me across the center console.

With a quick twist of his wrist, he gets the cuffs in his hands and slaps them back on. "You aren't gonna behave, are you?"

There's enough play in the chain I could wind this around his neck. If only the angle were better. "Nope." And I lunge forward to try, anyway.

Once again, he out-moves me, and the scuffle ends with the chain wound around the door handle and the cuffs still tight on my wrists. I jerk on them in frustration.

"Stop being a brat," he says, the violence in his eyes belying his mild tone. This time when he scrutinizes me, it's like I'm trapped behind glass at the zoo. "You're a hit man, and you know nothing about the criminal underworld. How is that possible?"

"It's the way I was trained." I squirm around in the seat. The car's suddenly confining, the metal frame compacting and compressing, squishing down. My palms itch and my legs twitch. "The less you know, the easier it is to compartmentalize." Lock it away, or it'll eat you alive. I only inherited a fraction of Turner's coldness. It enabled me to train, to complete the jobs I took. In the end, my conscience wouldn't shut up. It kept telling me this wasn't who I was.

It's why everything fell apart.

Fatigue crawls in and wraps itself around me. "Just…go." I wave a hand at the empty lot. "If you want your answers, we'll need to catch him before he leaves work." I go back to staring out the window, at the broken pavement, the crumbled buildings, the fence someone knocked down. Such an apt and pathetic metaphor. Come off hiatus to find I'm as wiped out and torn up as I was a year ago.

Something buzzes, and I glance over to see him pulling out his phone. "Kosta," he barks. His scowl deepens as he listens to the voice on the other end. "Send Isaiah." The longer he listens, the colder he gets. When he hangs up less than a minute later, his expression has smoothed out, bearing no hint of the anger lying beneath. "Slight detour."

I know that face. That's the face Turner has on all the time. That's *my* face on a job. My heart rate kicks up. I'm trapped in a car with a killer.

He spins the car in a slow half circle and pulls out of the lot. Another twenty minutes of driving takes us to a non-descript, one-story building. Surprisingly, he uncuffs me, then pushes me ahead of him through the front door.

The guy behind the front desk leaps to his feet and stammers out a greeting, one Nick ignores in favor of clasping my elbow and propelling me down a brightly-lit hallway. The door at the end is shut, and he pushes it open. Seated behind a monstrosity of a desk is a pudgy guy with a comb over. His eyes widen. "Mister Kosta. I-I-I wasn't aware you'd be picking up the deposit in person."

Nick locks the door and releases my elbow. "I was in the neighborhood."

Gone is the seductive, sinful voice. In its place is a tongue as quick as a blade, cold and steely and designed to remind you who, exactly, you were fucking with. The man behind the desk nods so hard I swear I hear something snap, and he starts digging through desk drawers. "I have it right here. It'll just take me a minute to—"

"Step away from your desk so I can inspect it myself? Excellent idea. Then we can discuss the rumor passed on this morning that the deposit was short for the past three weeks."

The sickly stench of piss fills the room, and I wrinkle my nose and turn away. Impressive, though, that Nick scares someone badly enough to wet himself.

I find a chair and settle in to wait. I've never watched someone intimidate another person into giving answers. Unfortunately, it's not as interesting as I hoped. Nick asks a question, the man gives a stuttering, fumbling response, Nick asks the same question, and the man gives a shorter, higher pitched response. After a while, the repetition gets boring, and I pull out my phone to check my e-mail.

"Time to go." Nick startles me out of my phone-induced stupor, and I lurch out of the chair as he pulls me to my feet, propelling me toward the door. I limp along, trying to match his long-legged stride, and I can't. My ankle still hurts too much.

"Nick, slow down. Please." I tug at his hold. He glances at me, and I point at my foot. "Bum ankle, remember?"

He nods once and slows, his fingers flexing and softening on my arm. "You think your contact will still be there?"

"Should be."

He helps me into the car, though he leaves the handcuffs off. How nice of him.

Somewhere around the tenth minute of silence, my anger returns. I just had a graphic display of what he was capable of, despite the lack of violence. His hands are probably bloodier than mine, and he's sitting there being all judgey.

He unlocks the doors, and I climb out, almost moaning with relief. I stretch my arms over my head, arching my back, the crack of each vertebrae a little shock of pain down my spine. Feeling looser, I limp onto the sidewalk in front of the low-slung building. Doesn't look like they've given the sign its annual paint job yet. Bird crap dripped all over the *M* in *MassTech Solutions*. It must be driving Turner nuts. "Come on. Might as well get it over with."

He trails behind me a few steps as I head for the side door. Inside, it's cool and dim, the air slightly stale. I wave at a few people as we walk down the hall, fighting to push the guilt and sadness into its tiny box. Once I tell Turner it's over, I'll never see them again. I've known some of them since I was little and would go from desk to desk, begging for candy. Anxiety's a knot in my chest, waiting to expand and choke the life out of me. The last year hasn't been a good one for my relationship with Turner. I never outright told him my decision to quit, and I can't bring myself to actually do it, so it's festered. We argue about it periodically, and it makes everything more strained.

If he knew I accepted Nick's job because of the last fight we had, he'd be extremely pissed off. The minute you're emotionally motivated, the job goes sideways.

Never allow your heart to rule where you mind should, Cass. That's the moment you make your first mistake, and that's the mistake that will get you caught.

Turner's where I thought he'd be, tinkering with something in the sterile room in the back of the building. The room has its own airlock to prevent any outside particles from traveling in, and anyone who goes in has to don a white suit and mask. The machinery inside is all top of the line. They repair and clean some of the country's most sophisticated technology in this room.

He's bent over a table, the top of his head obscured by a white hood. We walk into the airlock, but rather than pulling on a suit, I step over to the intercom system. I hesitate with my finger over the button, watching him. An interruption could mean damaging an important scrap of equipment. Best to wait until he lifts his head.

There's also the benefit of delaying the inevitable. Once Turner meets Nick and finds out what's going on, there's no going back. I'll have to admit I don't have what it takes to continue the family legacy, not anymore, and possibly never did.

"That him?" Nick's murmured question makes me jump, his mouth close enough it wouldn't take much to have his lips brush the curve of my ear. Warmth pools in my belly, temporarily blanketing the nerves. What would happen if I leaned into his chest? Rested my head on his shoulder?

Stupid question. He'd smirk and nudge me away.

Turner puts aside the tool he's using, and I push the button on the intercom. "Hey. Got a minute?"

My skin pricks and breaks out in goose bumps, my mouth dry as he nods and makes his way over to the airlock. The door unseals, and he steps through. He removes his mask and pushes the hood from his head. His blond hair, so much like mine, is mussed and needs a trim, his grey eyes flat as he regards me. "Cass. This is unexpected."

I swallow and dig down for the strength I'll need to get through this. "Turner, this is Dominic Kosta. He's got some questions I can't answer." A drop of sweat beads and slips down my spine. "Nick, this is my dad, Caleb Turner."

Chapter 5

I always thought the cliché "you could have heard a pin drop" was overused. No more. It's so quiet I'm scared to breathe because it'll be too loud. Nick and Turner regard each other steadily, neither moving, their faces perfect blanks.

Nick breaks first, which is strange. Usually the weaker person is the one who acquiesces, and he has so much more power than my dad does. But he holds out his hand, and after another beat, Turner shakes it.

Turner doesn't waste time with niceties, either. He turns to me, annoyance glinting in his eyes. "Explain."

Nick opens his mouth, and Turner holds up a hand to stop him. "I want to hear from my daughter what's she's doing with one of the most notorious men in LA's criminal world."

I straighten my shoulders, reach in, and pull out the detachment he prizes, then wrap it around me like a cloak. "I was contacted less than a week ago for a job. Compressed timeline, no schedule, recon limited to what I could find a few hours before the hit. I was sent a picture, a date, a time, and a location. I decided to take it. I arrived ahead of schedule, took a look around, and realized it wouldn't work. Too many possibilities for things to go wrong. No place to hide, and no guarantee he'd actually be alone. As I was leaving, I spotted him and an SUV tailing him. Something about it didn't jibe, so I went with my instinct. I was right. The men in the SUV followed us into the restaurant and opened fire on the other diners, chased us through the kitchen and into the alley. I helped him get away, and he showed up at my apartment three days later, demanding I help him, even after I told him I wouldn't be able to."

Turner's face is just as impassive at the end as it was at the beginning. "She's correct," he says, glancing at Nick. "She knows nothing about the networks and gangs and other organizations in the greater Los Angeles area. You still don't follow the news?" he asks me.

I shake my head.

"Good girl."

The praise does nothing for me. No blast of warmth, no bubble, no fizzy, happy feeling.

Turner's gaze flits over my face. "Do you still have the e-mail?"

"Yeah. I had to contact them again to send the deposit back."

It's on the tip of his tongue to lecture me. I recognize his tells, the way the skin around his eyes tightens, the slight flaring of his nostrils. I could have found a way to complete the hit, if not that night, then when Nick broke into my apartment. Or today. I've had enough training drilled into me I should have been able to improvise.

But I'm not Turner. And we're past the point where I have to keep trying to be what he wants.

He gestures to the door, and we follow him to the cramped, tiny room he calls an office. "I'd like to see the e-mail string."

Using Turner's computer instead of my phone, I bring it up and get out of the way. Turner brushes by to sit at his desk. I doubt he'll find anything of use. It's bare bones, less than what I usually get.

He studies it with the same intensity he shows all his work, legal or otherwise. Then he makes me go over the evening again before asking Nick for his version of events.

Nick leans against the wall and slips his hands into his pockets. There's a casual grace to him, all sleek movement waiting to uncoil. "I had a meeting with a contact on a new line of product through Sinaloa. We used all our standard vetting procedures, and I set up the meet myself. Chose the day and time after the contact picked the location. Did a run through the neighborhood, found the alley, plotted an escape route. I'd noticed the SUV and figured if things went sideways, I'd use the back entrance. When Cass came up and offered to help, I thought I might be able to make it to the alley without being shot at."

So he *did* have a plan. I'd thrown myself into the middle of a firefight for no reason.

"Cass was able to point us to a route I'd missed. Not all of the spaces between the buildings are very visible, especially in that alley. If she hadn't come along, I might not have found the one we ended up in."

I don't know if I'm pleased or embarrassed. Saving lives isn't my thing, and I didn't actually do a very good job of it. But it seems to be annoying the crap out of Turner, so I go with pleased.

Dad clicks a few keys, and the e-mail disappears. "I don't see what information I could provide you. Cassidy was contracted for the hit. While the timeline does raise some questions, it's not entirely outside the parameters of what she'll accept. Your likeliest suspects are members of your own organization or a rival intent on taking over a portion of your business."

"Are you aware of anyone who would be willing to make a hit look like a gang shooting rather than a targeted hit?" Nick asks.

For the first time since he's come out of the repair room, Turner's face shows something other than its cold neutrality. One corner of his mouth tips up. "We generally work alone." The smile is there and gone in a blink. "Some of the newer ones might, especially if they aren't picky."

"Would you be willing to give me some names?"

Turner drums his fingers on the desktop. "No," he says finally. "I may not approve of their methods, but neither will I roll over on them." He stands.

My part here is done. Good. All that's left is several hours' worth of reaming by Turner, and it'll all be over with. "I'll get my bag out of Nick's trunk. Can I catch a ride to the house with you?"

"You will stay with Dominic and help him figure out who wants him dead."

Did that—did my dad just throw me to the wolves? "Dad—"

He cuts me off with a frown. "You've involved yourself in a potential turf war. However cautious you may have been, you made a mistake. I will not have you bringing that danger near your mother."

"But—"

"No."

The finality of the word snaps the last strings tying me to him. I am done. I'm not playing his game any longer. "I'm out." No need to elaborate. Turner will understand. His head bobs in a curt nod, but I'm not finished. "I'll tell Mom I won't be home for Thanksgiving." Or Christmas. Or any other family holiday.

I spin on my heel and stalk out of the room, down the hall, and out into the bright sunshine.

He didn't used to be this way. He didn't used to insist I call him Turner. Up until I was six or seven, he was a normal dad, or as normal as a man like him can get. He came to my T-ball games and read me bedtime stories, drove me to swimming lessons, and taught me how to ride a two-wheeler. But as I grew older, the distance between us stretched. He wanted a child he could train, same as his father had trained him, and his father before him. And like the desperate fool I am, I tried to be what he wanted. It was the only way I could think to get my dad back.

I don't need to pay a shrink to tell me I have daddy issues.

He adores my mother, though. He's also right. If I'm in any danger at all, I can't risk having it get back to Mom. She's under enough stress already with Turner and I fighting, and this final break will only make it worse.

I wander out to Nick's car and lean on the trunk, slipping my phone from my back pocket to call Mom. She doesn't answer. I leave her a message that I'd like to get together for lunch tomorrow if she can and end the call.

Nick walks up and settles himself on the other corner of the trunk, arms crossed over his chest. "I don't know who's more fucked up, you or him."

The comment blows fresh air over the embers of my anger. "Hypocrite much? I bet you've got more deaths on your head than I do." I straighten and thump a hand onto the trunk. "If you could open the trunk for me, I'll get my bag." There's a bus stop not too far from here. I'll find a no-tell somewhere and hide out for a few days. I should have brought my textbooks. Then I won't fall behind.

He stands so fast the back end of the car whines as it springs up. "Get in the car."

"I'm not going to help you."

"Cass, *get in the car*."

Something in his voice sparks my attention, and I scramble into the passenger seat, gripping the door handle as he shoves the car into gear. Tires squeal as we roar out of the parking lot. "What's going on?"

My seatbelt snaps taut as we take a corner too fast. "We've been found," he says grimly.

A bullet bounces off the rear window with a thud, and I sink down in my seat, hand still closed tight around the handle. "Bullet-proof glass?" Please let it be bullet-proof glass.

He whips the car around a corner, tearing through an alley. Another thud, followed by two more, and we zip around another corner, drawing horns and shouts. My heart is somewhere in the vicinity of my mouth with my stomach not far behind. Sweat slicks the door handle, and I tighten my hold, my fingers aching.

"Know how to shoot a gun?" He wrenches the wheel to the left, and the velocity throws me against the side of the car.

"I am not sticking my head out the window. I'm not sticking *any* body part out the window." Yes, I know how to shoot a gun. Hello? Trained killer?

He leans over, eyes still on the road, and fiddles with the latch on the glove compartment. After a second and a few more swerves, it pops open. A 9mm pistol slides out and lands on the floor between my feet. A couple of spare magazines tumble out after. I reach down and pick up the gun, testing the weight. "Loaded?"

We bounce over a speed bump, and I look up. We're in a parking garage, tires screaming over the polished concrete. He pulls the car in a one-eighty spin and races up the ramp to the next level, screeching to a halt in the far corner. "Out. Behind the car." He grabs a spare magazine and shoves open the door.

I barely have enough time to crawl out and flick the safety off before the next bullet pierces the side of the car. Nick's crouched next to the front tire, and he jumps up and fires a couple rounds at the next pause in the shooting.

"Two of them," he says. "Behind their car."

The world slows, sound coming from the end of a tunnel. My hand curls around the grip in a perfect fit, as though this gun is as familiar as my own. It's me or them, and I'm not the one leaving in a body bag today. Easy. Steady. In this moment, I am perfect.

Turner's training clicks into place, and I scan the nearby cars for cover. We'll have to get behind the shooters if we're going to get out of here alive. I scoot closer to Nick. "Cover for me? I'm going to see if I can come up from behind."

He springs up and fires again. I duck walk to the next car in the ensuing racket, pausing when the shooting stops. The wall behind us is a blessing and a curse. No one can sneak up on us, but it blocks us in, too. Hunched over, trusting Nick can distract them long enough not to notice my footsteps, I run between the line of cars and the wall until I'm far enough away they shouldn't see me crossing into the open.

The wound on my leg protests as I crouch next to the front bumper of a truck, waiting for the next round of gunshots to cover me. I peek around the car. They're about fifty yards away. Too far for me to get off an accurate shot.

More gunfire, and I run across the open space to the next row of cars, not stopping until I'm between a dark sedan and a bright red two-door. The noise doesn't last long enough to cover my footsteps, and they're unnaturally loud in the cavernous building.

I shift my grip on the gun and draw in a breath, let it out, count my heartbeats as I wait. One second. Two. Heavy footfalls approach, slow, slow, each one ringing in my ears. I haven't fired yet. I shift my stance as quietly as I can.

It's like watching a movie advance frame by frame. He's tall. Dark hair. Hard jaw. The gun looks tiny in his hands. Mouth a bit too wide for his face, narrowed eyes. He's not expecting me. He's not expecting the bullet that lodges itself in his eye.

The shot echoes long after he's on the ground. My hand is numb. *I'm* numb. Blood pools and spreads under his head, deep, deep red on the dirty garage floor.

More footsteps running toward me, and I bring the gun up to fire again, squeezing the trigger on instinct. It's only by sheer luck the shot misses Nick, and he stumbles to a halt. I drop my hand and take a step forward. Another. Then another. "Police will be here soon."

He nods. "I'll get your bag. We'll take their car. You injured?" His gaze skims over my body.

"They didn't hit me. You?" Blood seeps through his shirt, high on his bicep. We have matching wounds. Nice. I tug the fabric up and inspect the graze. It's not as long or as deep as mine. "You won't need stitches." I pull his sleeve into place and move past him, heading for his car. We have to wipe it for prints and get out of the garage before the cops show up.

Sirens wail in the distance, and I sprint for the SUV, Nick on my heels.

Chapter 6

"Cass?"

"Mmm?" I glance over at Nick. Something about his expression, carefully and totally blank, makes me wonder if I've missed something.

He gestures to the door. "You want to get out of the car?"

I guess I did miss something. The entire drive. We're on a mostly empty street, shaded by tall buildings on either side, a few cars parked along the curb. A faint hum of traffic vibrates through the car. Downtown. I think we're in the business district. I unclip my seatbelt and get out, retrieving my bag from the back seat. "What time is it?"

"Almost three."

I called my mother just before noon. Assuming the shootout lasted only a few minutes, we've been driving around for over two hours, and I haven't spoken a word. The numb feeling's settled in, familiar and calming, distancing me from the violence. "Which way?"

He points left, and I heft my bag onto my shoulder and start walking, the pain in my ankle a dull ache. After a few steps, he falls in beside me. Traffic noise increases the farther we get from the SUV, and we turn onto Grand. "Are we going any place in particular, or no place special?"

"Safe house." He stares down the street, peering toward the next intersection. "Come on."

"If the hit was ordered by your own family, wouldn't your safe houses be compromised?"

He reaches out and takes the bag from me. "Not this one."

And that's all the answer I get. He hails us a cab at the corner of Grand and Seventh and gives the driver an address out near Manhattan Beach.

Nick's "safe house" is a condo in a multi-story complex about five blocks from the beach. The complex is new and unremarkable, the outside done in shades of tan and white. Rather than take the elevator, we hike the stairs to the third floor, and he lets us in to a unit somewhere in the middle of the building, facing away from the ocean.

The place is furnished. Barely. There's a couch covered in a dark gray fabric and a coffee table that looks like an IKEA cast-off in front of it. A small flat screen is on a stand in the corner. The blinds are drawn, leaving the interior dim. A set of French doors open on to a balcony. I rattle the handle. Balconies compromise safety. I thought everyone knew that.

"Bedroom's through there." He jerks his head to the far side of the living room.

The short hallway is dark with two doors on one side. I open the one on the far end, farthest from the balcony. Inside is a small bedroom. Does that mean the bathroom is elsewhere? Because the other door has to lead to another bedroom. I study the furnishings, such as they are. The queen size mattress is bare and still has the tags on it. "Are there blankets?"

"Should be some in the bathroom closet." He tosses my bag on the floor and leans on the doorjamb, hands in his pockets.

The bathroom is one of those pass-through ones with doors on both ends. I find the closet he's talking about and grab a set of sheets and a couple of pillows. He hasn't moved as I make my way over to the bed and begin making it up. "Is there food, or do we need to go get some?" The top sheet doesn't want to center. I tug it this way and that, the creased line stubbornly remaining a few inches off.

Heat and cinnamon invade my senses, the long, hard line of Nick's body flush against my back. "Cassidy." A shiver tiptoes down my spine at the way he says my name, my full name, lush and decadent, cracking the ice encasing my mind. He glides his hands along my forearms and closes his hands around mine, pulling them away from the sheet.

I'm dreaming because there's no way this is happening, not after the way he looked at me today, after he blew me off so many times already. But it is, and his hands shift to my hips, following their curves, urging me around. He presses his hands into the small of my back. One hand comes up and wraps around my ponytail, tipping my head back, his mouth inches from mine.

The softness of the kiss wakens my mind from its slumber, bringing me out of the cold. This isn't supposed to be how it happens. He's supposed to take, demand my surrender, weaken my knees with the fierce possessiveness of it all.

His lips are a featherweight on mine. Sweet, barely there, warm enough to turn my body liquid and flow against his own, let him mold me however he wants. It's wrong, this way, but it might be the only way I'll get to touch him. It might be the only way he'll touch me.

I don't care. I need this sweet warmth, this flickering desire, need to feel it curling and sending out tendrils to wrap around any part it can touch. I cup the back of his neck, then slide and fist my fingers into his hair, the strands silky soft on my skin. Amazing. Amazing and fantastic and impossible, this kiss, his tongue seeking entry, stroking and teasing and demanding more.

Then he eases back into the softness and the tender brush of lips that threatens to leave me in pieces.

When the words come, it's like a tidal wave breaking over me.

"Good to know one thing hasn't changed," he whispers, his lips against my mouth. "Not sure I like cold, calm Cass."

Cold? He thought I was cold before? I'm freezing now. I'm ice. I sidestep him and pick up a pillowcase, tucking a pillow under my chin. "Was that an experiment? Did you think I'd freak out at the sight of a dead body?" I toss the pillow onto the bed. "I don't remember agreeing to play your little game. I do kill people for a living, remember?"

He sucks his lower lip into his mouth, and I wish I was the one doing that. "Fuckin' A. You're so damn calm, like it's nothing. Okay? You tell me you kill people. Seeing you do it is something entirely different."

His frustration is kind of adorable. It doesn't change the fact he took advantage of my attraction to him and kissed me solely to get a reaction. The pain scatters the ice, and I clutch the shards closer. I grab the other pillow and wrestle it into the case. "Now you know. Curiosity satisfied." Leave. Dear God, leave before I do something stupid and girly. Like cry.

I will not cry in front of him.

My phone buzzes in my pocket. I fish it out, grateful for the distraction. I get a glimpse of the screen as I thumb off the lock to answer. "Hi, Mom."

"Hi, sweetie. How are you?"

I throw the other pillow on the bed and sit on the edge, my back to Nick. It's a really broad hint, and I hope he takes it. "Not so good. Can we have lunch tomorrow?"

Nick makes a grab for the phone, and I twist away, scrambling across the bed and dropping to the floor on the other side. "Sure. I've got a deposition but should be done by around one."

"That'll work." I crawl under the bed to get away from him.

"Cass? What are you doing?"

Flat on my belly, I kick out as he grabs my ankle. "Trying to keep my phone from being stolen. Do you want me to come in, or meet you some place?"

"Come in. Deposition might run long." I tell her I love her and I'll see her tomorrow, then use my elbows to creep along to the other side. Dust clings to my shirt as I crawl out, phone in hand.

He's waiting for me at the foot of the bed, and I brush wayward strands of hair out of my face, then swipe at the dust bunnies on my shirt. "Personal space. Stop invading it." I slip the phone into my back pocket and back into the wall.

"Stop making stupid mistakes, and I'll consider it. You're not going anywhere. And give me the phone."

"The GPS is disabled." I disable it whenever I get a new phone. "It's just lunch."

He plants his feet on either side of mine, trapping me with his body. Not fair. Not fair at all. "Give. Me. The. Phone."

"No."

Wait for it. He won't be able to resist. He can't. It's so easy. So tempting for him to just slide his hand in there, palm the phone. Palm my ass. His hand is at my hip, almost to its destination, and I ram my elbow into his stomach. He stumbles backward, and I duck around him, heading for the door. "Learn the word 'no,' Nick. Because when I say it, I mean it." I'm leaving this place, first chance I get.

The kitchen matches the rest of the condo. Barely furnished. A length of counter closes the space off from the living room, forming a U and connecting to another counter broken up by the stove. I open cupboards at random and find plates and a couple of pots, along with a drawer full of silverware and other kitchen utensils. There's no food. Great. I haven't eaten since the toast this morning, and my stomach's growling like an angry tiger.

"Cassidy."

I open the fridge again, unwilling to look at him. "Is there a grocery store nearby? If we're going to be stuck here for a few days, cooking would be easier." I glance over my shoulder. "Or are we not allowed outside at all?"

"Quit being a brat."

I shut the fridge and slump against it, tired of fighting. Tired of fighting my attraction to him. "We need some rules. Or rule. A single rule." His face is blank, eyes dark and watchful. "You don't touch me. Simple, right? You don't touch me unless there's no ulterior motive behind it. You should be able to remember that. I think you're hot. You know it. You use it against me and I *will* hurt you. Someone paid me to kill you. Piss me off enough, and I'll do it for free."

"You wouldn't." His declaration is quiet and sure. "All you get is a picture and a schedule, right? Don't follow the news. You don't know anything about your hits because it humanizes them. Once they're people to you, you can't bring yourself to pull the trigger."

His assessment is frighteningly accurate. Turner always warned against allowing emotion to influence your kills. His advice flies right out of my brain the longer I stare at Nick. I arch a brow. "Do you really want to try me?"

He smirks.

My fingers twitch, aching to close around one of the kitchen knives. Calm. I need to calm down, wait for the rage to pass. Because as infuriating as Nick is, he's also right. If he dies, it won't be by my hand.

"You win," I mutter. "Food?"

The smirk is gone. "Grocery store about three blocks up."

I nod and head for the door.

"Wait."

I pause, hand on the doorknob, eyes trained on the door. "I'll be fine by myself." I'm out in the hall and the door's shut before he can respond. I take the stairs to the lobby and walk outside, blinking into the bright sunshine.

The store is where he says it is, and I wander the aisles, filling the cart with more food than I can carry, but it gives me time to think. I have two options: leave Nick or stay and help him.

The problem with leaving is I have nowhere to go. I can't go back to my apartment; he'll just find me there. I can't stay with my parents. I don't have a Charlie to lean on, like Denise, and I don't want to run through my savings on a motel, even a rent-by-the-hour one. Plus, ew.

Staying brings up a whole different set of problems, starting and ending with Nick. Nick and his ridiculous hotness, Nick and his aggravating way of doing things, Nick and the severe lack of information.

He couldn't have kissed me like that if he didn't feel something too. Right? All sweet and slow and coaxing.

Of course he could. He said so himself—he did it to prove a point.

I pick up a six-pack of beer on the way to the check out and watch with dismay as the checker loads bag after bag. It's three blocks. I can make it.

My arms are screaming in protest, and the pain in my ankle's increased by the time I reach the front door to the complex. I ring the buzzer for Nick's unit, and he lets me in.

Produce spills out of one of the bags as I dump them on the floor of the kitchen. I pull a beer out and pop the cap off using the edge of the counter as he empties the grocery bags.

"There's a bottle opener, you know," he says wryly.

"Shut up. And if you drink one of my beers, I'm sending you out for another six-pack." It won't get me oblivion-wasted, but drunk sounds good right about now.

I put the food away while I finish the first beer and crack open a second as I cook dinner. Nick has made himself absent from the kitchen. I take a plate of chicken and rice out into the living room and unlock the balcony doors.

There's no patio furniture, so I grab two of the wooden bar stools and set them outside before putting my plate and beer on one and climbing up on the other. I swallow my whimper as I prop my foot up on the bottom rung of the stool. I'll have to ice it tonight. The neighborhood is quiet except for the occasional shout from a kid or a barking dog. Cool evening air sneaks under my shirt. I gulp the rest of my beer. I'll give this much to the balcony—it's giving me space to think.

"Thanks for making dinner." Nick appears in the doorway and hands me another beer. I take it and return my gaze to the darkening street. The silence between us grows and stretches tight, snapping like a rubber band when he breaks it. "I'll come with you tomorrow."

I shake my head and drain half the bottle. "I'd rather you didn't. You don't need to see all my dirty laundry."

He says nothing, reaches out and tugs the end of my ponytail, fingers playing with the strands. I stare at him until he drops his hand and tucks it into his pocket. "He never should have trained you."

I polish off the rest of the beer and stand. He doesn't move from the doorway, so I have to edge around him to get another. "He didn't force me to do it." The beer's taking hold. My head's a little woozy, and I stumble a little as I pass the coffee table. By the end of the six-pack, I should be pleasantly goofy. I pull my fourth bottle from the fridge and pop the cap after missing the first time.

"How did he get you to do it, then?" He's back inside, blocking the way out to the balcony. No matter. Those places are dangerous, anyway.

"I asked." And I lift the bottle to my lips and drink.

Chapter 7

This is interesting.

I've managed to shock Dominic Kosta. Full-stop surprise on his face, lips parted, eyes unblinking, brow creased. Someone's hit pause, his body locking up, thoughts frozen. "You asked him to train you." A muscle jumps and twitches in his neck.

I lift my beer in a toast. "Yup. Family business. You're familiar with those, right? Have to carry on the tradition. He was trained by his dad, who was trained by his dad, and his dad was some kind of goon." Beer slops against the sides of the bottle as I wave it around. "I just wasn't quite up to dear old dad's standards."

I am not nearly drunk enough for heart-wrenching confessions. "Tell me abutt yer famly." I take another long pull from the bottle.

He slouches onto the couch, legs kicked out in an elegant sprawl. "Like I said, we own most of the city. Biggest chunk of the legit side is technology, though. We own the company your dad works for." His smile is humorless, more a spreading of lips than an actual happy expression.

I scrunch my nose. I don't want to think about Turner. "I don't care about the business part right now." Won't be able to remember much if I finish the beer. "I mean your family. You know, mom, dad, brothers, sisters? Do you have any?"

"What, moms and dads?"

I wander over and flop onto the opposite end of the couch, licking up droplets of beer that splashed onto my hand. "Ha ha. Brothers and sisters. Sometimes I wish I had a brother."

"Three sisters. Two of them are married with kids. Youngest sister's younger than you." He nicks the bottle from my hand and drains it over my protests. "She's at FIDM studying textile design."

I glare at him and haul myself upright. The room wobbles a little as I stumble to the kitchen for another bottle. Rather than resume my place on the couch, I plop down on the floor near the kitchen and point at him. "Stay."

One side of his mouth quirks up, his half smirk somehow not as irritating as the full-on version. "You're cute when you're drunk."

I scowl harder. "Shut up. You don't get to say shit like that. And I'm not drunk." Not nearly drunk enough. If I was, I'd be plastered to him, begging him to bend me over a table. "Whass her name?" I can barely taste the beer; maybe I am drunk.

"Liana."

"Liana." I purse my lips. She's probably drop-dead gorgeous. His whole family probably is. Does she taunt people with it like he does? "What's she like?"

He smiles, bright and full and sweet, and I blink slowly. He just got even better looking. It's kind of not fair. "Smart as hell. Kind of shy, takes her a while to open up to new people. Too nice for her own good. Stays out of trouble."

I snort. Right. Stays out of trouble. This is not the age to stay out of trouble. This is the age to get *into* trouble.

"What?"

I lick beer off my lips. "You're delusional. Your baby sister is totally gettin' into trouble."

He gets up and prowls toward me. I twist away, shielding my beer with my body.

"Lemme guess. Second year, and she said she wanted to move out." I giggle. "That's what happened with Denise. And me." My eyes widen as he comes closer, and I scoot back until I run into the counter, trying to hold on to the slippery bottle. "Don't party in high school. Don' wanna give mommy and daddy the wrong idea." He's on his knees, crowding me. "You're nothing but a bully, aren't you?" I can't breathe. I'm dizzy and fuzzy-tongued and the beer's humming through my system, urging me to lower my inhibitions. To lower my guard.

"You're drunk," he growls. "You've had enough."

I shake my head, the ends of my ponytail slapping my cheeks from the frantic moment."Buzzed. Definitely buzzed." He's in my face, hovering over me, and I choose to sacrifice my beer to the greater good. I upend the bottle over his head and scramble out of the way as he sputters. "You're ruining it," I whine. "God, I just wanted to drink the fucking beer, okay?"

He wipes moisture from his face and glowers at me. "Brat."

I gain my feet, swaying a little from the effort. "Look, it's been a shit-tastic day. Now I've got one beer left, and I want to drink it in peace."

He's dripping all over the carpet, his hair soaked, the shoulders of his T-shirt wet. "Fuck it," he mutters and yanks the shirt over his head. He rubs it over his hair and stalks out of the room, giving me an excellent view of his ass.

He returns a minute later, wearing a clean shirt, a set of keys clenched in his fist. I watch him leave, wincing as he slams the door behind him. Huh. Okay. I pick up the empty bottle and toss it in the garbage, then blot the carpet as best I can.

I gaze mournfully at my last beer. A six-pack would have gotten me fully drunk, especially if I pounded them. But Nick's little tirade has cost me a bottle. Hopefully this last one will do the trick.

Somewhere in my addled brain, a tiny voice speaks up, wanting to know what crawled up his ass and died. I drown it in beer. Tiny voices can shut up. I weave my way to the couch and sit carefully so I don't spill the beer.

I'm down to dregs when he storms back into the condo. Two six-packs get slammed onto the counter. He yanks one free, pops the cap, and stalks over to the couch, pushing it into my hand. "Since you're intent on getting yourself wasted."

Passing up free beer isn't high on my list of things to do, so I raise it to my lips and drink deeply. Mmmmph. This is the good stuff, the stuff I can't afford. Another one of these, and I'll toddle off into oblivion. "Wanna tell me what's crawled up yer ass?"

He retrieves a beer for himself and slumps into the opposite corner. "You really think she's out there partying?"

I frown. Is that all this is? Worrying about his sister? He is *way* overreacting. "Uh, yeah. She's what, twenty? On her own? Yeah, she's partying."

His brows draw down, mouth tight, and I fight off a sigh. He's gone all broody. He's never looked sexier than he does right now.

Or maybe that's the beer talking.

"I can't see her doing that. Lia's really quiet. Got bullied when she was a kid."

You could bully a crime boss's daughter? Really?

The muscles in his forearms flex as he turns the bottle around in his hands. My fingers twitch with the urge to trace those sinuous lines.

"Poor baby." I set my bottle on the floor, crawl across the couch, and wrap my arms around his neck. I lower my head to his shoulder and shut my eyes.

He stiffens. "You're violating your rule."

"Nuh-uh." My voice is muffled by my own arm, my mouth pressed against it. "Rule is *you* can't touch *me*. Doesn't mean I can't touch you. It's a hug. You look like you could use a hug."

The next ice age dawns before his arms come around me, but once they do, it's tight and warm, and I want to snuggle in and sleep here forever. "Besides," I mumble, "it's not like you want me, so it doesn't mean anything."

He skims a hand along my back, shifting me closer. "Right," he whispers.

* * * *

Drummers have taken up residence in my skull.

My mouth is full of cotton, and opening my eyes takes all my energy. A glass of water sits on the table by the bed next to a bottle of aspirin. I knock the bottle to the floor reaching for the water. It's room temperature, but it's wet, and that's what counts. I swallow the contents before I lever myself off the bed and onto the floor, searching for the wayward bottle.

I find it and take it into the bathroom along with the glass. One very long shower, three aspirin, and another glass of water later, I feel marginally better except I can't find my damn phone.

It's not in the bedroom. It's not in the living room. I even look under the couch and remove all the cushions. It's not in the kitchen. I knock on the other bedroom door. Nick's "Come in" is muffled.

Tech is everywhere. Cables crawl across the floor, waiting to trip someone. A laptop sits open on a low table, a second laptop in a corner. There's a desktop computer, the CPU heating the small room, three monitors spread out across the top of a desk. The desk is so massive it takes up most of the room. I spot my phone lying in front of one of the monitors, mixed in with four others of the smartphone variety. Nick's hunched over a keyboard, the speed of his moving fingers putting Turner's skills to shame. His hair sticks up, and his shirt is rumpled, his feet bare. His beer-soaked shirt is crumpled in a far corner.

Obviously, there is no second bedroom.

"Um. I'm leaving to go meet my mom." It's not even noon, but without a car, public transit is my only option. And public transit in Los Angeles takes forever. "Can I have my phone, please?" I feel ridiculous, asking politely for my own property, deferring to him like he's a much older adult.

He straightens and pushes the keyboard away. "What time are you meeting her?"

"One. It'll take a while to get there from here."

"I need to shower, and then we can leave." He gets to his feet and glances around absently. His gaze lands on a duffle bag near the door to the hallway.

I lift a brow. "'We?' I'm meeting my mother. There's no need for you to tag along."

"Non-negotiable, love." He hauls the bag onto the chair and rifles through it.

"Stop calling me that," I say, irritated. "And why can't I have lunch with my mother all by myself? Last time I checked, I was a grown up too." Though I certainly don't sound like one right now. Apparently Nick brings out the petulant toddler in me.

"Because you won't come back, and we still have a lot of work to do. I've started a list"—he gestures to the computer workstation—"but there's a fuckin' lot of data to go through."

I want to tear out my hair. "I never agreed to help you. That was my father, being the overbearing jackass that he is. I'll be fine on my own."

He pauses at the door leading to the bathroom. "Your apartment was broken into last night."

I stop breathing.

"Denise wasn't there. She must have taken your request seriously and spent the night at her boyfriend's. Someone else in the building called the police," he adds.

I snatch up my phone the minute he shuts the door and call my friend. She answers on the second ring. "Cass? Are you okay? Please tell me you're okay." Her voice is pitched high and wavering, and I know she's about to burst into tears.

Two seconds later, she sobs into the phone.

"Denise? Hon, are you okay? I heard someone broke into our apartment last night. You weren't there?"

I hold the phone away from my ear as she gulps air, trying to calm down. "No," she sniffles. "I stayed with Charlie last night, like you asked. The police called early this morning with questions. Are you coming to class today?"

Shit. Classes. I can't afford to skip classes indefinitely. "Not today. Do you think they'll let me into our apartment? I left some of my books there." Like all of them.

The sound goes fuzzy and faint for a moment, then clears. "Charlie thinks if you contact the officer in charge of the investigation, they'll let you in. They need to know if anything's missing. I told them it didn't look like it. All my stuff was still there."

Whoever had broken in was either very, very stupid or didn't care the police could put two and two together and get it to equal four. "Text me the number? I'll call them."

She promises to do so, and after another minute, she says she has to go. Class, most likely. What I'd give for a normal day right now.

The water's still running. With one eye on the bathroom door, I work my way across the room. I'll be long gone by the time he's out. The knob's smooth and cool under my hand. It also won't budge. I try it again, rattle it back and forth. Desperate, I try the other door, the one leading to the bathroom.

The bastard's locked me in.

Chapter 8

"What are you doing?"

I click on the next little envelope. "Checking my e-mail. I figured since you left everything on, you wouldn't mind." Someone wants to pay me five hundred K. Job to be completed within the next two weeks, picture and schedule attached.

I delete the message without responding.

He blows out a breath, the sound ending on a growl. I twist around in the chair. His expression is stony, eyes sparking with anger. "My family is incredibly tech-savvy. It wouldn't take much for them to track down our location." He stalks over. "Move."

I abandon the chair. "Give me some credit, Nick. I know how to cover my tracks, and it's a lot easier to do on a full size keyboard."

He drops into the chair. "Out." His shoulders are as tight as his voice. Whatever crawled up his ass last night must have set up camp.

I keep my mouth shut and exit through the bathroom, stopping in the bedroom to pick up my wallet. Given Nick's current mood, it might be best if I gave him some space. I pull out my phone to search for a bus schedule. The nearest bus stop is several blocks away and the next bus leaves in ten minutes. If I run, I'll probably make it. Casting one last look at the hallway, I hurry to the door and flip the deadbolt.

"I asked you to wait."

I whip my head around. Nick's dressed, dark hair damp and brushed away from his forehead, jaw as tight as his shoulders. I shrug. "I figured you'd want some time alone. Since you're in such a pissy mood."

A muscle near where his jaw meets his ear throbs. "Sorry." He rakes a hand through his hair. "Sorry," he repeats. "You did a decent job of covering your tracks, and I should have figured you'd know how to do that." His body is still rigid with tension, so I nod and turn the knob.

"Cass."

Cinnamon tickles my nose as he steps in close. He smells so damn good. "What?" I whisper.

A hand on my shoulder, and he nudges me around. "You going to be okay?"

I hesitate and give him the truth, shaking my head. "The last thing I want is to cause Mom pain. But I can't—" The ache in my throat makes it hard to talk. "I can't keep fighting with Turner about this. It's never going to get better."

He sighs and tips up my chin with his finger. "For what it's worth, I think you're doing the right thing. I need to put on some shoes, and then I'll drive you."

He follows me out and down the stairs, stopping me before I can push through to the lobby. "This way." He jogs down the next flight of stairs and opens the door at the bottom.

The small parking garage is poorly lit, and he clasps my elbow, telling me without words to stay close, something I would have done anyway, considering what happened in the last parking garage we were in.

No one jumps out, no guns fire, and he unlocks a boring sedan. The whole moment is anticlimactic, and we drive out of the garage without fanfare.

Aside from asking me for the address for Mom's firm, he doesn't speak. Neither do I because, with each revolution of the tires, I'm closer to telling my mom I've fought with Turner for the last time. Although I wouldn't call it fighting. Fighting would mean there's some give and take, and all Turner does is decree with absolute certainty, and his word is law.

Traffic is backed up, as always. It gives me a chance to figure out what to say and how to say it. It also gives me more time to work myself into a state of anxiety and sadness.

I love my parents. I don't want to break them apart, force them to take sides, but that's exactly what I'm doing.

Nick finds a parking spot a few blocks away from Mom's office. We sit, silent as stone guardians, staring out the window as the world passes by.

"You ready?"

His voice is unnaturally loud. My throat's too tight for words. I shake my head. "I'm about to make my mother pick a side. No more family dinners. No holidays, no birthdays." Unless Turner changed his mind, which he wouldn't because he was Turner and changing his mind went against everything he stood for, I would never set foot in my childhood home again. My interactions with Mom would be relegated to meetings like these, fit in around busy schedules. And that was only for as long as I remained in LA. If I moved after college, I'd see even less of her.

I always knew that was a strong possibility. I just assumed if my mom came to visit, so would my dad.

Strong, warm fingers lace through mine. Startled, I stare at our entwined hands before lifting my head.

His lips quirk in a small smile. "You look like you need it."

I did. I do. The simple gesture centers me, and I squeeze his hand once before letting go to get out of the car. He surprises me again when he takes my hand as we walk toward my mom's office.

He holds it tight the entire way while we wait at intersections, while we dodge other pedestrians. He uses it to pull me closer as we wedge ourselves into the elevator with people returning from lunch.

It's perfect, and it's too much. This is why I have my rule. To protect myself from sweet gestures that make me long for more.

We step out of the elevator, and I tug my hand free. "Thank you," I say quietly. "We'll probably just end up ordering sandwiches or something. Could you give me a few minutes alone with my mom?" This could get ugly, at least on my end, and I already feel vulnerable. Having him there as a witness would only make it worse.

He leans against the wall next to the elevator and jerks his head toward the door, expression shuttered. It's as if the gentle, kind man he was a minute ago never existed.

The firm's long-time receptionist, Mrs. Davis, greets me with a smile and a wave, answering the phone at the same time. My own smile falls away the second I pass, nerves clumping in my stomach.

"Hi, dear." Mom hurries around her desk and wraps me in a hug, and I bury my face against her shoulder, wishing I was five again, and all it took to make me feel better was a hug, a kiss, and a couple cookies.

"Hi, Mom." The clamp on my throat has me choking on the words. Swallowing is damn near impossible. "Um, could we talk for a minute? Before lunch?" I doubt I can stomach anything, anyway.

"What's wrong?" The lines on her forehead deepen with her frown, and we sit in the visitor chairs in front of her desk.

It's medicine. Swallow it in one gulp. "It's Dad. You know we've been fighting." It's not a question; she's seen the tension between us whenever I come home. "He wants something different for me and—" God, this is hard. Harder than it should be. "I can't do it," I say, my voice cracking.

"And he's so stubborn. You know when you tell him 'no,' that's it. He cuts you off. I'm sorry."

She shuts her eyes and rubs her hands over her face. "No, I'm sorry, Cassidy. I should have tried harder to stop him." She drops her hands, sorrow shadowing her eyes.

She should have tried harder to stop him. I'm hearing things. "What?"

The smile on her lips is a mockery of the expression. "I know what your father allegedly does. And I know he trained you to do the same."

I can't feel my lips. "You knew."

Her hands flutter, a useless movement that's completely out of place. "We argued constantly when you were younger. Your father said it was what you wanted, and up until you took your first job, he said it was just training. Harmless. You were a lot happier, and you were spending more time with him, so I figured everything worked out for the best."

My own mother let me down. She failed me. "*Why*? Why didn't you stop him?" I would have lost my dad then, but at least now I wouldn't be constantly fighting the shadows waiting to seep in.

"I did," she argues. "I filed for divorce. We were in the first stages of negotiations when you started…perking up. I knew how upset you'd been that he wasn't being much of a father to you. Around the time you were sixteen, things seemed to be a lot better between you two. If I made a mistake, it was assuming he'd come to terms with having a child who wouldn't carry on the family tradition."

I made my first hit when I was sixteen. Cyanide poisoning.

Everything is far away. Mom peers at me, waiting for a response. I don't have one for her. The woman I thought was strong and capable and fierce is nothing but a coward.

My heart shatters under the strain, the shards sticking into my soul and leaving it bleeding. I stand. "I'm your *child*. You could have talked to *me*. If I was old enough to do what Dad does, I was old enough to listen to reason, and you were supposed to be that voice of reason." The door isn't nearly close enough. Each step is like wading through concrete.

"Cassidy. Dear. Please let me explain." There are tears in my mother's voice. Strange, but it's the thing I need to shut down my emotions. Turner's training is a blessing, holding me together, holding back the pain and the chaos. If taking lives hasn't broken me, losing both my parents won't, either.

I glance over my shoulder. "We're done."

Her protests go in one ear and out the other as I stride out of her office and down the hall to the reception area. Nick's in the same spot by the elevator, leaning against the wall, and he straightens when he sees me. I walk past him and push open the door to the stairwell.

Mom knew all along. She knows what Turner does, knows what he's done to me, never mind I asked for it. She didn't try hard enough, didn't fight hard enough, and there's no reason why that will ever make me understand. She's my *mother*. She fights for me when I can't fight for myself. It's what parents *do*. And she didn't. She chose my father over me.

Shut it down. Lock it away. Don't think about it.

The sunlight's blinding, and it takes me a minute to reorient myself. We cover the distance to the car in half the time it took us to get to the office, and he's easing the car away from the curb within minutes.

My therapy bills are going to be outrageous.

We get caught in another snarl of traffic, the drive stretching on forever, the silence heavy with unasked questions. The moment Nick puts the car in park, ensconced in the underground parking garage, I'm out of the car and heading for the entrance. I need the ocean. Even in the cheery light of day, I need its constancy.

It takes a while to find a deserted patch of beach away from late season tourists and locals walking their dogs and toddlers. The waves roll in and draw back, in and out, in and out, always changing, always staying the same.

I burrow down, wiggling my butt into the sand, staring hard at the glinting water, waiting for it to work its magic. Waiting for those soothing tendrils to twine themselves around me.

Instead I get Nick plopping down next to me, handing me a pair of sunglasses. I slip them on.

"I take it things didn't go well."

"Shhh. This is the part where we don't talk." C'mon, waves. Do your thing. Break down the other Cass and replace her. His hand slides up my back, cups my nape.

"Nick." The warning in my voice is a bright red flag.

He ignores it. Tugs me closer.

I jerk backward. "Stop."

He turns my face toward him. "If I'm reading subtext correctly, you told your father you weren't going to be taking any more jobs yesterday. Since you didn't stay for lunch with your mother, I'm guessing shit didn't go well there, either. My sisters are tough, and if this happened to any one of them? They'd be wailing banshees right now." His hand slides along my jaw. "You don't need permission to fall apart, Cass," he says softly, his words almost lost to the crash of the ocean. "It just happens."

I don't have that luxury, but the need for it, to collapse, to crumble, to become a violent, whirling mess, vibrates through me, setting off alarms and bells and tripwires, cracks fissuring and spreading, creating canyons. "I'll be fine," I say, the first sob rising and falling in my chest, dying before it can be released.

I scoot away, wishing the waves would consume me whole.

Chapter 9

The names on the screen blur together. I blink, and they separate. "I think if I stare at this monitor much longer I'll go blind."

Nick sits back in his chair. "Probably ought to eat something, anyway."

The thought of food makes my stomach clench in protest. I haven't eaten a thing all day. I should be starving.

Nick spent hours compiling a list of possible suspects, rivals in business, legal and otherwise, people he slighted or maybe felt they were slighted. The names mean nothing to me, but staring at them gives me something else to focus on. I yank the tie out of my hair and reorder my ponytail. "Can we go back to my apartment tonight?" Studying would be a better use of my time.

"No."

"I need my textbooks. I'm not talking about staying."

His mouth stays shut, his eyes on the list. "I feel like Mexican," he says at last.

Mexican?

"El Dorado. You know what you want?"

El Dorado's a restaurant a few blocks from my apartment. Denise and I eat there probably every other week, always ordering the same thing: enchiladas. Their mole sauce is incredible. My stomach perks up at the thought of guaranteed tasty food. "Chicken enchiladas with mole sauce."

He reaches for the phone sitting on the desk to call in the to-go order. Crap. To-go order. We can't sit around in a restaurant enjoying our meal. The targets are still on our backs. Being out in public is an unnecessary danger, but I have to get to class. I'll go crazy otherwise. The normality of it is one of my last tethers. I've given up too much already.

I gnaw on my upper lip, Nick oblivious as he mutters to himself and scrolls up and down the list. "Nick?"

"Hmm?"

"My first class is at ten tomorrow."

"No."

"No what?"

He shoots me a look as he pushes away from the desk. "Don't give me that shit."

I draw up my knees, heels resting on the seat of the chair, arms tight around my legs. He's more likely to let me go if I play nice. "I have an exam on Friday. I can skip tomorrow." I lace my fingers together, bone on bone.

"Cass."

"Please," I whisper, hoping he won't hear the wobble in my voice. I'm teetering on the edge, grasping at threads so slim they pass right through my hands. "I need this. I need *something*." The last shred of my carefully constructed life. It's all that's holding up my faltering house.

His scrutiny is painful, burning through my skin to scorch the bones below. In this moment, I am the girl he says I am, one wrong move away from being laid out and flayed until I've got nothing left to bleed.

When his head bobs up and down, I almost burst into tears. I swallow hard. "I'll need my textbooks. My notes. I'm not quite ready for it. I've got another paper due Monday, so I'll either need to borrow one of your computers or bring mine back." I'll e-mail my profs. Make excuses. It's only for a few more days. It has to be.

He stands. "Food'll be ready soon."

* * * *

The place is a mess. Furniture overturned, books and papers mixing with plates and pots. A quick search shows nothing is missing. My laptop is on my desk where I left it. I gather up my books and computer and fit them in my bag while Nick rights the couch.

I flop down. "I can't decide if whoever did this is supremely stupid or very dedicated."

He hands me my take-out carton. "Nothing's missing?"

"Nope." My appetite's returned, though, and my stomach growls in anticipation. Delicious, delicious mole sauce, all for me. I slide off the couch and sit cross-legged on the floor, then set the carton on the coffee table,. "So explain the list to me."

He sets his own carton on the table and settles in. "It's everyone I can remember the family has crossed paths with business-wise."

"That's a really long list," I say around a mouthful of enchilada. "Seriously. Can't you narrow it down? Who did you piss off a few years ago?"

Sauce clings to his bottom lip, and he licks it up with a quick swipe of his tongue. "A few years ago? Why not recently?"

"Huh?" Tearing my gaze from his mouth, I meet his eyes, find there's no smirk in them. Only curiosity. "If someone in your organization crosses you, do you always take care of it immediately, or do you sit back and wait to see if it happens again?"

"Usually immediately. On occasion it's smarter to wait."

I swallow a bite of enchilada. "People who hire an assassin to do their dirty work for them typically wait a while. It takes planning and finesse. Revenge is a dish best served cold and all that. You're looking for someone who won't do it themselves and likely crossed your path at least a year ago." I uncap my bottle of water and drink. "Were there any of your own family members on that list?"

His face goes blank and smooth as a wall. "My family has given me no reason not to trust them. We make an effort to play to everyone's skills and give them plenty of opportunity to prove themselves. Having me killed is counter-productive. Moreover, any grievance that would cause someone to want me dead would be handled within the family, not farmed out to a hired hit."

"It's also incredibly naive and trusting to believe none of them would wish you harm. You've probably done things not everyone agreed with one hundred percent. And now that I think about it, they'd be *more* likely to get someone else to make the hit. It puts distance between them and the act, making it harder to trace it to them. That is, of course, assuming they're smart enough to cover their tracks." There's been more than one story in the news in the past few months of regular people paying good money to have someone else knocked off.

He narrows his eyes. "There's something wrong about you saying that. Very calm and matter of fact."

I shrug. "It's matter of fact for a reason. I may have told Turner to suck it, but he did train me to do this. I know the mindset. I may not have the experience he does or the depth of knowledge, but I know who hires out for something like this, what jobs would throw up warning signs. He drilled it into my head. Frankly, if you want to know who hired me, who those men were, you're going to need to figure out who in your past wants you dead badly enough to send backup along just to make sure the job gets done."

He points to my enchilada. "You sharing?"

I cover the container with my hands. "You had your chance. You should have ordered the mole sauce yourself." He opted for shredded pork with traditional enchilada sauce.

"That was before you started whimpering like the enchilada was fucking you hard...and you liked it."

I do *not* make sex noises when I eat. The tips of my ears burn, and he grins. "One bite," he cajoles, inching over.

Not fair. So not fair, not when he's invading my space, all sexy and slick talking, his lips close enough to bite. Hands shaking, I cut off a piece and spear it with the plastic fork, swirling it in the mole sauce before holding it out for him to take.

He doesn't.

He closes his lips around it instead, and my heart explodes. I tug the fork free of his lips, fast enough the prongs probably scrape across the roof of his mouth, and scoot away until I'm on the opposite side of the table. "Your family?" I concentrate on cutting up the rest of my enchilada, body vibrating with sudden tension.

When he doesn't answer, I glance up. His hands are fisted on the table, jaw tight. The hunger in his eyes stuns me. It's desire and anger and madness, swirling together and coating his features, thick and sticky.

"You lied," I whisper. Because what's on his face is too real to be faked. Too tangible.

He snaps the plastic knife in half. "I told you the truth the other night. I don't mess around with girls."

The last sticks propping up the remains of my pride crack and collapse. He doesn't mess around with girls, yet he sees fit to flirt with me. Taunt me. If I don't break this cycle before it starts, I'll continue throwing myself at him, rejection be damned. "I see." Monotone. I'm as neutral as Switzerland, as barren inside as a desert. With quick, efficient movements, I pack up the rest of my food and carry it into the kitchen. "I'd like you to leave."

"Your place hasn't been cleared by the police, and we haven't figured out who those men are."

"You're under no obligation to protect me. I don't need it." Nor did I need his surprising wordless confession and the verbal arrows that came with it. Any other day, I might have been able to handle it. Today? Not so much.

"The men are after you," I say quietly. "We've been operating under the assumption that they saw me with you and, for some reason, would come for me as well. I can't see it. I have nothing to offer. By now they've found I'm just a college student."

He unfolds himself and gets to his feet. "They broke into your apartment."

"That's *if* it was them. If it was, they likely assumed you were staying here. Looking for you, not me." Step, step, step. The counter's the only thing separating us. "The rule still stands."

"I really fucking hate your rule." But he doesn't move any closer.

"Yeah, well, you don't have to live with it anymore. Go home, Nick. No one's coming after me."

I edge past him and pick up my messenger bag to carry it back to my bedroom. It's as bad as the living room, sheets and blankets tangled and lumped together, clothing littering the floor. I dump the bag on the floor and get to work, stripping aside the sheets to wash, picking up clothes, throwing pillows on the bed.

"You can stay with me until the police clear your apartment."

Snorting, I continue my clean-up efforts. "Thanks, but no thanks." I drop to my knees to retrieve more clothes from under the bed. "Figure out who in your family you can trust. You're better off asking one of them for help, anyway. They've got all the information on who you've done business with." My knife is missing. I'd hoped the long, wicked blade was hidden in the mess, but with everything picked up from the floor, the bed stripped bare, it's not anywhere.

I crawl out from under the bed and brush my hair away from my face. "If you could bring my clothes back tomorrow, I'd appreciate it."

He rocks on his feet, hands in his pockets. "I don't feel comfortable leaving you here."

I smile in spite of myself. "That's probably the big brother in you talking. Do I need to remind you I almost sliced through your throat the other night?" He's downsized the bandage on his neck. "How's your arm?"

"How's your leg?"

Tight and itchy. My ankle's mostly back to normal, though. "Fine."

The air between us grows heavy and tense, the weight of it threatening to crush the air from my lungs. Once, just once, I want to know what it's like to kiss him on my own terms. To memorize the taste and feel of him, to know his response isn't a calculated act.

Idle thoughts are bad for you. Idle thoughts lead to bodies in motion. The distance between us shrinks, his gaze locked with mine. I lay a hand on his chest, heart stuttering. The line of his jaw is as hard as I imagined, rough with stubble. It's perfect. Warm and real and perfect.

He clasps my wrist and pulls it away, lifting it to inspect the bruising. It's almost gone. "Lock the door behind me." He doesn't release me.

I lick my lips, my gaze flitting from his eyes to his mouth and back again. "You have issues with my age."

He lifts a brow. "I'm thirty-two. Yeah, I've got issues with your age. I've got issues with your past choice of employment too."

"I don't." And I rise on my toes and press my mouth to his.

His lips give under mine, firming, answering my unspoken question— yes, he wants me. His head and body are in disagreement, and it doesn't take much for his body to overrule the brain. I control this, control this kiss, and I want slow and thorough and hot, very hot. I want tongue and teeth and low moans, hands skimming and roaming, the feel of his body against mine.

I get it. He gives it to me, gives it all, parts his lips and allows me entry, and I want to devour him. This is all I'll get because there's nothing left to hold us together. Just his mouth on mine, as eager as I am, his hand wrapped around my ponytail, holding my head at such an angle he can take over. He shifts us so I'm whimpering and clawing at him, shifts so I'm giving him everything he's asking for, and he's doing it slowly, tauntingly, drawing it out. I want his mouth on my skin, my jaw, my neck, lower, much, much lower, because if I had any doubts before, they're gone now. Sex with Nick would be the most mind-blowing experience I'd ever have.

Except he stops. Leaves it at lips on lips. It's how it should be, the two of us panting, propping each other up. I can take this one perfect moment and tuck it away for safekeeping. Anything more will lead to regret, and regret has a taint you can't get rid of.

I don't want my last view of him to be his retreating back. I duck into my closet for clean sheets. A minute later I hear the front door open and shut.

Now I can fall apart, mourn the loss of my parents. It's better this way. Free of the need to please my father, to hide from my mother, I can finally be whoever I want.

I finish in the bedroom and wander out to the living room. The deadbolt is still in good shape, and it locks fine. I flip it, push in the button lock, and drag over a chair and prop it under the knob for good measure. It won't do jack to keep someone out, but it might make enough noise to alert me. The pots and pans and plates go back in their places, the broken pieces in the trash, and I move on to Denise's bedroom. I strip aside her sheets and throw them in the wash with mine, then pick up her clothes and straighten the books and papers strewn across the room.

By the time I've run out of things to clean, my body's stopped throbbing with a need I can't indulge. I grab a kitchen knife, sharpen it, and slip it under my pillow. Old habits and all that shit.

I stare at the ceiling as the hours pass, hoping I haven't made a mistake.

Chapter 10

I don't make it to class the next morning. I drag myself out of bed around eight, go for a run, shower and eat, and pack up my bag for a day spent on campus before I remember Nick stole my car.

I call my insurance company and report it. I figure it'll take maybe a half an hour, tops, and I might still be able to make my other morning class.

Two hours later, I'm standing in the garage with one of the representatives from the insurance company, attempting to explain how someone could get into an underground locked garage and hotwire a Honda unnoticed. Fortunately, the property manager comes through—the security cameras aren't actually turned on.

Since I've wasted the morning, I might as well finish it off. I call the number for the police officer Denise gave me.

He answers on the third ring. "Officer Gregory."

"This is Cass Turner. I'm calling about the break-in at my apartment?"

"You're difficult to get ahold of, Ms. Turner."

I squirm a little, even though he can't see me. He tried to call me yesterday. I'd been too busy dealing with my personal version of hell to answer the phone. "I hope you got everything you needed from Denise."

"She didn't report anything as missing. I'd like to meet with you as well, take your statement."

Crap. I glance around the neat and tidy living room. "That's fine. I've been staying out in Woodland Hills with my parents. It'll take me a little while to get there." The lie rolls off my tongue with practiced ease, my brain working overtime to come up with a solution.

The officer agrees to meet me in two hours, and I set about undoing some of what I'd cleaned up the night before. I shut the door to Denise's room, upend the couch and coffee table, and stand in the doorway to my bedroom, studying the space. Police officers are trained observers, and I have no way of knowing whether this guy is one of the super observant ones who'll notice every detail, down to the placement of a wayward sock. Finally, I pull the sheets and blankets free of the bed, throw some clothes around, scatter papers on the floor, and dig my laptop out of my bag and put it on my desk.

In the kitchen, I get out a few of the dishes and pans and dig the pieces of broken porcelain out of the trash. It's less than perfect. It'll have to do.

I grab my wallet and head out, carefully replacing the yellow tape across the door. A new deadbolt will help both Denise and I feel better, though I doubt we'll be staying in the building much longer. I've seen the way Charlie looks at her. If he hasn't thought about asking her to move in with him yet, he will be soon.

I hope he does. He makes her happy, and I like the two of them together.

Purchasing the deadbolt takes longer than I thought it would, and I hurry back, digging my phone out when it starts buzzing against my hip. "Hello?"

"Ms. Turner, it's Officer Gregory. Just wanted to let you know I'm running behind. I should be there in twenty minutes."

Excellent. More time to mess up my apartment. "That's fine."

I take the stairs, the paper bag containing the deadbolt clutched in my hand. I unhook the tape, open the door, and survey my little rental kingdom. Were the cushions from the couch lying on the floor? Or were they jumbled up on the couch?

The door clicks softly, and I freeze. "I thought—"

A rough hand slaps over my mouth, a blade biting into my neck, hot breath on my ear. "Not so tricky to find." The voice is low and as rough as the hand, dull, without inflection.

Ice slicks over my skin as my brain shuts out the extraneous noise, focuses on the essential information. He's taller than me and quiet, so he's got some skill. His arm feels strong, as does his chest. First step is to get away from the blade. He's already made his first mistake; he didn't slit my throat immediately. Give him enough time, he'll make more. Ignoring the steadily growing pressure of the blade on my skin, I swing the hand holding the bag with the deadbolt in an arc toward the side of his head. It's not heavy enough to do any damage, and I'll likely miss, but the idea is to distract my assailant enough that he moves the knife.

It connects with something solid, and he grunts, the knife moving a precious few millimeters. I grab his wrist and stomp on his instep, pushing out and twisting forward.

If I maintain my hold, I risk him trapping me again. If I let him go, he'll just come after me.

Both options suck. I choose the second one, dart to the other side of the room, and immediately realize my mistake. All the sharp implements are behind him. My only defenses are my own hands.

Except one. The knife I slept with under my pillow last night. All I have to do is get into my bedroom somehow.

I've taken self-defense classes, but Turner didn't spend a lot of time on hand to hand combat, instructing me instead to cut my losses and get away. His way of proving he does care, I guess. At any rate, assassins aren't meant to engage their targets. They just take them out, quick, clean, simple. Interaction leads to too many questions and too many eyes looking in the wrong place.

Blood trickles from the cut on my throat as we stare at each other. He looks remarkably similar to the man I shot the other day. Dark hair, dark eyes, and supremely pissed off.

The flight instinct's growing stronger with every passing second. Rather than continue our Mexican standoff, I race for my bedroom then yank the knife from under the pillow as he stalks into the room. He blocks the door and smirks. I'm trapped, and he knows it.

I do the first thing that comes to mind—I throw a pillow at him. It hits him square in the face, and I throw another one. Two more pillows later, I'm out of missiles and he's growling and ready to charge.

He lunges forward as I crouch to scoop up a shoe to throw at him, his blade slicing along my upper arm. Pain blooms and spreads, and I fumble my grip on my knife. My pathetic kitchen knife. He whips his arm back to strike again, hummingbird quick, and I stab upward, my knife lodging in that weird space where leg meets torso.

It won't come out.

I'm tugging while he stumbles back a step, and I finally free the knife. Blood seeps through his pants, the dark stain spreading across his groin. It looks like he's pissed himself, and I've got the hysterical urge to giggle. If I managed to hit the artery, he'll bleed out in a minute or less. That's a mighty big *if.*

It's not a chance I can take.

Fingers flexing on the handle of his knife, he feints left, and like an idiot, I fall for it, his blade landing on my hip. The sharp edge slices through my jeans like butter and into my skin, leaving behind a searing line of heat. I jab toward his stomach, tearing the material of his shirt and nicking his side.

He recovers first, caging me against the wall, knife digging into my neck. But he's made another mistake.

He left my arms free.

As his knife slices my skin, I ram mine into his gut, pushing him away at the same time, hoping the maneuver will work.

It won't kill him. Not right away. Stomach wounds bleed slowly, giving the victim a chance to get to safety and seek medical attention. I either need to retrieve my knife again, or disarm him and finish the job.

Exhaustion drags me down, makes me weak, makes me want to walk away. Blood clings to the handle, my fingers slipping a little as I pull it free. His knife sneaks in under my arm, the tip digging into my stomach, but there's no power behind it. It gives me the time I need to plunge my knife into his neck, hot blood now flowing unabated.

Over. Finally over. He trips backward, slides down the side of the bed, and lands on his ass, tipping to the right in a drunken slouch.

I take off my bloody shirt, press it to the wound on my throat, and make my way to the bathroom. Blood swirls down the drain as I wash my hands, and I dampen my shirt to wipe away the worst of the mess. I hope we have butterfly bandages. The second cut on my neck is bleeding more than I'm comfortable with.

There is a God, and He provided butterfly bandages.

My fingers are cold on my skin, trembling slightly when I try to get the bandages to stick. I cover it with a thin strip of gauze and deal with the rest of my cuts. The one on my arm is by far the worst, blood oozing from the wound. I remove my jeans and deal with the cut on my hip, checking my bullet graze for good measure. The skin's split in some places, bleeding anew, and I plaster over it with gauze until I have time to deal with it.

I'm running out of time.

I snatch up my pants and fish my phone out of my pocket. Ten minutes have passed since Officer Gregory called. Which means if I'm lucky, I've got another ten minutes to get the hell out of here.

I gather up my bloody clothes and dash back to my bedroom, ignoring the flat, unseeing eyes of my attacker. I grab a bag from my closet, toss the clothes inside, and hunt through the mess on my floor for something to wear. I need a scarf, a turtleneck, something to cover the bandage on my neck. A violently pink floral thing catches my eye. Denise tries, she really does, but the girl needs help if she thinks bright pink flowers will look good on me. I slip on a black long -sleeve shirt, grimacing as the fabric snags on the tape holding the gauze in place. I drag on a pair of jeans, then wrap the scarf around my neck, taking precious seconds to adjust it to ensure it covers the bandage.

I ignore my increasing jitters and focus on the next steps. My fingerprints are all over the knife. I wipe off the handle, smearing blood, and stow it in my bag. His is next, and I pry his knife from his hand. I wrap the blade in the shirt I used to wipe off my kitchen knife and stow it in the bag. Another couple of changes of clothes, an extra pair of shoes... I glance around the room, unable to shake the feeling I'm forgetting something. Something tells me I'll never see this place again.

At the last second, I snap a picture of the dead guy's face, then shut off my phone and stuff it into my bag. I snag a couple of bobby pins from the bathroom and hurry to the door.

No one's in the hallway. I don't bother with the tape this time, pinning my hair into a messy topknot on my way to the stairs, my bag heavy on my shoulder. But the hair pinning is essential—people automatically register hair length, and an easy way to fool them is to put it in a bun.

My legs are wobbly as I reach the bottom of the stairs. I have very little cash in my wallet. Using my debit card to make a withdrawal is out of the question. I need water, sugar, and a place to hide.

The side entrance dumps me into a shady alley, and I walk to the back of the building. There's a bus stop a few blocks away. I don't know where the bus goes, but it'll get me out of here. The distant sound of sirens fills me with panic and quickens my step.

A bus is rolling down the street as I approach the stop. Perfect timing, too, because those sirens are closer. I dip my head, dig out some change, and climb on to the bus, relieved to have a place to sit for a while. A place to figure out where I go from here.

An hour later, I've changed buses twice, downed a bottle of orange juice, and I'm no closer to a solution. I can't drag Denise into this or any of my other friends. My parents are out. A motel will require use of a credit card. I need to get some place where I can tend to my wounds, since I'm pretty sure the one on my arm hasn't stopped bleeding.

There's one place left.

It takes another hour, and by the end, I'm worn out and painfully aware of the aches popping out in my body with every passing second. He might not be home. He might not let me in. But this place, this condo no one knows about, is the only refuge I can think of.

My hands are shaking so hard my finger slips off the buzzer several times before I manage to press it in. Sweat rolls down my spine. My head is pounding. And no one answers the buzzer.

I prop my head on the front door, willing my mind to clear, to think. I push the button again.

Nothing. Just seagulls and the distant rush of the ocean.

"Hello?"

The sudden greeting jolts me upright. My hands are fat and clumsy as I fumble with the intercom. "It's Cass."

More silence.

There's a clicking and a metallic buzz as the front door is released, and I walk into the lobby and sway in front of the elevator, poking the button repeatedly in an effort to make it come faster.

It takes its damn sweet time, the doors sliding open with an agonizing slowness, mocking me. The hallway mocks me, too, stretching on forever, the distance between me and Nick's door never growing shorter.

Each rap of my knuckles on his front door has pain singing up my arm, and I clutch the doorframe so I won't fall over. The sight of him when he opens the door is the most beautiful thing ever. His brows rise in question, the look on his face one of mild interest.

Please let me in. I'll beg if I have to. I'm not too proud to do it. I try to smile and fail, searching for the words that will move him out of the way and allow me entry. The truth. I can tell him the truth.

"I didn't know where else to go."

Chapter 11

I'm going to fall over. My legs can't hold me up any longer. "Nick? I'm sorry, but I really need to sit down. Can I please come in? Just for a minute?" The edges of my vision are fuzzy with fatigue. I let go of the door and lurch forward, shooting out a hand to grab the frame again. The hollow of my throat is damp, from sweat, from blood, I don't know.

He narrows his eyes, peering at my neck. "What the fuck—" He pulls the scarf away. "You're bleeding."

So that's blood then. Good to know.

"Jesus, Cass. How long have you been walking around like that?"

"A few hours. I caught a bus. Then another bus. I didn't know where else to go." His hold on my arms is all that's keeping me upright, my duffle bag hanging off my shoulder. I shrug, and it falls, catching on his hand. He drops it and leads me over to the couch, his hand pressing on the wound on my hip. I bite the inside of my cheek to stifle the hiss of pain. "Is it bleeding badly?"

He helps me onto the couch. "Lie on your back." He reaches up and pulls the pins from my hair himself, then peels away the tape and gauze to inspect the wound. "Not too much. Shit job you did here."

"Gee, thanks."

"One sec." He disappears, returning a minute later carrying a red plastic tackle box.

"What the hell is that?"

He opens it and pulls out gauze, tape, antiseptic wipes, a pre-packaged syringe, and a few other things, but I stopped paying attention after the syringe. "What's the syringe for?"

He holds up a packet containing a needle.

I struggle to sit up, to get away from him. "Oh, no. No no no no no. You are not coming anywhere near me with that."

He drops the needle into the box and reaches for me. "If the cut on your neck is deep enough, it'll need stitches. Either I do it, or we go to the emergency room."

Hospitals have security. Hospitals ask questions. I scoot down, my gaze trained on the ceiling as he snaps on a pair of latex gloves. The gentle touch of his fingers calms me further as he cleans the wound. "Verdict? Stitches or no?" The answer had better be no.

"Don't think so." My skin stretches and pulls as he pinches the edges together. "Hold still."

Heart thudding loud enough he has to hear it, I do what he asks, seconds slipping into minutes while he works. "There's more," I say when he's smoothed gauze over my throat.

One side of his mouth tips up. "Of course there is." He sits back on his heels. "You need help?"

I might be able to handle the ones on my legs, but I doubt I did a good job on my arm. It's too high up for me to see well. "One on my stomach, one near my shoulder. There's another on my hip, and the bullet graze reopened."

A line appears between his brows before he shuts his eyes and mutters something unintelligible. When they open, they're dark with worry and anger. "How close to your shoulder?"

I arch my back and pull up my shirt, wriggling slightly to get it over my head, careful to avoid his eyes. I roll onto my side so the wound is visible. He swears softly and pulls off the bandage. "Still bleeding." He goes through the routine of cleaning the wound and inspecting it. "Cass?"

I'm not going to like this. "What?"

"Needs stitches."

"No."

"It's too deep—"

"No. Use the butterfly bandages."

"The one on your throat—"

"Didn't need them. Neither does this one."

He strips off the gloves and nudges me onto my back. "The one on your throat isn't as deep but probably should be looked at by a medical professional anyway. The cuts on your arm and hip *will* require stitches. You don't get them, they won't heal right, and you run a higher risk of infection." His eyes never leave mine. "Do you trust me?"

"No." However much I want to, I don't. Trusting someone without knowing them leads to stupid decisions.

The only sign he's pissed is a muscle jumping in his jaw. "Too bad. I can stitch up the cut on your arm and the one on your hip. If the cut on your neck needs stiches, it'll require more skill. You have two options. You can leave the one on your throat, risk infection and a nasty scar, and I'll take care of the others. Or you can trust me, and I'll take you to someone who will do a better job than I can."

"No hospitals."

He smooths the hair away from my forehead. "Not a hospital."

Vain as it sounds, I don't relish the idea of a thick, ugly scar on my throat. I'll likely have one anyway, but if it can be minimized...

"Okay," I whisper.

He redoes the patch job on my arm and helps me into a shirt. In a moment of perfect symmetry, he bands his arm around my waist and helps me out of the condo and into the elevator, mimicking our long, labored walk the day we met.

I fall asleep. I don't mean to, but fatigue and hunger and my horrible aching body demands it, and I wake with a kink in my neck. I glance at the clock on the dash. We've only been gone fifteen minutes. "Where are we?"

Nick eases the car to a stop at the curb. The street outside is a residential one, the dying evening sun casting long shadows. A couple of kids are playing what looks like a mean game of tag a few houses over, running from the yard to the middle of the street and back again.

"Hermosa Beach." He gets out of the car and walks around the hood to the passenger side. Cool air rushes over me as he pulls open the door. His gaze lands on my arm, the line reappearing between his brows. "Shit."

Without warning, he unclicks my seatbelt and gathers me up, carrying me from the car. "Nick. Put me down." My protests sound weak, even to my ears. Damp warmth covers the skin below my wound.

He ignores me, stalking up the front walk and around the side of the house. The door rattles in the frame as he kicks it in lieu of pounding on it with a fist.

The man who opens it is dark haired and dark eyed like Nick. That's where the similarities end. He's shorter, slimmer, and kind of forgettable looking. He's also glaring up at Nick. "Try knocking next time."

"Hands full. You ready?"

The other guy catches sight of the blood soaking through my shirt, and he steps aside. "You sure it didn't nick a vein?"

"No."

He leads us through the house, down a flight of stairs, and into a brightly lit room. It's mostly white. In fact, it looks like a hospital room. Glass encloses the rear half, a table, and a metal tray covered in one of those blue papery things sitting under a big, round light. An IV stand is next to one end, a bag of clear liquid already hanging from it. There's other equipment, but I'm not given a chance to examine it.

Nick sits me on a counter and maneuvers my shirt over my head, then plants his hands on either side of my hips, his dark eyes intense. "You're going to be fine." Quiet words, meant to soothe.

They don't. Being around all this sterility is nerve-racking. I'm about to let someone I've never met near me with a needle. Needles rank higher on my list of nightmare objects than spiders.

I fist the front of his shirt. "Don't leave." I don't care how much it sounds like begging. If begging is what it takes, I'll do it.

"You stay, you scrub in." Nick's friend looks over from the sink where he's washing his hands. "Tish will be here in a minute. Wasn't sure if I'd need her for this."

On cue, a short blond woman rushes in. "Anesthesiologist," Nick says. "Hey, are you going to use a local anesthesia?"

"Makes the most sense, unless she's going to be a difficult patient." He shakes water off his hands and snaps on the gloves Tish gives him.

They're going to keep me awake? Oh, hell no.

It's pathetically easy for him to stop me from sliding off the counter. "Cass. Hey. Look at me." For the first time since I showed up at his condo, I do. I really look at him and see worry and fear and anger, one right after the other, darkening his expression. "He can use general anesthesia instead, if you want. Your arm wound hasn't stopped bleeding. He needs to get in there to find out why, and it'll be less traumatizing for you if they put you under. I'll be here," he murmurs. "Let them fix this."

Vulnerable doesn't sit well with me. "I hate needles," I confess.

He grins. "Figured that one out myself, love." He picks me up off the counter and sets me on my feet, hands on my hips to steady me. "I think Tish has one of those embarrassing gowns for you to change into."

I nod, and Tish comes over, a wad of blue in her hand. Nick busies himself washing his hands while Tish helps me into the gown. I manage to get my jeans off on my own, and she walks me into the glassed-in room.

The last thing I see is Nick, his hand clenched around mine as the IV slides in and the drugs rush through my veins.

* * * *

I've swallowed burning coal. My eyelids have been replaced by anvils, but something's prodding me to lift them anyway.

The amount of effort required to open my eyes isn't worth it.

"Cass."

I like that voice. I like it a lot. I still don't want to open my eyes. If the voice could keep talking for a while, I'd be quite happy.

"Cassidy."

Fine. I slit open an eye and immediately shut it again. "Too bright," I whisper.

Click. "Light's off."

I try again, raising a single lid a millimeter. No bright lights. I force my eyes open. "Need sleep." God, I need more sleep. I could sleep forever and still be tired.

Nick's in a chair next to the bed, hair mussed, forearms braced on his thighs. "Need to get out of here first. Simon promised to keep this under the radar, but if someone else calls in, he can't turn them away without raising suspicion."

Simon? Simon must be the doctor. "We can't hide here for a few more hours?"

He shakes his head. "We could. But if you're right, and it's someone in my family who wants me dead, that's not a risk we can take."

He's taking me seriously? Goody. I think. Moving might be a problem. "Can you move the elephant?"

"Elephant?"

"The one sitting on my legs. I'm not sure I can get up."

His laugh brings a goofy smile to my face, or maybe that's just the drugs. Probably the drugs. He slides one hand under my back to help me into a sitting position, and I push back the blankets, sucking down air to fight off the wave of dizziness. I'm still in the hideous blue gown. "Clothes?"

He hands me my jeans, and I stare at them. Somehow I'm supposed to get them on my legs. Hard to do, what with the elephant and all. Plus my fingers have been replaced with shrimp.

In the end, Nick has to help me dress because my limbs are weighed down with sandbags. Tish sticks her head in as I'm putting on my shoes. "Got another call. Tried to delay them so she'd have more time to sleep off the anesthesia, but they're almost here."

"Fuck." Nick grabs my hand, pulls me to my feet, and cages me against his side, his hold like titanium. It's necessary, unfortunately, since I'll likely trip over my own feet if left alone. We follow Tish out of the room and along the darkened hall.

Voices drift down the stairs ahead of the clatter of feet on the hardwood floor overhead. Nick swears again. "That one," Tish whispers, pointing at a closed door to the right. Nick pushes it open and drags me inside. He shuts the door with a soft click as the stampede hits the stairs.

The room is pitch black. Even after my eyes should have adjusted, I can't see. But he's there, bracing me against the wall, chest rising and falling as we listen to the shouts coming from the other end of the hall.

"Nick?"

"Shhh." He cups my head, cradling it to his chest, and I will my heart in my throat back down to my chest.

We're never getting out of here. We're stuck, trapped by the shouts coming from the sterile room. Long minutes pass, the shouts growing in volume, and someone starts wailing. Another set of feet race past our hiding spot. More waiting, more time for panic to coalesce and ball in the pit of my stomach. Nick eases the door open a crack and sticks his head out to check the hall. He slips into the hallway, pulling me with him, and we creep up the stairs.

The adrenaline's doing funny things to my head. I'm dizzy and tired and my hearing's all wonky, my pulse thudding and racing like a greyhound. The distance to the side door we came in is miles long and takes an eternity to cover, but once we're outside we're not in the clear.

We still have to sneak out of the yard.

He pulls me toward the neighbor's house when I try to veer toward the front yard. "Moved the car," he mutters, and I want to cry. My body doesn't want to keep moving. It wants to curl into the fetal position and wait out the rest of the anesthesia.

Step by step, staying to the shadows, my head throbbing in time with my heart, the aches in my body roaring back to life, we skulk like thieves through the neighbor's yard to the next street over, and he picks up the pace, heedless of my stumbles. His car is near the opposite end of the block, and I fall into the passenger seat as he climbs in behind the wheel. "You okay?" he asks.

I nod mutely. I don't have the brainpower to do anything else. Certainly not talk.

The drive to Manhattan Beach passes in a fog. Hunger, thirst, pain, and exhaustion battle for dominance, and I don't know which to give in to. Hunger, maybe. I can satiate hunger and thirst at the same time. Hopefully he hasn't eaten all the food I bought the other day.

Nick's got other ideas, though. Ideas that don't include me eating and drinking and collapsing into bed. As soon as we're behind the closed door of his condo, he rounds on me, all cool and arrogantly demanding. "What," he says, pointing at my throat, "the fuck happened?"

I burst into tears.

Chapter 12

I am not a crier. It never solves anything, and when it's over, I feel awful, my head stuffed up and achy, eyes burning and dry. Worse, I feel weak. Like my soft center is exposed. Everyone has their breaking point, and this moment, with Nick standing in front of me demanding answers to questions I don't want to address, is mine.

"Shit. Cass. Cassidy." He draws me to him, ignoring my feeble attempts to shove him away, and I drop my head onto his chest. The worn cotton of his shirt soaks up my tears. They won't stop. No amount of deep breaths or fisted hands halt the flow, and the strength drains from my body as I give in and accept that it'll be over when it's over.

Hours or days or years later, the flood's subsided to the occasional sniffle and, as expected, my head weighs a ton, I can't breathe, and my entire face feels swollen and hot.

I'm also on the couch, squished up against Nick with my head on his shoulder and my legs across his lap. He moves first, carefully shifting away and getting to his feet, and my head lolls to the side, resting on the back of the couch. I'll be embarrassed in a moment. Promise. Right now, my brain's not engaging.

"Here." He hands me a box of tissues before resuming his previous position, his hand warm on my knee.

I wipe my face and blow my nose—a honking, unattractive sound—and lower my head to his shoulder. "Sorry," I mumble.

"I grew up with sisters. I'm used to it."

Laughing hurts, but I do it anyway, the sound trailing off into a soft moan. "I was attacked in my apartment this morning. I was supposed to be meeting one of the police officers to go over the place, you know, because of the break-in? I went out to buy a new deadbolt to install. When I got back, I went in to see what else I could mess up since I cleaned the place last night. I didn't think about locking the door, and he came up behind me."

He slides his fingers under my chin and tips it up. "He got your neck. How'd that happen?"

I grimace. "He screwed up."

"He screwed up."

"Yeah. He had me solid. He was behind me, knife at my throat, but he hesitated. Said something about being not so tricky to find. When I hit him with the deadbolt, he lost his hold. We fought. It was sloppy, mostly because I didn't know what the hell I was doing and he was pissed. I killed him, and then I left."

He rubs the ball of his thumb over my lower lip. "I thought you'd be able to defend yourself better."

I draw back, his touch unwelcome, mostly because it makes my stomach flip inside out. "I've taken self-defense classes. That's different from actively engaging someone in a knife fight, which I was not trained to do. Some assassins will engage their targets if it's necessary. Turner always structured my training to maximize my skills. Going on the offensive was never one of them."

My stomach rumbles. "You didn't eat everything I bought, did you?" With the crying out of the way, I can get to the eating and drinking portion of the evening before I end it with sleeping for twelve hours straight.

He squeezes my knee. "You bought a lot of food. No, I didn't eat everything." His mouth curves in a wry half smile. "Can't cook worth a damn, either. I can handle eggs. That's about it."

"I can fix something. Don't worry about it." After I wash my face. It feels grubby. I'm grubby all over. I wonder if I can take a shower.

He leans in, nose practically touching mine. "No," he says quietly.

My blood heats, and my hands twitch with the need to touch him. Sweet Jesus, this is the last thing I need. "The rule stands."

"I really fucking hate your rule."

Space. Please, please, *please* give me some space. "You've said that. Has anything changed in the last twenty-four hours? You still have issues with my age and past choice of employment?"

His gaze drops to my mouth. "Yeah," he mutters. He gets up and stalks into the kitchen.

Uncertain if I've dodged a bullet or done myself a disservice, I slide off the couch and head for the bathroom. I wash my face, which is awkward because I'm trying to keep the gauze on my neck dry, brush out my hair, and discover there's dried blood on the ends. Fantastic. I yank it into a ponytail to deal with later and sort through my clothes to find some different pants to change into.

The scent of burning bread greets me as I make my way to the kitchen. Nick's in front of the stove, manning it like it's about to attack and he needs to brace himself. I pop the lever on the toaster and flick the two partially burnt pieces onto a nearby plate. With a lot of butter and jam, they should be palatable.

Hopefully his egg-making skills are better than his toast-making skills.

One look at the frying pan confirms my worst fears. I reach around him and turn down the burner. "Move over."

He scowls, but doesn't argue. The eggs are runny around the edges and bubbling in the middle. I pick up the spatula he was using and push the eggs around in the pan, moving the runny parts toward the middle where most of the heat is.

Less than a minute later, I have a plate of scrambled eggs and burnt toast piled high with raspberry jam, and Nick's scowl has turned into a look of chagrin. I pat his cheek as I walk past. "It's the thought that counts."

I sit with my legs straight out in front of me on the couch, plate balanced on my knees, and fork up egg. I pause before I shove the food into my mouth. "Any progress on your list?"

He sprawls on the other end, beer in hand. "No. It's a fucking long list, and going only by my impressions isn't helping much. I pissed off a lot of people over the years. Don't know which of them are angry enough to want me dead."

Crap. He's going all broody again. As dead tired and miserable as I am, I can't handle sexy, broody Nick, because sexy, broody Nick makes me forget about the stitches on my throat and the blood in my hair.

I give the food on my plate my full attention. The sooner it's gone, the sooner I can escape. "I know I warned you against being too trusting when it came to your family, but maybe one of them can help. Someone with enough knowledge of the deals but wasn't too close to them? Is that even possible?"

His prolonged silence makes me glance up. He's still broody and sexy, but his brow wrinkles as he considers my question. I dive back into my eggs.

"Yeah," he says finally. "Constantine."

Constantine. A very Greek name.

"You don't have a very Greek name." I hunch over the plate, biting into a piece of toast, crumbs falling on the last of the eggs. "I mean, your last name is, but Dominic?"

He snorts and lapses into silence once more. I crunch through one piece of toast, finish my eggs, and eye the second piece.

It disappears, along with the mostly empty plate, and I'm left staring at my lap. Strong hands grab my waist and drag me across the couch that ends with me on Nick's lap and bearing the full brunt of his broody, sexy frown. He traces the edge of the bandage on my neck with the tip of a finger. "It's easy to forget how young you are."

I am not up for having a serious conversation. "Can we save this discussion for another time?"

"You should be partying. Pulling all nighters, going to study groups, freaking out about what you're going to do after graduation," he continues. "Not figuring out the most efficient way to end a man's life."

I cover his mouth with my hand to keep him from saying anything else, and the warmth of his lips on my palm sends tingles up my arm. "One. I *do* do all those things. I stayed up until three in the morning the other night writing that damn paper. I have no idea what I want to do with my life, because hello, liberal arts degree? It's just a really expensive piece of paper. Although sometimes I think I might want to be a teacher. Two. I haven't plotted a man's death in almost a year. You were my first job in eleven months." The date of my last hit is burned on my brain. It's the one that convinced me to reconsider the choices I made, the choices that did nothing to earn me the affection I craved. "Three. You're taking this entirely too seriously. It's just sex. Four. I'm fuckin' drained. Can we please stop this conversation and continue it some time when I haven't been bawling my eyes out and getting stitched up?"

Mouth thinned with displeasure, he slips his arm under my knees and stands. "Hey. Put me down." I've been carried around more today than I've been since I was a toddler. It's embarrassing. He moves down the hall and into the bedroom. I take in the rumpled sheets and bunched pillows. Did he sleep there last night?

Where is he going to sleep tonight?

"Seriously, Nick, you can put me down. I'm capable of walking. I just need to sleep." Well, first I need to wash my hair. I'm not sleeping when I can get dried blood on my pillow.

He releases my legs, letting me slide down his body, and I swear he's done it on purpose to torment us both. Pressed close to him, his hands splayed across my back, one hand wrapped around my ponytail, he holds me a while longer, his gaze intent on my mouth.

My body's out of control. It wants kisses and sleep and to be free of pain. More than kisses, it wants to be fucked. Hard. Hard and long. It wants sweetness and dirty words, and it wants the skilled hands only someone with experience would have. Lots of experience.

Someone like Nick.

I like sex. A lot. I like everything about it—the connection, the exploration, the dizzying highs and the mellow lows.

The flip side, the darker side, where it's boring and too fast and unenjoyable or followed by a "Thanks, babe, I'll call you," I can do without, thank you very much.

I think, if I wasn't so tired, I could talk Nick into fucking my brains out. I also think, given the war his brain is currently waging, it will end in a "Thanks, babe, I'll call you." Not something I want if I'm going to be staying with him for a while.

On cue, my jaw cracks in a huge yawn. I push at his chest. "Go. I need to wash my hair and go to bed."

"Right." He releases me and rubs a hand over his face. "Why don't you just go to bed?"

"There's blood in my hair." I tug the end of my ponytail forward to show him the crusted strands.

"You're limited to sponge baths for a few days. The wound on your neck needs to stay dry."

I slump onto the bed. "Fine. I'll just…bend over the tub or something. Is the showerhead detachable?"

He takes my hand and pulls me to my feet. "C'mon. The sooner you get it washed, the sooner you can sleep."

"Wait. What are you doing?"

The showerhead is, indeed, detachable. He ignores the question and digs out a couple towels from the linen cupboard, then throws them on the floor. "Ass on the towels."

Too worn out to argue, I sit, slouching so my head tips over the rim of the tub with minimal difficulty.

You'd think having a big, strong, sexy as hell man wash my hair would be amazingly romantic, but it's actually pretty weird. We don't talk; Nick seems more concerned with getting my hair free of blood as quickly as possible. Five minutes later, he's rubbing it with a towel, and my swollen eyes are getting heavier by the second. Not being able to sleep off the rest of the anesthesia didn't do me any favors.

He helps me to my feet. Resting a hand at the small of my back, he guides me into the bedroom. I get rid of my jeans and crawl onto the bed. My eyes droop shut as my head hits the pillow.

"Cass?"

With effort, I open one eye. "What?" I mumble.

"What did the guy who assaulted you say again?"

I search my muddled brain, pushing at the edges of sleep. "Something about how I wasn't tricky to find. Oh! I took a picture. It's on my phone."

He stares, then shakes his head. "You took a picture." The bag's on the floor near the door; he must have tossed it there earlier. "You mind?" He jerks his head toward the bag.

If it means I get to sleep, he can do whatever he wants. "Be my guest." I shut my eye and snuggle deeper into the blankets to the sounds of Nick going through my bag. The phone chimes as it powers on.

"*Fuck.*"

Nick's curse is loud enough to jolt me out of twilight sleep. "Now what?"

He shoves the phone under my nose. "He's one of mine."

Chapter 13

I screw my eyes shut. This couldn't have waited until tomorrow? When I was awake and had the energy to deal with it? "That's nice," I mumble. In the back of my brain, it registers that this is a big fucking deal, that someone in his family tried to kill me, and it'll just add to all the issues Nick's currently piling on himself.

But I've been stabbed. I'd really like to go to sleep.

I roll onto my back and open my eyes. "Who is he?"

Nick's pacing the floor now, one end of the bed to the other. "His name is Josef." He pauses, glances over at me. "I've used him on occasion. For deals."

"As in, you use him to ensure you get what you want?"

He shoots me a glare before he resumes pacing. "You got lucky. Extremely lucky. If he's given an order to kill, he follows through, and he's not worried about being subtle. He likes it bloody."

I rub my hands over my face. "I think I just pissed him off. I threw a couple of pillows at him. He didn't seem to like that." I peek through my fingers. "Could you stop with the pacing?"

He does, only to sit on the edge of the bed next to my hip. "Pillows?"

I yawn widely enough to bring tears to my burning eyes, and I shift onto my side, facing him, cuddling deeper into the pillow. "I needed to distract him. We were in my bedroom, so I threw a pillow at him. It hit him in the face. He got my arm when I bent to pick up a shoe to throw at him. I guess he got tired of having things thrown at him."

A strand of hair slips over my cheek, and he pushes it back, fingers trailing along my skin. "Why aren't you trained in hand to hand combat? Thought that was standard protocol for assassins."

His touch feels good, too good, good enough to loosen my tongue and say things I probably shouldn't. "Some might be. I used to practice Wushu, but my skill lies in stealth, not brute force, like I told you. It's more effective for me to take someone by surprise. Crowds are good. Easy to conceal your actions." A wandering thumb rubs along my jaw, fingers tangling in my hair. "Stop it."

"Can't," he murmurs. "I can't figure you out."

I can't figure him out, either. Can't figure out why he's so bent on torturing us both. "Josef?" I prompt.

He withdraws his hand. "He's a member of the family, not someone on the outside we might bring in. Probably need to apply that question you asked me to yourself. Who have you pissed off in the last few years?"

My head starts to pound. "Don' know. Never knew their names." Their faces are buried under layers of memory, shrouded over and locked tight. I doubt they'll remain that way for long. "Are they going to try again?"

"You're still breathing. They'll keep trying until you aren't."

A lance of pain spears my left temple, and I wince, lifting my hand to rub it. "Great." Turning my head a little, I squint up at him. "I'm sorry, Nick. I know we need to talk about this, but I'm falling asleep."

Gaze intent, he combs his fingers through my damp hair a few more times. "We'll talk about it tomorrow."

"Goody," I murmur, already halfway to dreamland. Not even the touch of his lips to mine can bring me back, though it does make me smile. And have uncomfortably erotic dreams of Nick doing more than giving me chaste kisses.

A rumble of voices wakes me the next morning, the sound too muted to make out the individual words. I push my hair behind my ears, stumble out of bed, and shamble for the door like a zombie. Coffee. I need coffee. Possibly breakfast, but definitely coffee, followed closely by painkillers.

Mind focused on a huge cup of bitter, life-giving caffeine, I don't notice the voices are louder and more distinct, forming actual words, until my nose is buried in a mug, coffee scalding my tongue.

I lower the mug. Nick and someone I've never seen before are watching me, Nick's expression furious, the other guy amused. And appreciative.

Oh fuck me, I'm not wearing any pants.

Cheeks and ears burning, I mumble a greeting and hurry back to the bedroom and retrieve a pair of pants. Instead of putting them on, though, I sit on the bed and wait for my skin to return to normal while I sip my coffee.

I pull on my pants and find the bottle of aspirin Nick left for my hangover. I pop three and carry my half-empty cup out to the kitchen for a refill. Nick and his friend are no longer in the living room, so I wander over to the French doors and push them open before stepping onto the deck and squinting into the sun. The morning carries some of the chill from last night, and I shiver, wrapping my fingers around the mug for warmth.

Sunlight dances over the streets, shadows retreating, kids shouting to one another as they wait for the school bus. The balcony is my little window into the world I can't inhabit. I wish balconies weren't so dangerous.

I wish it faced the ocean. I want to see it waking up.

"Cass."

Shivering for an entirely different reason, I glance over my shoulder. Nick no longer looks furious, but from the tight line of his jaw, he's definitely still angry. He's wound too tight over this age difference. Who cares that he's ten years older than I am? It's not like I want to marry him or have his babies or anything.

He just needs to get used to me.

Before I can talk myself out of it, I walk up to him and give him a quick kiss. "Morning. Sorry about"—I wave my mug around—"earlier. I thought the TV was on." Wait. "Who is that guy, and what is he doing here? I thought you said no one knew about this place?"

Nick's eying my mouth as if it's the best dessert he's ever tasted and he's just been told he can't have any more. "Constantine. He's one of my cousins. And no one knows. I told him the address this morning." He snakes an arm around my waist and dips his head, stopping an inch from my mouth. "If you're going to kiss me, do it right."

Coffee breath. Morning breath. Neither are conducive for the kind of kiss I want. I close the distance anyway and fit my mouth to his, his hand splayed over my lower back, pressing me to him. Heat flares and travels from my mouth to my belly, igniting everything in its path. The man is a fantastic kisser. Makes me forget I'm the one in charge.

Who am I kidding? He is in charge. The moment his mouth met mine, I relinquished control.

But I yank it back when he tries to deepen the kiss. His dark eyes burn into mine, and I can't help it—I shiver. Again. "Don't make promises you aren't able to follow through on," I warn. I want him naked, but I want him naked without reservations, and I need to keep my head. Quick kisses aside, I'm not letting him drive this anymore.

His mouth quirks up in a wry smile. "You sure you're only twenty-one?"

"Yup. I'll be twenty-two in December if it makes you feel any better." I edge around him and head for the kitchen. Now that my brain's mostly awake, my stomach's coming through loud and clear, and it's saying *feed me*. I slip a couple of pieces of bread in the toaster and start going through the cupboards. "Did you move the peanut butter?"

"I didn't put any of the groceries away. You did. No, I didn't move the peanut butter." He comes up behind me and reaches over my head into the cupboard. Metal and glass clank together as he shifts things around, then withdraws his hand and passes me the jar of peanut butter. "Need to work on your observation skills."

I stick my tongue out at him and unscrew the cap. "So Constantine." He wouldn't be here if Nick didn't trust him. That doesn't mean *I* should trust him.

"Get your breakfast and join us." He pours himself another cup of coffee and walks out of the kitchen.

I take my time spreading peanut butter on my toast, fill a glass with water, and carry everything into the office. There's no place to sit; Constantine has commandeered the single chair. Nick's standing to one side, legs spread, arms across his chest. I take a bite of toast, smearing peanut butter across my lip.

They ignore me, arguing about one person or another. It gives me a chance to watch them together. Their back and forth rings of years of collaboration, picking up threads and nuances, finishing thoughts. A partnership, a friendship with that much depth, helps me trust Constantine more than Nick's assertions ever could.

Finally Nick's frustration gets the better of him. "I need more coffee," he growls and stalks out of the room. I drain my glass of water and put the half-finished piece of toast aside.

Constantine spins the chair around. "We haven't been introduced. Constantine." He holds out a hand, and I get to my feet to take it.

"Cass." I blush as he lifts my hand to his mouth, a sly smile playing over his lips. "Nice."

"You're unexpected. Younger than Dom's usual women." He tightens his grip on my hand when I try to tug it free.

"He's pointed that out numerous times. And I'm not his woman." Wasn't sure I wanted to be.

Constantine studies me a moment longer, his mouth staying shut. He releases my hand and turns back to the monitor. "Dom mentioned one of the family attempted to kill you yesterday. He seems to think you've angered someone. Why would he think that?"

"Don't know," I lie, the words flowing off my tongue. "He didn't explain that thought to me, either."

He shoots me a look that says he knows I'm lying through my teeth, but lets it go. "This is the list Nick's put together. I've added some names. Figure we can start here, see if there's any that cross over to you. Any of them ring a bell? "

I lean over his shoulder for a closer look. "Are they all still living?"

"Why would a dead man want you dead?"

Why didn't Nick think of this himself? I deal with dead people, not live ones. I don't have any way of tying the people on the list to my hits. "Excuse me a minute." I pick up my glass and half-finished toast and escape to the kitchen.

Nick's out on the balcony, mug in hand. He doesn't look at me when I join him. "We have a problem," I tell him, keeping my voice low.

"We have several. Which one are you referring to?"

"The one where Constantine doesn't know who I am or my SOP."

"I know who you are." Constantine's in the doorway, leaning on the doorjamb. "Not your standard operating procedure. Dom didn't get that far."

It would have been nice if someone had clued me in before we got started this morning. I rub my arms, the chill hanging in the air pricking my skin. "Pictures. I don't do names. I get pictures and basic schedules."

Constantine's brows come together. "Shit."

I don't want this. Don't want to dredge up those locked down images, don't want to open myself to the deluge of guilt and remorse and whys each of those hits will bring. If they stay battened down, I'm fine.

I can live with it as long as it doesn't come back to smack me in the face. I chew on my lower lip.

"Cassidy." Nick's gone all cold and blank on me again. "If you've got an idea, say it."

Is that how he wants to play it? Fine. "You're going to need to make a second list. Everyone in your organization who's died in the past five years. You can eliminate anyone who was killed in the last eleven months." I brush past Constantine. "I'm going to take a shower."

"Sponge bath," Nick calls out.

Right. Can't shower yet, not with my wounds still healing. I make my way to the bedroom and gather up clean clothes, then lock myself in the bathroom. Thanks to the wounds on my legs, a bath is out of the question. I turn on the tap anyway and root around for a clean washcloth, pin up my hair, and step into the tub.

Taking a sponge bath is an unpleasant experience. My skin doesn't stay wet, and the bubbles from my body wash make my skin itch.

It takes a while, much longer than a shower, and the end result is I'm clean but cranky.

Dressed, I brush out my hair and twist it into a braid to keep it out of my face, slap on a little makeup, and steel myself for what comes next.

Nick's still in cool and distant mode when I emerge from the bathroom. "You ready?"

No. I'll never be ready for this. I don't have a choice, not if I want this to end. "Whenever you are."

When Constantine rolls his chair over a few inches, I tuck my hands into my back pockets and step forward, the sins of my past waiting for me in full color.

Chapter 14

"No." Click. "No." Click. "No." Click. "Just how many people in your family have died over the last five years? No."

Constantine shoves the keyboard away. "Babe, you're not doing us much good right now."

I squash the relief blooming in my chest. None of the pictures he's brought up so far are familiar. Key words being *so far*. There are more to go. "Nick's filled your head with bullshit. My hit list isn't that long."

"Dom hasn't said much of anything about your illustrious career." He flicks the screen to the next picture. "Want to fill me in?"

I study him for a moment, picking my words. There's nothing about him that outright says he's not to be trusted. But there's something about him that says I need to be careful. I just can't figure out what it is.

There's always a first time for my instincts to be wrong. I lick my lips. "There isn't much to tell. I was trained by my dad. It's a family thing. About a year ago, I started thinking maybe this wasn't for me. I stopped taking jobs while I tried to figure it out. Nick was my first job in almost a year."

"Hmm." He clicks to the next picture.

I lean in for a better look. "No."

Muttering a curse, he pulls the keyboard toward him and begins a new search. "What I'm more interested in is how you do it in the first place." He glances over at me. "You don't look like a cold-blooded killer."

This is the part I don't understand myself. How it's so easy to switch on and off, easy to distance myself, and know that it's all waiting to crash down around my shoulders. That if the wall I've erected crumbles, I may not survive.

After the last couple of jobs, the struggle to return to normal college-student, pulling all-nighters and partying Cass, took more effort than it should have. It would have been easier to become the cold, emotionless robot my father is.

I turn around and lean against the desk. "You don't look like one, either, but I'll bet your kill list is longer than mine."

He doesn't. He's as dangerously hot as Nick, the same dark hair and eyes, same strong jaw covered in stubble, and when he smiles, his dimple winks into existence. It's disarming, that dimple, and it's probably melted many pairs of panties. He uses his charm like a dagger, coming up under your guard, and you don't realize you've been taken until the point is buried in your stomach.

A sneaky reminder I shouldn't be so quick to trust.

"Touché," he murmurs. "What about this one?" He nods toward the screen, and I glance over my shoulder, prepared to give the same answer I've given the last twenty times.

A pudgy, pasty face stares back at me. Wide, guileless blue eyes, dark brown hair without style and in bad need of a trim. Thin lips, double chin.

"I remember him." Remember how much he'd thrashed around. I came away with bruises on my stomach from his elbows punching me repeatedly as he tried to free himself. Tying him down had been exhausting. "Overdose." The amount of heroin I had to score had gone a long way toward convincing me this wasn't the life I wanted, skirting the edges of pits I was in danger of falling into.

Constantine stares at the picture. "Fuck. Remind me never to piss you off." He regards me with narrowed eyes. "There was enough heroin in his system to kill him four times over," he says quietly.

"Then don't request the target die of an overdose."

He sits back in the chair. "Don't you do research?"

"Only enough to confirm the schedule I'm given and find the best way to get him alone. Insinuating myself into his life would have drawn suspicion, and that's what I would have had to do to confirm tolerance. My way ensured he was dead."

Nick's been quiet all this time, a laptop balanced on his knees as he sits in a corner of the room. He lifts his head. "Heroin habit? Is that Steven?"

"Yeah." Constantine clicks a few keys, oblivious to the earthquake trembling inside me.

He has a name. Target number six from roughly two years ago has a name to go with his violent curses, the bruises he left on my skin, and the disgusting smirk he laid on me when I cornered him.

I remind myself it's not my place to judge if he's deserving of death. He has a name.

Soon he'll have quirks and friends and people who miss him and people who despised him enough to wish him six feet under. He'll be human instead of a number.

Nick sets the laptop on the floor, rises to his feet, and wanders over to the desk before coming to a stop on the other side of Constantine. Considering he had to veer left to do so, it's obvious he's done it on purpose.

I shouldn't be surprised. Or hurt. He's been blunt about his issues with me. But I'm both, and I curl my fingers into the desk, scratching the surface. The guys argue over who would mourn for Steven, who would be smart enough to track me down.

"Cass? If someone wants to contract you, how do they do it? How do they know who you are?"

I blink, bringing myself back to the conversation. "E-mail. I've never met a client face to face. As for how to find me, it's word of mouth. You ask someone who might know something or who might know someone who might know something, and it spirals from there."

"Alias?"

I fist my hands on the desk. "Is that necessary information?"

Nick catches my eye. "If you're done, does it matter?"

They'll find out eventually. "Sydney Bristow."

Constantine frowns. "Why is that name familiar?"

"TV character."

He lifts a brow. "Oh. Going for obvious, then." He pushes away from the desk and drags a hand through his hair. "We've got a dead junkie that no one's particularly broken up over. I don't see the connection."

I cross my arms over my chest. "No girlfriend? Wife? Close family?"

Nick answers. "Kid brother who thought he walked on water, but he's not smart enough to figure out how to contact you and pull something like this off."

Assumptions will blow this whole business to hell. "It's the stupid ones you have to look out for. They'll take you by surprise every time." The walls are closing in. I don't like the way they're watching me, Constantine cataloging every word, every gesture, Nick's expression icing over until there's an inch of frost on his skin. I have to get out of here. "I'm going for a walk."

"You're staying inside. It's too risky."

I cross through the bathroom, Nick trailing behind me, and rummage around in my bag, locating Josef's knife. I hold it up for him to see before tucking the handle in the waistband of my jeans, the blade flat against my spine. "I'll be fine."

I walk out of the room and down the hall, grab Nick's keys from the counter, and head for the beach.

* * * *

I'm frozen. I can't feel my fingers. I'm sure my lips are blue. The wind cuts through my T-shirt, goose bumps springing up on my exposed skin.

I can't bring myself to go inside.

It's not working. The push-pull of the water, the billions of droplets breaking apart and reforming, isn't doing its job. I stare harder at the horizon, the sun a miniscule strip of light growing smaller by the second.

The faint crunch of sand has me reaching for the knife at my back. My body relaxes when I see who it is. Nick walks toward me, hands in his pockets, hair mussed from the wind. It'll storm tonight. "Cold enough?" He takes off his jacket and sits beside me, fitting the jacket around my shoulders.

I nip the edges with my fingers and pull it closer, wallowing in the warmth. "Thanks."

The sun sinks into the ocean, darkness creeping in to put out the light. The beach is deserted. We keep our gazes trained on the fading strip of sky, the distance between us mere inches and as wide as the Pacific. "Did you guys make any more progress?" I ask.

"You walked out before Constantine could show you the rest of the pictures."

I huddle into the jacket. "So you don't think Steven's brother is involved."

"I think you need to come back and finish what you started before we start jumping to conclusions." He gets to his feet and holds out a hand.

I shake my head. "I'll be there in a while."

The wind blows a strand of hair over my eyes, stinging them, but they're clear enough to see Nick's not moving. He bends over and yanks me up, the move knocking his jacket from my shoulders. "We finish this." His voice is cold and flat. "Then you can come back out here and freeze."

Doesn't he get it? Doesn't he understand what he's asking me to do? "I don't want to be her anymore." I thump a fist on his chest. "Every time it's harder to come back. Harder to care, harder to keep everything separate. I'm either going to end up like my dad, or I'll be locked up in the psych ward on suicide watch." I punctuate each sentence with another thump.

He holds my wrists together to keep me from hitting him again. "The quickest way to move on is to help us. Once we figure out who sent Josef after you and whether it's tied to the hit on me, we can deal with the threat."

I lower my head to his chest. "At least be honest. You mean eliminate the threat. And whose responsibility will that be?" It should be mine. He shouldn't have to take care of it for me.

"Mine."

"No."

"Cass—"

"No." I tip my head back. "There's a high probability he was sent after me because they know you're still alive. I took the job. I have to finish it."

"Someone in my organization sent him after you. I'll handle it."

More bodies. Either way, there'll be more bodies. I pull on my hands, and he releases me. Full dark has fallen, and the wind's picked up even more. Bending over, I pick up his jacket, and he holds it while I thread my arms through the sleeves. I study the sand, searching for answers. "I guess it doesn't matter," I say, ending the standoff. "You take care of it, people die. I take care of it, people die. What happens if we work together? Twice as many people die?" Could we pull it off without adding to the body count? The only way I can think to make that happen involves running away with my tail between my legs. It's appealing since it means there won't be any more deaths on my conscience. I'll only have to live with the ones I've already taken.

It also means I might be looking over my shoulder for the rest of my life.

"I'm going to have to drop out of school." Bye-bye degree. Bye-bye normality. It could be years before this cycle ends. I kill someone and there's a respite. I think it's over for good and then it happens again.

"Take a leave of absence."

I glance up at Nick. He shrugs. "One of my sisters did that. See if UCLA has any sort of
leave policy. Leave means you don't have to re-apply as long as you come back within a certain period of time."

A bubble of hope rises and expands. I can put my life on hold for a little while. There's an end date. I like that.

"Look." He steps forward and stops when he's inside my personal space. Close enough to touch. Close enough to set my body humming. "We don't have to figure it out this minute. We go back inside, have some dinner, and you go through the rest of the pictures. Maybe something will pop. Maybe Steven will be the only lead we'll get. But standing out here isn't going to get anything done. Like I said, we finish, you can come back out and freeze your ass off."

He has a point. Also, I'm hungry. I reach for his hand and lace our fingers together, ignoring his jolt of surprise. "This dinner you speak of," I say, as we head up the beach to the sidewalk. "Would I be the one cooking it?"

"You saw the extent of my kitchen skills. Unless you want take-out or something completely inedible. Constantine's worse than me. He can't even order a pizza without fucking it up somehow."

I slide him a glance. "How do you fuck up a pizza order?"

"I'll let him show you someday."

Someday. Like I'll be around. With him. Someday in the future. We reach the sidewalk, and the question I've been waiting to ask pushes out. "How do you do it?" I ask quietly.

"Do what?" He rubs his thumb in lazy circles over the back of my hand, the gesture absent-minded enough I think he doesn't realize he's doing it.

I choose my words with care. "You've killed. Whether it was justice or because someone told you to, you've done it. How do you keep it from crushing you?"

We dodge a couple of teenagers giggling behind their hands, eyes wide as they stare at Nick. "It's how I was raised. Always been like that, handling mistakes within the family. You put it in a place you can shut down or cover up, and you go on with your life."

That's exactly what I've done. And now he's asking me to tear down the walls. The admittedly shaky walls, but he wants them gone all the same. "Do you get it? Do you get what you're asking of me?"

He stops and turns to me. "Yeah, I do. I wish there was a way around it, Cass. But it's the only way this'll end. Otherwise, you'll never be safe."

I slap at a strand of hair. "You're sticking your neck out awful far for a girl you've known a few days. I think we've gone past *you owe me* and are firmly in the *I owe you* line."

He starts walking again, tugging me with him. "Maybe that girl's gotten under my skin. Maybe she did it the moment she walked up to me and offered to help me out."

Maybe his words will squish my poor, scarred, blackened heart.

"You can fall apart. Later. When this is over, if you want to drown yourself in remorse, regret the choices you made, turn yourself in to the police, whatever you want to do, I'll let you do it. For now, I need you to hold it together until this shit's straightened out and no one's coming for you."

I don't want to fall apart. I want those memories to stay where they are, encased in concrete. He's also right. I have to hold it together, somehow, long enough to figure out the next move. "We need to go to the grocery store." I'll worry about this later. Much later.

"There's still food in the condo." He pulls me closer as we walk around a wagon someone left in the middle of the sidewalk.

"Yeah, but I want spaghetti. So. Grocery store. And you're buying." I bounce up and give him a smacking kiss on the cheek.

After letting go of my hand, he slips his arm around my waist, fingers working their way under my shirt to brush over my skin. "You know, you've never asked me why our age difference doesn't bother me," I say, tucking my hand into his back pocket.

He squeezes my hip. "I'll bite. Why?"

It's my turn to stop and face him, and I slip my other hand into his pocket, palming his ass. "Because it's hard to relate to guys my age. Hard to relate to any guy of any age, really, who hasn't seen a lifetime of trouble. Sick, probably twisted, and I can't tell you the number of times I wish it wasn't true, but there you go. And I think, if you shut off your brain for a little while, you'll discover our age gap isn't such a big deal. The disturbing thing is, we're more alike than you'd think. Might as well turn a really big minus into a sparkly plus."

Before he can think about it, back away, before he can fire off a response he may or may not mean, I rise up and kiss him, using my mouth to silence his doubts. "It's just sex," I whisper against his lips. "It doesn't have to be anything more than that."

He kisses me harder, his tongue slipping between my lips. He swallows my moan and eases away with a nip of teeth at my upper lip. "Love, you don't know what *just sex* is yet," he whispers back.

Oh, *shit*.

Chapter 15

"What's this?" Constantine pokes one of the bags as Nick sets it down.

"Dinner." I shed Nick's jacket and lay it over one of the bar stools, pull Josef's knife from the small of my back, and set it on the counter. I move to the sink to wash my hands. Metal clanks as Nick removes the cans of tomatoes from the bags. "Put the meat next to the stove."

"You cook? Dammit, Dom, you always steal the good ones."

"No stealing involved this time," Nick says mildly. "She came on to me."

I take my time inspecting the selection of kitchen knives. "That was before I realized the error of my ways. He thinks I'm too young for him," I explain to Constantine.

His dimple makes an appearance. "I have no problem robbing cradles."

It's a sad, sad day when a wickedly hot guy fails to spark my interest. Under normal circumstances, Constantine's smile would have made me drool and trip over my own tongue.

Then Nick happened.

I take the chef's knife from the block and sharpen it, keenly aware of two sets of eyes on me. The sound of steel scraping steel always sets my teeth on edge, and I clench my jaw hard enough to see spots. "You two planning to stand there the entire time?" Nick and Constantine are both leaning on the counter, Constantine opposite me, elbows on the hard surface, Nick on my side, the edge of the counter biting into his back, his arms crossed over his chest. I wave the knife around. "Go do something evil. Take over a small country. Send someone to sleep with the fishes."

Constantine's brow wrinkles as the corners of his mouth draw down. "Are you even old enough to know what that means?"

I roll my eyes. "Mafia speak for killing someone who turned traitor or otherwise needs to be eliminated."

"Yeah, but where's it from?" Nick drawls.

The knife becomes the most interesting thing I've ever seen.

He laughs. "Someone's education has gaps. It's from *The Godfather.*"

Of course it is. "I figured it had to be either that or *Goodfellas.*"

"That comment implies you haven't seen either."

I shrug, set an onion on the cutting board, and slice off the ends. "Haven't gotten around to it. Too many other movies to see. And old TV shows." Which reminds me I was in the middle of watching one. "Any chance I might be able to access my Netflix account?" I blink away tears as I peel the skin from the onion.

"Dom'll set up a new one for you. How are you not cutting yourself?" Constantine's attention is focused squarely on the knife, flashing under the glare of the kitchen lights. "Last time I tried to cut something up, I ended up bleeding all over it."

"Curl your fingers under." I lift my hand to show the tips of my fingers bent inward to touch my palm, leaving my fingers straight to the second knuckle. "First thing I learned. You have fewer accidents that way."

"Trick from your dad?"

I shake my head. "Mom. She taught me how to cook. Nothing fancy, but she figured I'd eat better once I was on my own if she got me in the habit of cooking. She was right." I smile, forgetting for the moment how seriously angry I am with her. "When some of my classmates are down to ramen because they've blown most of their mad money on take-out, Neese and I are eating actual food."

Mom gave me that, and it was fun, sometimes, making dinner, her teasing me about boys, discussing my college plans and the schools I'd applied to, what Denise and I were planning for the weekend. She'd kick Turner out if he ever wandered into the kitchen.

She knew. All those nights I came in after running drills with Turner, the self-defense courses, the sneaking around to keep her in the dark—she knew.

And she didn't do a fucking thing about it.

The knife comes down in rapid thunks, the scent of onions stinging my nose, blurring my vision. I put the knife aside and shut my eyes, willing the fury and desperate sadness back into their boxes where they belong.

Strong fingers squeeze the nape of my neck, lips flutter against my temple, the warmth of him soaking into my skin, and the sting magnifies and spreads.

Then it's gone, and when I open my eyes, they've moved into the living room.

I finish chopping the vegetables for the sauce, turn on the burner, and toss the pepper and onion into the pot once the oil heats. Once the vegetables are mostly cooked through, I add the tomatoes. I leave the sauce to simmer and wander over to the couch. "Nick said something about more pictures?" Constantine nods, and I stifle a sigh. "After dinner. I'll look through the rest of them after dinner."

"Good. We need to move on this fast. And you," he says to Nick, "have to stop hiding out. That deal you wanted? Isaiah's about to tank it."

Nick rubs a hand over his jaw. "Shit. When's the meeting?"

"Tomorrow. One o'clock."

He pinches the bridge of his nose. "Fine. I'll be there."

Just like that, Nick's going back to his normal life with no mention of his safety. Though he's had plenty to say about mine. Bastard.

They continue to talk about the "deal" Nick's been angling while my thoughts darken. Regret and resentment clash in my chest. I've lost so much in so little time, and Nick hasn't sacrificed a thing. I return to the kitchen, locate a skillet, and open the packages of turkey and chorizo.

Constantine materializes next to me while I'm poking at the browning meat. "That smells incredible." He flashes his dimple at me. "What do I have to do to get you to leave him?"

One side of my mouth kicks up in a smile I don't feel. "Nothing. We're not together."

The incredulity on his face would be amusing if I wasn't wallowing in a pool of self-pity. "Get out of the kitchen before you ruin dinner." I nudge him away with my hip.

After a long, drawn-out, uncomfortable hesitation, he leaves, and I continue dinner preparations, adding the meat to the sauce, cooking the pasta, making a salad they probably won't eat.

I call them to dinner, and we eat at the counter, perched on stools, slurping spaghetti. They continue their work conversation while I concentrate on making my food disappear as quickly as possible so I can escape.

The rain hasn't started by the time I'm done eating, and they're still engrossed in the details of whatever's going down tomorrow. I leave them to it and walk out onto the balcony, pulling on Nick's jacket when I step outside.

Palm trees whip around as the wind chases itself up from the water, loosening more strands of hair and blowing them into my face. I wrap my hands around the metal railing, wishing it would bend, wishing I had an outlet for the oily black seeping through my veins. Life's not always fair, but do all the unfair things have to happen at once?

I have to take a break from school, if not drop out completely. Unavoidable, but it's not the end of the world.

I can't go back to my apartment.

I won't go back to my parents.

I have to lie to my best friend.

All I've got left is myself.

"You ready?" Nick's in the doorway, not quite filling it but taking up all the space anyway. He does that, I've noticed, takes up all the space, sucks the air from the room when I'm not paying attention, and then I'm dizzy and lightheaded. Outside, there's air. Space. The sky might promise rain, and it might be cooler than I'd like, but I'm not forced to sacrifice my air and space to him.

Sometimes I don't have a choice. Like now. The sooner this is done, the sooner we can all move on, and I'll be able to start on piecing together my new start.

"Yeah." I don't move, the cold metal soaking through the fabric of his jacket. "Would you drop me off on campus tomorrow before your meeting?" I can stop by the registrar's office and find out if a leave of absence is possible, at least. See Denise. Pretend everything's okay for a few hours. "I'll call you when I'm done. Or I can take the bus or something back here." I'll have the place to myself. Time alone, time to lay out a plan without distraction. The thought is wholly unappealing.

"Campus will be crowded," I add, when he doesn't say anything. "Plenty of people around, low chance someone will try to take me out." It's a thin, thin thread I'm clinging to, this last sliver of normal.

His response comes an eternity later. The interim he spent scrutinizing my face, my neck, my body, every part of me he can see. "Fine."

Relieved, I nod and move toward him, hoping he'll step aside to allow me to pass. He does, thank God, and I take off his jacket and toss it on the couch, heading for the spare room.

Constantine's already got a picture up on the monitor. I peer at it. "No."

He clicks on the next one, and we wash, rinse, repeat ourselves for the next few minutes. "Dom locking you in the tower tomorrow?"

"He's taking me to campus before his meeting. Got some things to take care of there. No," I say and point at the monitor. The picture on the screen is of a truly scruffy man, patchy stubble, hair that needs a lion tamer, bloodshot eyes.

Constantine sits back, his hand falling off the mouse. "You trying to make him crazy?"

"It's a side benefit. Look, he gets to go back to his life, no harm, no foul. Me? My apartment's a crime scene twice over. And that's the least of it. He's the one who decided I needed protecting. If it were up to me, I'd be long gone." I pull the elastic from the end of my braid and work my fingers through my hair. "Are there more?"

We spend another half hour staring at the screen, long enough for my eyes to start burning. Long enough for me to start thinking Steven, the heroin abuser, will be the only lead. Long enough for me to relax, secure in the knowledge that the rest of those memories will stay where they belong. Constantine brings up the next picture, and I open my mouth to say "no" when the face triggers a memory.

My throat closes over.

Dark hair and eyes, typical of this family I'm starting to think. Good looking.

He was so calm.

He knew. He knew and hadn't fought. Stilled the moment I jumped on his back and locked my knees at his hips. He'd lowered himself to the floor without the aid of my Taser. Slicing through his carotid was the hardest thing I've ever done.

"Cass?"

I try to swallow. The last job. Eleven months ago, the one that marked "The End" on my short career. "Him." The word comes out strangled.

Every Wednesday, he went to this little cafe in Silverlake. Had a cup of coffee, maybe read the paper. Fridays he'd cut out from work early. I trailed him to the beach once. I almost forfeited the job then, standing on the beach, watching him surf. He wasn't very good. Fell off his board more often than he remained upright.

I watched arguments and cold assessments, women sauntering up to him. He gave them a once over before he waved them off. He held stealth meetings in his car.

"Marc." Nick's voice rocks me out of my stupor. "He's a cousin. Second or third, I think. No immediate family. Parents both dead, estranged from his sister. Didn't dick around. Worked for me for a while. Good guy, well liked, close with a few of the members of the organization. No idea who ordered the hit?"

Please. We've been over this.

He gives me a small, humorless smile. "Right. Con, you remember what he controlled, what he ran?"

"Didn't have his own piece. Ran it for someone else, but didn't complain. Never seemed to want anything more than what he had. Escorts, mostly. Think he kept an eye on one of the supply lines, moved product when necessary."

I need to sit down before my legs give out. I lower myself to the floor. "You said he doesn't have family? No deals gone bad?" He was too accepting. When I use the knife, there's almost always a struggle. It doesn't last long, but it's there. It's a hallmark of the game. "He didn't fight me," I whisper. "It was almost like he knew it was coming." He had to know. If he hadn't been expecting me, wasn't ready to die, he wouldn't have gone on his knees before my blade met his skin.

An odd thought pierces the fog. "Do you have a high suicide rate? In the family?"

Nick stares down at me. "Suicide by assassin? People do that?"

"Probably. It's not like we keep statistics or anything. The Order is long gone."

"Order?" Constantine interrupts.

I pick at my thumbnail. "Order of Assassins. Dates back to around the First Crusade." I tuck my thumb into my fist to avoid picking at it. "It's possible he ordered the hit on himself. He knew I was there. He could have gotten away, defended himself, something, and chose not to." I stand, barricading the images of Marc into their corner. "I need to call Denise. The police have probably called her by now."

When I brush by Nick, he stops me, closing his fingers around my wrist, his hold tight and bruising. "The cops have likely figured out you're not staying with your parents."

He's right. Which means Denise probably knows, too, and is freaking out even more. My phone's been off all day. Knowing her, she's had a meltdown by now. "What do I tell her? The cops find out I'm with you, they'll just have more questions for her." Questions she doesn't deserve.

His lips spread in a humorless smile. "Give the police a little credit. They don't have evidence, and they're unlikely to question her about my criminal activities. Go ahead and tell her you're with me. She doesn't know my last name, so I doubt they'll connect me with you."

Josef's blank gaze flashes in front of my eyes. "I wonder," I say slowly, "if I ought to talk to them myself. It'd be pretty believable if I tell them I got to the apartment first, found the door open, and saw a dead guy and freaked out."

"And they'll ask you where you've been. No doubt they've talked to your parents already."

He's right. Again. I need an alibi, and I need one quick.

His hold loosens, his thumb rubbing soft circles along my inner wrist. An idea forms. I could do this. It would work since more than one person's already seen me panting after him. I paste on a cheery grin, bounce up on my toes, and kiss him, pushing the last thoughts of Marc from my head. "You'll just have to pretend to be my boyfriend, then."

As his gaze turns calculating, I free my wrist, walk through the bathroom to the bedroom, and shut the door behind me. I don't breathe until I'm sitting on the edge of the bed, air leaving my lungs in a long, shaky exhalation. It's a dangerous game we're playing with my sanity as the prize. The longer we play, the closer I get to a total shut down. It's either that or go insane with guilt. I need a lifeline if I'm going to stand any chance of holding on to the sunnier, cleaner side of myself.

I swipe my phone from the bedside table, lay down, and power it on. "Denise? It's Cass."

Chapter 16

The bandage is too noticeable. It's too warm out for a turtleneck, not that I own one, and the neckline of my shirt doesn't come high enough. Grumbling, I pull out more gauze and trim it down, then stare at it lying on the counter.

It's going to show. There's no getting around it. Denise will see it, she'll ask questions, and I can't think of a single lie that carries a hint of plausibility.

Stumped, I sit on the edge of the tub, staring at the gauze. The cut is small but still very pink, and I probably should keep it covered for a while longer.

"You almost ready?" Nick calls through the door. I get up and open it.

"Any suggestions?" I point at the offending gauze. "Either I need to cover it up, or I need a plausible story for Denise. She's scared enough as it is."

He washes his hands and picks up the gauze and medical tape. The sight of him kneeling on the floor in front of me makes my breath catch in my throat. He's just so…*gorgeous*. Competence has never looked so sexy.

"Scarf?" He holds the gauze in place with one hand, passing me the tape with the other. I rip off a piece and hand it to him.

"Only scarf I have is the one I showed up in, and it's in the trash. Too bloody." He smooths on the tape, fingers brushing my skin, sending tiny jolts of electricity racing through my body. I hand him another piece of tape, and he repeats the process on the other side.

He studies his handiwork, thumb rubbing the edge of the tape. Confusion simmers in the depth of his gaze. "We'll stop by Lia's. I don't think she's got class today."

I wrinkle my nose. "Is that a good idea?" The way he's described his youngest sister, I get the impression she doesn't know much about the family business.

His thumb drifts up my neck to my jaw, tracing the line. My heart skitters against my rib cage. "Lia has an ever-multiplying collection of scarves." The pad presses into my lower lip, the tip dipping inside my mouth. "You can borrow one of hers."

He needs to stop touching me. What was I thinking, getting him used to my kisses, trying to scramble his brain enough he'd forget the whole age difference thing? I killed his *cousin*. He should be furious. I have to get off this see-saw. Lusty, molten heat one moment, icy indifference the next, and that's just in my own body. Add in Nick's ability to switch on and off in a blink, and my brain's the one that's scrambled. Not his.

I'm pretty sure he knows exactly what he's doing. "We should go." The words come out breathy, and all I want is to lean forward and kiss him.

So I pull his hand away and stand. My legs wobble like a newborn foal's as I make my way to the bedroom. I stick my phone into my pocket and follow Nick into the hallway. We descend the stairs to the garage, ignoring each other as we take our seats and buckle our belts.

He slides his phone out of his pocket a few blocks away and swipes his thumb across the screen. Holding the phone to his ear, his eyes on the road, I tuck my hands under my thighs to squash the urge to soothe the jumping muscle in his jaw. "Lia? You at home?"

I stare out the window.

"Good. I'll be there in about an hour. I need a favor." The phone clatters against hard plastic. He's dumped the phone in one of the cup holders. "She's at home."

I go back to the window. "Any thoughts on what the next step should be?" Priorities, Cass. Reorganize your priorities. Learning who's the real target and resolving the issue should be mine. Nick and the manic lust he inspires should not be on that list.

The muscle's still ticking. I free a hand and brush my fingers over it. His skin's a study in contrasts, rough with stubble, but warm and smooth in places, that tic bumping under my fingertips. I want to feel it under my tongue.

"Con's checking out the piece Marc ran, see if anything unusual pops there." Nick clasps my hand and pulls it to his mouth, kisses the palm. The sweetness of the kiss confuses the hell out of me and ties my stomach in a big, fat knot. It tightens further when he brings my fingertips to his lips, kissing them one by one. "You always checked your e-mail from your laptop?"

"Or my phone." He sets the knot on fire by nipping into the sensitive pad of my index finger. Warmth pools between my legs, spreading to eradicate the soft, squishy feeling he'd brought on earlier. I bite my lip to hold in a moan.

"I want to see if there's any trace of Marc's job on your computer."

Which means breaking into my apartment. Again. Talk about a downer. It washes over me, sluicing away the desire and replacing it with something far more practical. Resignation. He laces his fingers through mine and lowers our hands to my thigh. I swallow a sigh. "Fine. I doubt you'll find anything, but you're welcome to try."

His grin blinds me, robbing me of coherent thought for a long, long moment. "Underestimate me at your own risk." Attention back on the road, he continues. "My sister, George, was close with him. Closer than I was, certainly. If you're right, and this was suicide by assassin, she might be able to tell us how fucked up he was toward the end. Though that wouldn't explain the attempt on your life."

Speak. I'm supposed to speak now, say something intelligent. Nick's hand is warm and strong and entirely too distracting. "It might if someone else didn't think he needed to die. I *do* have an M.O. You ask the right questions, you can figure out who handled what hit. As for who would have tried to kill me, it's the same question you asked about Steven. Who would have been angry about his death? Doesn't have to be family. Doesn't have to be for sentimental reasons. Could be business related."

Business. Steven was an addict, but he'd had a position in the family. "What did Steven do? Was he trusted with anything like Marc?"

He snorts. "Steven lost us more business in the last year he was alive than we'd lost in the previous five years. Everything was turned over to other people about three months before he was killed."

Traffic into the city is moving, for once, and the remainder of the drive races by. Nick finds a spot in a parking garage and I climb out, scanning the dim interior. No SUVs skid up next to us, no tall, grim-faced men pull guns and start firing.

Liana's apartment is several blocks away. Nick's shoulders are tense the entire walk over. The moment we're in the elevator, he rounds on me. "There's a car in the underground garage. Lia has the keys. Take that to campus. Text me when you're ready to leave. You know how to lose a tail?"

I nod.

"I'll send you the address I'll be at. Meet me there."

"I don't know how long I'll be," I hedge. When he opens his mouth to respond, I cut him off. "I need some time, Nick. Stopping at the registrar's office is on the list. I'm going to the police. Or at least calling them. And I need to see Denise." I don't know what I'll say to her, have no idea what sort of shape she's in, but I've fallen down on the friend job the last few days, and I have to make it up to her.

The elevator doors slide open, and he takes my hand, leading me down the hall to a door on the right. He knocks, and the door opens a few seconds later to a small, curvy dark-haired girl with a scowl on her face standing on the other side. "You suck, Nicky."

He drops my hand to give her a hug. "Nice to see you too, Lia."

"Sorry." Her apology is muffled by his shoulder. "Good to see you. You still suck."

I like this girl.

She peers around him. "Hi." Her gaze is lit with curiosity. "I'm Liana."

"Cass."

Nick shifts to the side and draws me to him. "She needs to borrow a scarf."

Her eyes stop at the bandage on my throat. "I sort of forgive you." She glances up at her brother. "You were rude. What if I was on my way to class?" She flicks a hand at him. "Never mind. Come on in."

She closes the door, and we head deeper into the apartment. Her place makes my apartment look dingy. Large windows line one wall, bright October sunshine streaming through. Dark purple pillows covered in a nubby-looking fabric are tossed carelessly on a dark brown couch, her laptop open on one of the cushions.

Nick strides to the window and stares down at the street. He swears softly before fishing his phone out of his pocket.

Lia snags my elbow and steers me into a short hallway, then through an open doorway on the right. Her bedroom is as bright as the living room, though it's a lot more cluttered. There's scraps of fabric everywhere. "He's probably going to be a minute while he growls at whomever he's getting to take care of whatever problem's going on."

I doubt the problem can be solved with a single phone call. "Right."

Nick wasn't kidding. She has a huge collection of scarves. Two laddered hangers meant to hold pants are covered in floaty, colorful scarves. She throws them on the bed and paws through the layers, tugging a couple of them free. Frowning over her choices, she doesn't speak as she holds them against my shirt. My brows draw together. "You're a textile design major?"

"Yeah," she says absently. "I like clothes, but not enough to design them. This one." She holds up a blue and white scarf, dotted with splotches, the blue fading in and out in places. She loops it around my neck, tucks in the ends, and adjusts the fabric before pushing me toward the mirror hanging on the back of the door. "Try not to move it so much. No one should notice."

"Thanks." Denise will. But lying about getting a new scarf is easier than lying about a gash on my throat.

"How'd it happen, anyway?" She gives me an expectant look, and I have to remind myself she's a mobster's daughter. I can get away with the truth here.

"Someone tried to slit my throat. He took too long, and I got away." Okay, not the whole truth. Just part of it. "I've been staying with Nick, and my best friend doesn't know what's going on, and I want to keep it that way. So"—I point to my neck—"the scarf." Nick was *so* lying about his sister. Shy? Slow to open up? Please.

"Cassidy. Time to go." Nick grabs my hand and tows me to the front door, Lia trailing us, protesting the whole time that he's taking advantage of her.

"Lia, thanks. I'll see you soon."

We're in the stairwell, clattering down the steps, when my brain catches up. "What's going on?"

"Called in a distraction. Someone's watching the building. We've got a slim window to get the car out of the garage."

"Oh."

Less than a minute later, our steps are echoing off the polished cement floor of the garage. Nick unlocks the driver's side door of a boring navy blue four-door and hands me the keys. "Drop me outside the other garage."

The garage entrance is in an alley, and he directs me to go left out of the alley. I zig and zag my way through the streets to the first garage, wasting precious minutes losing a tail I don't have. Idling next to the curb, Nick wastes even more time leaning over to kiss me hard. "Do me a favor? Don't get knifed."

The heat of his lips weighs heavy on my mouth as he slides out of the car and jogs through the entrance to the garage. If the man has a problem with me causing the death of his cousin, he's sure not acting like it.

Somewhere between Lia's Chinatown apartment and Westwood, I find an alley and park. The engine ticks quietly as I call Officer Gregory.

"Ms. Turner." Cool. Neutral. Officer Gregory must be good at his job. I'd be furious or insanely curious. Possibly both. "I'm afraid I'll need you to come in to answer some questions."

Twenty minutes later, I'm seated in a disgustingly hard plastic seat, my hands jammed between my thighs. Officer Gregory looks worn out, but that doesn't stop him from leveling a disapproving look at me.

I force a quiver into my voice. "I'm sorry. I panicked the other day."

"Why don't you start with where you've been staying?"

My stomach falls, and I study the dirty linoleum. "With my boyfriend," I whisper. "He's older than me. A lot older, and my parents don't approve of him."

"Your roommate seems to think your mother's received some sort of threat."

The problem with lies is you tell too many, they get tangled in your mouth. Officer Gregory saves me from having to tell yet another one. "Your mother confirmed it. But she didn't know where you were staying."

Gaze on the floor, I wait for the next question. In the ensuing silence, the sounds of the station fill my ears. Copiers spewing out papers, the low murmur of voices, a distant phone ringing. Finally he sighs. "Tell me what happened."

Relief trickles through. "I got there a little early and noticed the door was open. I figured you were already inside, so I walked in. I saw the body in my bedroom, freaked, and ran out."

He leans back in his chair. "I can understand forgetting to call the police in a moment of shock, Ms. Turner, but frankly, your behavior in general has been suspect."

I lift my hands, helpless to offer a plausible lie. "The last few days have really fried my brain. The break-in and now this… I haven't even been to class." And I wouldn't be returning.

Officer Gregory isn't buying what I'm selling, but he doesn't ask any more questions. Good thing, because I don't know what else I could say to make him believe my lies. He lets me go after another round of questions, and I get in the car and drive to campus.

After the police station, dealing with the registrar is a piece of cake. I fill out a couple forms, am promised a refund of the rest of my tuition for the semester, and then I'm outside a few minutes later calling Denise.

"Cass!" Hysterical. She sounds hysterical, and a vise clamps on to my lungs. It screws tighter at her next question. "God, where have you been? Where are you now?"

"On campus. Meet me at The Grateful Bread?"

"Ten minutes. Cass, are you all right?"

Out of habit, I scan the walkways and find nothing unusual. "Yeah. I'm okay. I'll see you soon, okay?"

I have ten minutes to figure out how to lie to my best friend. Again. The vise closes another inch.

Chapter 17

"Cass!" Denise stands up so fast her chair tips over, and she stumbles over her bag in a hurry to throw her arms around me.

Then she starts crying.

Her obvious worry has a lump forming in my throat, and I blink back tears of my own. I hate this. I hate having to lie to her. I hate how much danger being my friend has put her in, and she doesn't even know it. Best friends since junior high, and not being able to talk to her, to tell her everything about Nick and my parents, is killing my soul, one ugly second at a time.

"Neese. Hon, I'm here." It's hard to talk. My tongue is thick in my mouth, words foreign, a damn tingling in my nose, and burning in my eyes.

She eases away and swipes at her tears. "Why are you wearing a scarf?"

All at once I'm tired of lying. There's a lot I can't tell her, but I can leave it out. "Can we sit down?"

She rights her chair and sits, pushing an oversize cup toward me, and the tears I struggled against brim again. Chai, with tons of honey, exactly how I like it. Denise has been my friend long enough that the battlements I've erected to keep others out open to let her in.

I suck in a breath, let it out. Drink some tea. Suck in another breath. Tug the scarf away from my neck.

Her face goes sheet white, her eyes wide and stuck on the bandage on my throat. "What is that?" The question is wavering and full of fear.

"Someone tried to slit my throat a few days ago." I cup my hands around the mug, suddenly cold. "Mugging gone wrong, I think." Lie. "I managed to get away. The cut's not too bad, but I'm keeping it covered for a few days while it heals." When she doesn't say anything, I push on.

I tell her I fought with my parents and I'm not staying with them—both true statements. "They think he's too old for me," I say with a scowl. "I've been staying with him instead."

The number of truths, happily, outweigh the lies at this point, though I don't go back and tell her why I asked her to stay away from the apartment. Allowing her to think it's still because of the threat to my mother means she'll be worried for me, but I'd rather have her worried than in danger.

I'm scared to tell her the truth. If Denise were to judge me for the past I've kept from her, I'd slip into that cold, empty space and never come out. I'd lose the toehold on my sanity. She has no idea how important she is to me. How completely screwed I'd be if she wasn't around. Being this dependent on another person scares the crap out of me, but I don't know how else to *be*.

"Wait. Nick's your boyfriend? That totally gorgeous man from our kitchen is *yours*?" Denise's hazel eyes round in surprise. "I thought you said he was with your mother's firm."

Squirming would not be a good idea right now. "He is. It's part of the reason Mom and Dad don't approve. It's obnoxious, you know? I'm an adult. He's only ten years older than me. If I were just a few years older, no one would care. But they're treating it like I'm still in high school or something." I scowl into the cup.

"Well…"

I glance up, and Denise is biting her lip and staring at the table top. "Go on. Might as well say it."

Guilt colors her face. "I don't see how it could work. You're in two completely different places. I mean, he's got a job and a place of his own, and you're still finishing your degree. He's had, I dunno, life experience and stuff."

Plus the cultural references. Don't forget the cultural references. I make a mental note to watch *The Godfather* sometime soon. "I sort of get it. It's weird for me too. I figured we wouldn't have much in common."

As far as I know, we don't. I'm not interested in dating him. I just hope we can indulge in some good, sweaty sex while this whole mess is going on, then go our separate ways once it's over. It's been too long since I've seen any action, and I'm getting antsy.

"The maturity level isn't to be underrated, though." The guys I dated since starting college had ranged from douchebags to total sweeties, but none of them came close to the realm of care Nick has shown me, and we're not even a couple. "You know Charlie would do anything for you, right?"

Her cheeks flush, and she nods, lips curving in a small smile. Jealousy pierces my chest. I want that. I want the guy who looks at me like I'm the most amazing thing ever created. I want the guy who would stand in front of me without hesitation and fight off the bad guys.

Or in my case, the guy who knows my strengths well enough to let me fight the bad guys myself.

"Nick's like that." A lie, built off a kernel of truth. I think, given the right woman, Nick would go to the ends of the earth to make her happy and keep her safe.

I am not that woman. Yet he took me in when he didn't have to, got me help when I needed it, and kept me safe. It's far more than I'd expect anyone to give a stranger. "Given how new our relationship is, he didn't have to let me stay with him. We haven't even had sex yet."

"Whoa. Okay. Time out. Are we heading into TMI territory?" She leans forward. "And I was totally gonna ask you how he was in bed, because *yum*."

Brain to mouth: close now. I take a sip of tea. "It hasn't happened. Bad timing." Truth. We should be concentrating on the threats to our lives, and with a few detours, we have. Add in my desire to wait until I'm absolutely certain Nick will have no regrets, and I might get lucky sometime in the next few weeks. *Might*. I think he's leaning that way.

Sort of.

Denise studies me over the rim of her mug. "Are you sure you're okay?"

I'm not. My life is a whirlpool of chaos, and I can't find my way out. "No," I admit. "This thing with my parents hurts. I figured my dad wouldn't be okay with it, but my mom? I thought she'd be more sympathetic." Who would I have been if my mother had stood up to Turner? If she treated me like a human being able to process logical thought? If she tried to talk me out of it instead of standing by and letting the black eat away at the edges?

I wouldn't have those images shuttered and chained. I wouldn't know how to lose a tail. I wouldn't *have* to lose a tail, and I wouldn't have to lie to everyone under the sun.

I wouldn't have met Nick.

Somehow that one major positive isn't outweighing the negatives. Though it's getting there. Silver linings. I'll take them when they come.

I nudge the mug aside. "I'll be okay. Eventually. I'm not sure when I'll be able to go back to class, though. I just got done at the registrar's. Did you know you can withdraw after the semester's started, and it won't count against you?"

She shakes her head and swallows a sip of coffee. "You think you're going to be gone that long?"

"Everything could be resolved tomorrow. But there's so much else going on right now with my parents and Nick and our apartment. I can't go back there, not after everything that's happened."

Her hands tremble around the mug, and she grips it firmly to halt the stutters. "I sort of needed to talk to you about that." She peeks at me through her lashes.

I grin, twin sensations of happiness and jealousy smashing into one another. "Charlie wants to move in together?"

She blows out a breath. "His lease is month to month, and his roommate graduates at the end of this term anyway and already has a job lined up in Sacramento. He, um, said he wanted to ask me a while ago before classes started last month."

"Hey." I scoot my chair back and stand to give her a hug. "Charlie is fabulous and outstanding and I love him to death. I'm happy for you, lady. Go for it."

She gnaws on her upper lip. "You're okay with it? I don't want to leave you without a place to live."

I sit again and pick up my mug. "I'll figure something out. If I can't find someone who's looking for a roommate, I'll look around for a place of my own." That I can't afford to pay for, since I'm currently unemployed. "Can we talk about something else? Something not so depressing?"

She purses her lips. "Scott's roommate got arrested again. Drunk as three frat boys and hollering all over the place. He almost fell off a balcony."

The next few hours whip by, coupled with mugs of tea and coffee and the bakery's to-die-for cinnamon rolls. They smear them with chocolate frosting instead of the white stuff. Eating one is like getting a glimpse of heaven.

My ass can only take so much of their less than comfortable seats, though. When Denise's phone chimes with a text from Charlie, I use that as my excuse to leave. Bag of cinnamon rolls in hand, I wander outside and wait with Denise until Charlie shows up. A quick look around doesn't show any random goons lounging about, and I head for the car.

* * * *

The man pacing the seating area outside the boardroom has the same dark good looks as Nick and Constantine and probably well over half their family, but something about his demeanor makes him less drool-inducing and more approachable, despite the dark look on his face. I pull out the copy of *The Godfather* I stopped for and open it to the first page.

The book serves a dual purpose: to educate and to pass the time while I wait for Nick to finish up whatever he's doing.

We had a stunted argument via text. I didn't see the point in coming to his office to wait for him to wrap up his meetings. Even though I don't have a key to the condo, I could find other ways to occupy my time. Wander the beach, mostly. The strip of sand a few blocks from where we're staying is more inviting than what they have at Santa Monica. Nick said we were safer if we stuck together, and the hours we'd spent apart were long enough.

The thought he might actually be worried about me tied my stomach in its now familiar knots, and I gave in. I detoured by the bookstore first, then took a meandering route to his office in Century City.

The pacer stops, as though he's noticed me for the first time, and strides over. Too late, I bury my nose in the book. "Can I help you?" he asks.

I lift my head, tuck my hair behind my ear, and smile. "Nah. Just waiting for my boyfriend to finish his meeting." The knot tightens on the word *boyfriend,* and my fingers flex on the paperback.

He sits in the chair opposite me and nods to my book. "A classic."

I tip the book toward me, glancing down at the cover. "I've been told. I was also scolded for not having read it." Scolded for not having seen the movie, actually, but whatever.

One side of his mouth kicks up higher than the other, and I smile wider in response. It's hard not to be drawn in by a crooked smile, and his is one of the best I've seen. "I wouldn't worry too much. I doubt the average American has read it, classic or no." He leans forward and holds out his hand. "Isaiah."

His grip is that perfect balance between strong and soft, meant to reassure you rather than demonstrate his alpha-ness. "Cass. Nice to meet you." The name tugs a string. This is the guy Nick resurfaced for, the one who almost ruined his deal. "Any idea how much longer they'll be?"

He releases my hand and scowls over his shoulder. "With Dom in charge, probably not much longer." Hair already disordered, he rakes a hand through it, making it stick up more, and screws up his mouth. "He was about ready to walk out ten minutes ago."

I scoot forward to the edge of my seat. "Tough negotiator?"

"Yeah." He mutters something unintelligible. "Yeah," he repeats. "He's not afraid to walk away from a deal if he's not getting the concessions he wants." This time the smile is rueful. "I could stand to be better at that."

Something about his "aw, shucks" attitude makes me want to make him feel better. I put my book aside and open the bag of cinnamon rolls. "Want one?" I hold it out for him.

The way his face lights up has giggles bubbling, and I swallow hard. Less than five minutes, and I like this guy.

"Chocolate cinnamon rolls. Grateful Bread?" he asks.

"Yup."

He separates one from the pack, then pulls it apart and offers me half. The one I ate earlier sits heavy in my stomach, but I'm not saying no. Not to one of these.

We spend the next few minutes eating and licking frosting from our fingers, idle small talk easy despite the lies I have to tell. I'm starting to think pursuing Nick is a mistake, especially since Isaiah's much easier to relax around, when the door to the boardroom opens.

Isaiah's out of his chair in a heartbeat, striding over to the men leaving the room. Handshakes all around, and he ushers a small group of suited men to the hallway and the elevator, leaving Nick alone, rubbing a hand over the back of his neck. He pulls off his tie and unbuttons his collar before stuffing the tie into his pocket.

I close up the bag of cinnamon rolls and tuck my book into my bag, giving him time to come to me if he wants. Sure enough, he's heading my way, his expression dark, intense, and immediately tipping my radar to wary. It's a look I'm unfamiliar with. My body tenses with the need to run and save myself from the big, scary predator. "Ready to go?" I ask.

I guess not from the way he cups the back of my skull and kisses me, his tongue sliding over my lips in a way that has me thinking of dark rooms, tangled sheets, and sweat-slicked bodies. It's delicious, being kissed like this, and it's over far too quickly. "Why do you taste like chocolate?" he murmurs.

Kiss me again. Kiss me everywhere. For all the kisses we've shared, he's never ventured past my lips. "Chocolate frosted cinnamon rolls." The words come out shaky with need, and I fist a hand in his shirt to steady myself.

His smile is just this side of evil, and he slicks his tongue over my lower lip again. His fingers spasm on my neck when I moan. "Tasty." He kisses me again, softer, more thorough. "You're getting harder to resist, love."

Chapter 18

His gaze remains locked on my mouth, tempting me to lick my lips, push him further, push him to give me more. "You should stop trying. I don't bite."

He rubs his thumb down the back of my neck. "Maybe I should."

All at once, our first kiss replays itself in my head, and the doubts rush back in. "So can I revoke the rule?" Less than a week. He can't have changed his stance on something that important in less than a week.

The hunger in his eyes darkens them, turning them almost black. "I really hate that fucking rule," he mutters.

That's what I thought.

I trace the edges of his mouth with my finger. "It's there for a reason," I say softly. "I'm trying to avoid post-coital awkwardness here. I figured you'd want that too."

He kisses the tip of my finger. "I forget about it most of the time. Your age. Can't forget what you've done, but you're right. I'd be a hypocrite for holding that against you."

"But?" I prompt, sensing he's not done.

"But you're still twenty-one. I'm still thirty-two. Admitting I want you to strip, sit on the edge of my desk, and spread your legs is easy. Convincing myself you won't regret it when it's over isn't." His kiss is gentle, innocent, and leaves my knees as weak as if he'd assaulted my mouth with his tongue. "You're not your average college student, Cassidy. I get that. Give me enough time, and maybe I'll accept it."

If he takes any more time, this will become less about sex and more about feelings I don't want to have for him.

He turns me away from him and winds his arm around my waist. "Home. You can make me dinner." I elbow him in the side, and he grins down at me. "It's very domestic of you. Cute too."

We opt for the stairs, footsteps clattering on the concrete, the sounds bouncing off the cinderblock walls. "What were you reading?" he asks as we settle into the car.

"*The Godfather*. I thought it might be educational."

He smirks. "And is it?"

"Luca Brasi is pretty badass," I admit. "But I'm not so sure about Tom Hagen."

"Tom's the most badass of them all. Just wait."

The early evening sun spears through the windshield on the drive home. Nick picks a random, circuitous route that takes over two hours. I unwind the scarf from my neck as we walk in the door. "Any food preferences? Otherwise you're stuck with what I feel like cooking."

He grins. "I'm at your mercy." He jerks his head toward the bedrooms. "Be right back."

I open the fridge and stare blindly at the contents, picturing Nick with his shirt off, Nick in a pair of boxers, Nick in nothing but skin and that evil smile.

He is definitely not at my mercy.

I grab a package of chicken breasts and random vegetables, then line them up on the counter. Looks like we're having stir-fry. I bang pots around until I find a suitable one for the rice.

His hair is damp and brushed away from his face, wet spots dotting his T-shirt when he makes his way into the kitchen.

"Hope you like stir-fry." Crap. Soy sauce. "Can you run to the store and get some soy sauce? Oh, and hoisin sauce. And five spice."

He digs his phone out and passes it to me. "Write it down, or I'll forget." It rings in my hand. Taking it back, he frowns at the read out. "Kosta," he barks.

What is it with guys answering with their last names only? Scott's started doing it too. It doesn't make them more intimidating. Honestly? I have to stop myself from rolling my eyes whenever I hear it.

The glower on Nick's face is no laughing matter. He stalks the length of the living room and back, his words low and clipped, his face drawn tight with fury. I'll just go get the soy sauce myself. Good thing I stopped at the ATM on campus.

Nick's gone from angry to resigned when I return with the rest of the ingredients for the stir-fry. None of the food I pulled from the fridge is on the counter. "Did you change your mind?"

"I have to go back to work. Dinner meeting."

So why did he put the food away? "Okay. Do you think you could hook me up with a new Netflix account before you leave?" I suppose I could use the time to look through more photos, but an evening free of Nick and death and knife wounds is really appealing.

"Need a plus one."

I arch a brow. "You can't just go alone?"

He smirks. "You're the one insisting I'm your fake boyfriend. I need a fake girlfriend for the night. They're bringing their wives. I want them to sell me their company, so we're going to pretend this is a friendly dinner and not talk about business. They'll be more relaxed if they think I'm like them. Simple manners, Cass. Don't want to be the odd man out."

I'm not going to pretend I understand the world of business. "I don't have anything to wear. Also? Bandages are not attractive." I finger the gauze on my neck.

His eyes track the movement of my fingers. "Lia will have something you can borrow."

"Lia's a good four inches shorter than I am."

"Cass." The warning note in his voice is almost overwhelmed by weariness. "Please."

I do owe him. A lot. And there's always the possibility that being seen together will bring more clues to the surface.

I tug at the hem of my shirt. "Do you think Lia's shoes will fit?"

* * * *

Lia's shoes, surprisingly, do fit. Wearing them is like balancing on needles. Literally. The heels are twig-thin. I could never run in these. I'll break something. Probably the heel, then my ankle.

But Nick likes them. A lot if the kiss he lays on me in the elevator is any indication. Or maybe it's the skirt. Lia says it hits her around the knees, and most of our height difference is in the leg, so you can guess where the hem of the skirt ends up. She finished the look with a three-quarter sleeve scoop neck top and a thin scarf that's more like a necklace. I'm beginning to despise scarves. I'll spend the dinner worrying about the ends getting in my food. It's a necessary evil, though, and I have to admit it does a good job of covering the gauze.

We switch cars in a run-down garage, complete with spooky lighting and nefarious characters hanging around. The one we drive out in is flashier and likely recognizable as a vehicle belonging to the Kosta organization.

I sincerely hope the glass is bulletproof.

The reason for the car switch becomes apparent the instant we pull into the valet drive. The restaurant is a celebrity hangout. Photographers stand around in clumps, chatting, flocking toward each new entrant.

I step out of the car and resist the urge to fidget with the hem of the skirt. It's long enough to cover the bandages on my thighs if it doesn't ride up too much. Nick walks over and places a hand at the small of my back.

"What do you want me to do? Act dumb? Not talk?" I like the not talking option, although I probably ought to look at this as a learning experience.

You, too, can find out what it's like to dine in expensive, trendy restaurants with people who have more money than God!

I'm going to make an idiot of myself.

He slides his hand around to my hip when I stumble on a crack in the sidewalk. "Be Cass. And you're not giving those shoes back."

"Oh?" Please don't let a flash go off in my face.

The photographers mostly ignore us at first, making more noise the closer we get to the door. "Liana should not have those shoes. They're inappropriate," he says.

Mentioning his sister and I are practically the same age would be a bad, bad idea. "I have a feeling I know what she'll say to that."

He holds open the door and motions for me to precede him. "Yeah?"

Warm air rushes over us, and I shiver. "Yeah. She'd say I'm her age, and you have no problem with me wearing the shoes. Then she'd tell you she doesn't like you." His step falters, and his arm drops away. Biting back a groan, I nudge him over to a corner of the waiting area. "Look. Your dinner guests are probably going to say the same thing, only they'll use big words and snooty voices. Do you really want me there?" Say no. Say yes. Tell me we can forget about this whole dinner thing and go home and get it on like a pair of rabbits.

He stares at my shoes. "It's different," he growls. "I didn't know she had them. I see them on you, and I see you wearing them and nothing else. You give them back, and I see them on her, I'm going to be seeing men doing the same thing to her. Which will happen over my dead body."

Poor baby. I grin and wind my arms around his neck. "Is this like the other night when you got all broody over your baby sister out causing trouble?" He growls again, and I inch closer. "Go. You have a business to buy."

He sobers, one hand sliding up my back. "Thanks for this. For tonight."

Feelings. Feelings are bad. Worse than bad ideas. Feelings don't happen after, what, four days? Five? Swallowing hard, I nod and duck under his arm.

The hostess falls all over herself, batting her eyelashes at Nick like something's stuck in her eye. I'd roll mine except Nick *does* bring on the eyelash flutters. She leads us to a table tucked in the back, two couples already seated. Given that there are two empty seats left, our dinner party must be complete.

Nick introduces me as his girlfriend, and I spend more time fighting my blush than remembering everyone's name. When a server comes around and asks what we'd like to drink, Nick orders me a glass of wine. I can count on one hand the number of times I've had wine.

"Trust me," he says, leaning in close, his words for me alone. "You'll like it."

He's right. Tart, very tart, and heavy, and dry. Delicious.

I curl my fingers around the stem and nod politely or smile at intervals, unsure how to insert myself into the conversation flowing around me. It mostly involves children and the trouble they get into.

I am so very, very out of place here in this dimly-lit, high gloss restaurant. From the black linen table cloths to the flickering tea lights, I've never been anywhere this fancy. The only thing that keeps me from wincing at the prices on the menu is the reminder that Nick can afford it.

"It's Cassidy, right?"

Startled, my hand jerks on my wine glass, red threatening to slop over the rim. One of the wives, blond hair sleeked away from her face, is smiling at me in the way of indulgent mothers. C'mon. I'm not *that* young. "Yes. But please call me Cass."

"Cass, then." She kicks her smile up a notch, then lets it slip down gradually. "Are you a student?"

I clasp my hands together in my lap, fingers tapping my knuckles. "I'm at UCLA. It's my last year."

"How nice. Any plans for after you graduate?"

Everyone's attention is on me, their eyes burning holes in my skin. I tap harder. "I'll be applying to graduate school and Teach for America."

"Teach for America?" The blonde's eyebrows don't quite draw together, and I stifle a snort. Botox much?

"It's a sort of intensive program. Think of it as doing a master's in education through hands-on experience rather than confined to a classroom for the first year. Most of the schools are in lower income neighborhoods and hurting for teachers." I reach for my wine and take a long swallow, my hand caught by Nick's as I set the glass down.

Someone screams.

The sound is from the front of the restaurant, and Nick's halfway out of his seat, dragging me with him since he's still holding my hand.

Crack.

A gunshot.

There's more, a rapid *crack crack crack* accompanied by more screams, some shouts. Without waiting to see what his dining companions do, Nick pulls me away from the table. I trip forward and almost fall to my knees, my ankle re-twisting itself. "Wait." Gritting my teeth against the pain shooting up my leg, I pry off the shoes and toss them away.

It's not as bad as when I twisted it in the alley. I'm able to put weight on it, and as the noise and gunfire increase behind us, we wind through the tables, heading for an entryway on the far side of the restaurant.

Chaos rises in waves, people scrambling away from their tables in a mass of humanity rushing to the front of the restaurant and the exit. Chairs are overturned, plates shatter on the floor, and another spray of bullets rips through the dining room. I point toward the darkened entry. "Think that's the emergency exit?" I shout, and he grunts in response, continuing to tow me through the crowd.

The screams multiply along with the gunshots, and when a woman goes down in front of me, so do I, the hard floor bruising my knees. Nick's down, too, and we start crawling along.

Someone steps on my hand. Feet are everywhere, clattering on hardwood, punctuated by bullets. I lose sight of Nick and sit up on my aching knees, glancing around. With the tables at the same level as my head, it's difficult to see anything else.

The doorway we were aiming for is close. Close enough I could stand and run for it. I opt to continue crawling, heedless of showing the restaurant my underwear. Personal safety wins over decorum.

The mouth of the hallway is empty, and I crawl in until I'm confident no one can see me. A green exit sign glows at the end, and I hobble toward it. A bullet slams into the door above my head as my hands hover over the crash bar. I drop to my knees, hissing at the pain singing through my legs.

But nothing else happens.

I glance over my shoulder to see Nick holding a blood-slicked knife, an ugly, barrel-chested man going to his knees, hands clasped at his throat, blood seeping past his fingers.

Nick jerks his chin at the door, and I push it open without a word. I get a glimpse of his expression as he passes through. Calm. I recognize the calm. It's the place you go when destruction stares you in the face.

We dash through the gathering shadows to the parking lot, away from the madness inside.

Chapter 19

Some gods must be smiling down on me because we both manage to escape without injury. Well, unless you count my bruised knees and twisted ankle. I hand my scarf to Nick and swipe the keys from his pocket to open the door for him. It went without saying we'd abandon the car as soon as possible, and while our fingerprints would be all over it, someone else's blood shouldn't be. The scarf, as narrow as it is, only helps clean him up so much. He clenches it in his fists as I zoom out of the parking lot.

I don't have the patience for the zigzaggedy driving needed to ensure we're not followed. Lapses lead to stupid mistakes, though, and I force myself to do it anyway. Twenty minutes later we're switching cars, and I'm as amped as I was when we ran out of the restaurant.

The feeling doesn't fade the longer I drive. Nick holds himself rigid in the seat beside me to prevent any random blood from transferring. A little over a half hour later, we're at the condo in Manhattan Beach, and he yanks his shirt over his head on the way to the bathroom.

I follow him without thinking, startled when the door slams shut in my face. The shower turns on a few seconds later.

Nick naked. Nick naked and wet. The adrenaline high I'm riding spikes. Mistakes, regrets, and uncertainty can all kiss my ass. I know exactly how I want to work this off, and dammit, I'm going to get it.

I shed my clothes, peel off the bandages, and open the door quietly before slipping inside and nudging the shower curtain away from the wall.

He's facing away from me, one hand braced on the opposite wall, head down. I step into the tub and wrap my arms around his waist, yelping as cold water pelts my skin.

"What the fuck?" He spins around and pins me to the wall, the cool tile as much a shock as the water.

"Surprise?" I smile weakly. "I understand the shower, but cold shower?"

He's not paying attention. Undisguised hunger gleams in his eyes, tracking the length of my body. I glance down.

Oh. Cold shower. I get it.

The water is no match for his half-erect cock, stiffening the longer he stares at me. This is it. This is my moment, my chance, the opening I've craved. I reach around and flip the warm tap on, plastering myself to Nick in the process. His dick is trapped between us, and he groans, sinks his fingers into my hair, and kisses me.

Kiss is the wrong word. *Assault* is more apt the way he storms through my shoddy defenses and past my lips, his tongue demanding I surrender, and believe me, that's no hardship. Licks, nibbles, the way he slants his mouth at just the right angle to coax a deeper response free, his hands roaming, his tongue flicking and rubbing against mine.

I want everything. I want his mouth on my skin in the places it's never ventured to before. I want him laid out before me like a feast. I want his hands on my breasts, on my ass, between my legs, his fingers inside me.

He loosens his hold, tilting my head to one side; he moves his mouth to my jaw, tracing the line of it with his tongue, then retracing his path to place searing kisses along my neck. He's careful to avoid my scar, licking the water from the hollow of my collarbone.

When his dark eyes meet mine, my breath catches and my knees weaken with desire.

I've lusted before and have been lusted after. I lost my virginity at sixteen to a boy I was with for a year and thought I loved. Sex has always been an outlet—for joy, for anger, an escape from reality.

Nick's not just lusting for me. It's a craving, a twisted, dark thing born of that hidden spot we both don't talk about. Something in me recognizes the same in him, and he knows it.

And he's ready to stop fighting it.

He slicks his hands down my sides and up again, cupping my breasts, his thumbs rubbing slippery circles around my nipples. "Ready for bath time?" he asks, arching a brow.

No. No, I am not. Not in the least.

He plucks the bar of soap from the holder and lathers his hands, suds foaming. "Back first. Turn around." I do as he asks, bundling my hair on top of my head to get it out of the way.

His mouth finds my nape as his hands stroke and glide over my back, teeth nipping at the curve where neck meets shoulder. His hands never stop moving, following the dip of my waist, the curve of my hip, delicate touches as he cleans the wounds on my thighs. He steps aside, allows the water to rinse my skin clean, and then urges me around, lathering his hands once again.

I'm out of my depth here. I'm fumbling this like an innocent, hands trembling, legs trembling, everything trembling hard enough I'm surprised I'm still upright. I dig my nails into his shoulders, desperate to ground myself as he soaps my breasts. The water chases away the soap, and he lowers his head, cleaning forgotten as he latches on to one of my nipples.

Fuck.

He uses everything at his disposal, tongue, lips, his teeth. One hand occupies my free breast so the onslaught of sensation is never ending. Every scrape of his teeth sends a jolt to my clit, and my inner thighs are damp from more than water.

He abandons my tormented nipples and kneels. Water streams over his face as he picks up the soap, and the look he shoots me is so hot I'm surprised I don't catch fire. Without taking his eyes off me, he runs his hands down one leg, then up the other, inching closer and closer to the maddening ache between my legs.

The first touch of his finger draws a gasp. The contact is tentative, deceptively so because he follows it with a long, assured stroke. He brings his finger to his mouth, his gaze trained on mine, and sucks it clean.

His challenge demands a response, a quip, some snarky remark, but he beats me to it and eases my legs apart, the teasing portion of this little display over. He dives right in with a flat, broad swipe of his tongue. I swallow the first moan, and the second. The third one breaks free, followed by whimpers and pants, his tongue doing wicked things, circling my clit, fluttering over it, tracing random designs. Everything in me compresses and arrows in on that taut, tiny bundle of nerves. His clever fingers get in on the action, and my whimpers morph into a high keening sound, taking all the air in the room with it.

The orgasm is so strong it about knocks me over, robbing me of strength. Wave after wave of it breaks over me, and I struggle to remain upright. He lets me fall, catching me as I crumple to the floor of the tub, his smile smug. I want to wipe it off his face. I want to see him delirious with pleasure. Narrowing my eyes, I give him a once over. "Your turn."

We switch places, and I lather up, then skim my hands over his back. The muscles twitch and shift under my touch, and I follow it up with my mouth, licking the water beading on his skin, scratching my nails over his ass.

My knees protest as I kneel on the floor of the tub, soaping his legs, my hands wandering up his inner thighs. I brush the underside of his cock with my knuckles. "Turn around." The command comes out husky, the voice not mine.

It's there, *right there* in front of my face, so I do the smart thing. I kiss the head of his dick and grasp the base, uncertainty elbowing its way in. I want so badly to do this well, and I've never been concerned with technique before. It's never *mattered* before, either.

Shoving the doubts aside, I treat it like my toy, flattening my tongue and running it the length of him, licking the tip before sucking it into my mouth. I trace every vein I can find, pump him slowly, swallow him inch by yummy inch. He's quiet, the thrust and jerk of his hips doing the talking for him.

Why does this feel new and powerful and right? I never saw oral sex as a display of dominance. I do now. For once, Nick's completely at my mercy, and he's enjoying it.

Not for long, though. "Enough," he growls, hauling me to my feet. But I'm not done. He's got this nicely defined chest I have yet to explore, and I'm not leaving this shower until I've learned every inch. Rubbing the soap over his abs to his pecs, I lean in and flick my tongue over a nipple.

He nudges me away and shuts off the water. I squeak in surprise as he picks me up and carries me into the bedroom. Skin wet, hair dripping, he lays me on the bed and stretches out above me, his jaw tight with desire. Lust like thick, molten honey slides through my veins. That quick display of strength silences the last of my qualms; he wants this as badly as I do.

"Someone's impatient." I stretch up and suck more water from his throat, smiling against his neck as he curses and fumbles with the bedside drawer.

He sits back and rips open the condom, then rolls it down his length. Braced on one forearm, his eyes locked on mine, I spread my legs wider and hold my breath.

That first moment, the first push of entry, especially the first time with someone, is my favorite part of the whole act, and with Nick it's the same and different. It feels incredible, and it feels *more*: harder, thicker, a tighter fit. When he's seated to the hilt, I wrap my legs around his hips, pressing him closer.

"*Fuck*, Cass."

Yes, please. Please fuck Cass. Fuck her now. "*Move*."

The perverse bastard moves, all right. He moves slower than slow, withdrawing, then pushing in, each stroke taking an eternity. "Faster. Nick, move faster."

"No." He takes my mouth as he rolls his hips forward, and I fall into his rhythm, a sinuous, filthy dance made dirtier when he picks up my hand, sucks on my fingers, and works them between our bodies, finding my clit and pinching it.

I bow up, the jolt of electricity stringing me taut. Our hips rock faster, jerking out of time, as he pinches my fingers around my clit a second time. "More," I whine. I'm chasing that elusive unicorn—the female orgasm during sex. It's going to happen, the pressure building to the shattering point. Not much longer.

Not.

Much.

Longer.

I throw my head back and see spots, my heels digging into his butt, muscles locking into that painful pleasure of release. He goes rigid above me, tendons standing out on his neck as his face twists with the climax pulling him apart.

I'm useless. Boneless. The only thought in my head is *again*. Bodies sticking together, I tangle my fingers in his wet hair, pressing my lips to his roughened jaw.

He pushes himself up, stares down at me, and rolls off, off the bed and onto his feet, retreating to the bathroom. I wait, shivering as the flood of heat from sex dissipates, the damp sheets uncomfortable under me.

Right about the time my stomach grumbles with hunger, I realize he's not coming back. I get up, open the bathroom door, and find it empty. The door to the office is shut and locked. I clench my jaw against the surge of hurt, shutting my eyes and holding my breath to keep it inside. Fine. If this is how he wants to play it, that's what we'll do. I got what I wanted. I have to deal with the consequences.

I finish drying off, replace my bandages, and towel-dry my hair, brushing it out and winding it into a braid. We missed dinner. I put on some clothes, strip the sheets from the bed, and hunt down the washing machine.

He emerges from hiding when I'm scooping rice out of the pot, then topping it with the stir-fry. I point to the stove. "Food if you're hungry."

The buzzer on the washer goes off, and I transfer the sheets to the dryer. He's tense, that tic jumping in his jaw, lines around his eyes, his mouth crimped at the edges. Regret rolls off him in a heavy, desolate wave, ready to swamp everything in its path.

I ignore him. I pick up my plate of food, find my book, and climb up on a stool. Immature, I know, but I'm past caring at this point. This is very much a "thanks, I'll call you" moment, awkward as hell and pissing me off too.

He hasn't moved from his spot near the hallway. "Since you're standing, would you mind getting me a beer?" I ask, attention on my book.

A rustling, and then he's at the fridge, opening it and handing me my beer. "Thanks." I put the book down and use the edge of the counter to remove the cap.

"You know, that's what bottle openers are for."

I shrug. "Counter works for me." I go back to my book and my stir fry, anger a low rumble in my belly.

"Cass—"

The anger spills over, and I choke it into submission. "No." I meet his gaze. "I am not having this conversation. You could have stopped at any time, and you chose not to. You wanted that as much as I did, and honestly? We'd still be there if I had my way. You're the one with the problem, so you deal with it. You do, maybe we'll do it again."

The sooner I finish eating, the sooner I can get out of here. Anger, hurt, and humiliation are all simmering below the surface, and I want to escape to the beach, wait them out until they've faded to nothing. I stare at my plate, willing it to empty.

I am keenly aware of him, his eyes on me, his body across the counter, just out of reach, the heady connection still arcing between us. This *sucks*. I anticipated awkwardness, but nothing like this. Nothing like a longing so physical it's painful. I would have been happy to stay in bed, wet sheets and all, until hunger drove me out of it. Instead, Nick's remorse threatens to smother me.

I have never felt more alone.

I drain half the beer and pick up my fork, only to have it taken from me. "I was using that."

"Not anymore." Nick's mouth is a thin line, little more than a slash above his chin. He comes around the counter, picks me up, and throws me over his shoulder in a fireman's carry.

"Nick. Put me down."

"Sure." He stalks down the hall into the bedroom and tosses me on the bed hard enough to make me bounce. He frowns. "Where'd the sheets go?"

I glare at him. "Washing machine." He catches my ankle as I try to crawl off the bed. "Whatever the hell you're doing, you're going to want to stop."

He pulls his shirt over his head. "Nope. We're going to do this until we get it right." He makes a "hurry up" motion with his hand. "You want to keep the shirt, you might want to take it off."

I cross my arms over my chest instead. "What exactly do you mean by 'this'? Because if you're talking about sex, I'm not all that eager to repeat it." Parts of it, yes, absolutely yes. After the ending? No, not so much.

He drops to his knees on the bed, crowding into my space. "I am," he says quietly. "I fucked up, and I'm sorry." He moves forward, farther into me, pushing me onto my back. "So let me try it again."

I bring my hands up to his shoulders, ready to shove him away. "Why should I? How do I know you won't react the same way?" It hurt the first time. I don't want to know how it'll feel the second time.

His gaze softens, and he rubs his thumb along my bottom lip. I twist my head to the side to get away from his touch, but all he does is move to stroke my jaw. "I'm sorry," he repeats. "If you don't want this, I'll leave."

No, don't leave. I don't want to be alone. I'm tired of always being alone.

I can't think straight with him touching me. I stroke my hands up from his shoulders to his hair, lace my fingers through the strands, and bring my mouth to his.

Chapter 20

I wake alone the next morning, the pillow beside me cool. The room's empty, and I pull on the first thing I find, which happens to be Nick's discarded T-shirt from the night before. The man himself is seated at the kitchen counter, a cup of coffee in front of him, attention on the phone in his hand. He looks up, his scowl giving way to a faint smile before he drops his gaze again. "We're leaving in a half hour."

So much for a good morning kiss. "Is my presence required at the office?" I pour myself a cup of coffee and take a cautious sip. I twist my mouth in a grimace at the bitter taste. A little over boiled. I dump a couple of spoonfuls of sugar into it and stir.

"I don't know who they were after last night, you or me. Or both of us. But there's data stored at the office I can't access here."

I frown. "Really? You store that information on your secure server? Where anyone can access it?"

"It's all the aboveboard stuff," he says wryly. "Marc and Steven both held positions in our businesses over the years. It's a good place to start, and you can use the secure connection to access information on the family's remote server. You know, where we hide the bodies."

Considering we've made next to no progress, I don't have much ground for complaint. I finish my coffee and head to the bedroom to dress, locking down the memories of last night, wondering if we've taken a giant step back instead of forward. His regret after the first time was tangible. It's not there now.

So what the hell is going on? His behavior doesn't provide any more clues when we leave the condo and walk downstairs to the garage. No matter how many sidelong glances I sneak as he focuses on the road, his expression doesn't change. His face is like a blank wall, and while I want to break it down, I'm a little afraid of what might be on the other side.

"Do you do this all the time?" We've been driving for twenty minutes with no sign of a tail. The way Nick's been going, turning left or right at random, doubling back, our forward progress gradual, only someone who's been right on our bumper the entire time would be able to keep up.

"I don't normally have to worry about whether someone in my family wants me dead." He makes a sudden right turn, throwing me into the door. "You okay?"

I rub my elbow. "Yeah. Did you see someone?"

He glances in the rearview, hands clenched on the wheel. "Not sure. Hang on." He whips the car through a series of tight turns, ending in an alley so narrow the light of day barely penetrates. He stares at the rear view mirror as one minute becomes two, then three, then four. On minute five, he cracks open the door and slithers out of the car with a terse "stay here."

Oh *hell* no.

I unhook my seatbelt and follow him to the mouth of the alley, back the way we came. There's a gun in his hand, held close to his leg. "Back to the car, Cassidy."

"No. Got a spare?"

"No, which is why I told you to stay in the car. Because otherwise you're going to have to start running *now*." He fires a few rounds, and I sprint back to the car as a loud *pop* sounds over shouts and screeching tires.

I've barely made it into the passenger seat, intent on scrunching down as low as possible, when he squeezes through the driver's side door and slides in behind the wheel. He shoves the car in gear and races for the opposite end of the alley.

"Tail?" I ask, fumbling for my seatbelt.

"Tail. Hold on." He spins the wheel hard to the left, and we shoot out into traffic, narrowly missing getting hit by an oncoming bus. "Managed to blow one of the tires on their car, but there might be more of them."

I grip the door handle as he weaves through traffic, tearing around a corner, then another and another until he slows several blocks later and pulls to the curb, scanning his rearview for signs we were followed. Me, I sit and try to remember that I need to breathe in order to live.

Apparently satisfied we lost the tail, Nick glides out into traffic and continues toward his office, circling and backtracking, dragging it out another hour. By the time we roll into the underground garage, my nerves are gone and I'm staring out the window at the passing scenery as if he didn't just abort some high-speed chase.

From my last visit, I know his company occupies most of the twelve-story building. The boardroom I sat outside yesterday was on the top floor. The seating area was slick and modern, the chairs and loveseats covered in a dark gray material, the walls a lighter shade of the same gray. The rest of the floor was taken up by offices, and I assumed his was one of them.

Today he punches the button for the ninth floor. He mentioned something about finding a place for me to work undisturbed. Maybe there's an empty office or cubicle on that floor.

The place is quiet. A low thrum of chatter and ringing phones and humming machines prevents total silence. He leads me through a short maze of cubicles, and I half expect someone to pop their head up like a prairie dog. He stops in front of one of the doors, the nameplate on the wall bearing his name, and fishes out his keys.

"I would have thought your office was on the top floor."

He unlocks the door and ushers me inside. "More accessible this way. Top floor is conference rooms and a break room, a couple of offices for contractors or temps. Constantine's office is next door."

The room reminds me of the condo—kind of boring. One wall is made up of windows with a view of the building across the way. His desk is covered in papers and folders. Two sleek monitors sit in one corner. A row of bookshelves hold some books, a few pictures, and what look like awards. A couple of visitor chairs are positioned in front of the desk, and I flop into one of them. "So where will I be?"

"There's an empty office on the other side of the floor, next to one of the server rooms." He sorts through a stack of folders and tucks one under his arm. "Come on."

Other side of the floor? Frowning, I trail after him through the cubicle maze, last night's doubts creeping in. When we'd finally fallen asleep, he was right there with me, my heart stuttering when he curved his body around mine and pulled me close. The last thing I remember was his arm tightening around my hips, his whispered, "Good night, love" sending me into dreamland. I was so certain we finally landed on the same page. My own fault for believing he'd made his peace with our age difference.

Stupid Cass, always wanting what she can't have.

"This is it."

It is an empty office. There's a desk, a chair, and a computer. Swallowing my hurt, I walk around the desk and boot up the computer. "What are you going to be doing?"

He leans over and types in a password. "My job. Where do you want to start?"

I purse my lips. "Your business." Nick personally owns, or owns part of, at least ten technology companies of varying sizes. We're in the offices of his largest company. "Did Marc and Steven both work for you? Aboveboard?"

"Not at this office, but at others, in some capacity or another." He points to an icon on the screen. "Portal's here. I'll write down the password for you."

"Any ideas on how far back I should start?"

Someone passes by the open door and waves at Nick, giving me a curious look. Nick waves back. "Marc started ten years ago. Steven started six years ago. Steven's brother, if you want to dig into that, is Vincent and started seven years ago."

"And Marc?" His name, his face, both still close off my throat, allowing the bare minimum of air to pass.

He spins the chair away from the desk and crouches in front of me. "Marc was an only child," he says quietly. "Tons of cousins, some friends and friendly faces within the company and the organization at large."

I stare at my hands, images of Marc bombarding me. The man wasn't clean. I saw enough of his life to know he was in something dirty. But I hadn't trusted my instincts, either, though they screamed at me that what I was doing was very, very wrong.

I went through with it anyway, because proving to my father I deserved his attention was worth more than another person's life.

"Cassidy. Look at me." Nick tips my chin up. "It happened. There's nothing you can do about it now."

"It didn't *have* to happen." The words are bitter on my tongue, all the more so for the truth they bear. "Turner always told me to trust my gut, and it said 'don't do this,' and I did it anyway." I want to curl into a ball and hide under the desk. "Why aren't you mad at me? He was your family. You liked him. You and Constantine both."

"Just because he was family doesn't mean I knew him well. His role in the organization was pretty far removed from mine. You can't control most of LA with a small family." My mouth twists with doubt, and he sighs. "Okay. Different example. Does Denise have any close friends you're not close with?"

She doesn't, but I understand what he's saying. "He's *family.* You grew up with him."

He slides his hand around to the nape of my neck, the gentle touch a shock. "I've had a year to come to terms with Marc's death. Being angry with you won't do me any good. You might have wielded the knife, but you weren't the one who killed him." He hesitates. "And I know what it's like to follow orders you don't agree with. To do something your instincts tell you isn't a good idea. What'd you call me the other day? A hypocrite? I won't lie—I was angry when you first told us. But staying angry would have made me exactly what you'd called me."

I let out a derisive snort. "Since when does my opinion of you matter?"

His gaze hardens, and he drags my head down to his. His kiss is a punishment, harsh, flaming heat, the rough scrape of teeth on my lower lip. "You've almost got me convinced we aren't so different on the inside despite the age gap. Don't try to change my mind now."

A new regret pops into my head, and I'm shocked I didn't think of it before. "I can't help it. I finally got you naked last night. Don't you think it's possible that's blinding you?"

"I'd like to think I'm past the stage where I think with my dick all the time, Cass."

I slide out of the chair, needing one of the most basic of human connections—comfort. On my knees, I wind my arms around him and bury my face in his neck. "I'm sorry," I whisper. I'm sorry for so many things. For agreeing to kill him in the first place. For doubting him. For putting doubts in his head. For taking his cousin's life. For the target on my back, which always seems to lead back to him.

I stiffen at the thought. It does, doesn't it? Those attempts on my life hadn't started until the job where I met Nick.

I draw away, sliding one hand into his hair to play with the strands, grounding myself. "What if they're connected somehow? Your hit and the people trying to kill me? No one's come after me before, not until you."

To my surprise, he groans. "Shit. I should have thought of that." He runs a hand down my back and up again, moving both hands to my elbows. He cups them and lifts me into the seat. "Stick with the original plan. See if anything pops on Steven or Marc. Chances are if you find something, it'll be easier to follow a trail to me."

I brush my hair away from my face, his hand catching mine before I can tug at the hem of my shirt. "You know you do that when you're nervous?" He squeezes my hand and lets go. "Come find me when you're hungry for lunch."

I suck my upper lip into my mouth and nod. "I'll need last names."

"Marc was Marc Pappas. Steven and Vincent are Kosta."

Marc Pappas. I can do this. "Go." I wave a hand at the door. "Be a big, bad businessman."

He smiles, a dark, wicked curving of lips that goes a long way toward chasing off the shadows and walks out the door.

Chapter 21

"I know you."

I glance up from the document currently giving me a headache. Isaiah stands in the door, brows drawn together. "It's Cass, right?"

"Right. And you're Isaiah." I minimize the screen and stand, needing an excuse to stretch. I've been at it for three hours, and the words are running together. The notepad I found in one of the desk drawers is half full.

He grins, his gaze darting around the room. "You didn't bring any more cinnamon rolls, did you?"

"Sadly, no." My stomach rumbles, reminding me it's been even longer since I've eaten. "Probably could use something more substantial than a roll at this point, anyway." I step around the desk.

Isaiah doesn't move, his face clear, a question still in his eyes. "You an intern as well?"

Huh? "As well?" My mind races for the next lie, the next story I'll spin. "Oh, you mean why am I here? Temporary employee. My work study position for the term didn't come through, and I needed extra cash. Nick needed some help sorting through old files and offered to pay me to go through them."

"Nick? Oh, Dom. Weird hearing you call him Nick. His sisters are the only ones who call him something other than Dom." I remember Lia calling him Nicky. Isaiah stares over my shoulder. "What are you looking for? Anything I can help with?"

I poke him in the shoulder. "Yes. You can help me find some lunch." Nick didn't say anything about not talking to his employees or other family members, and Isaiah might be able to help me cull out a number of years without actually having to read through the files. I edge past him and head for the elevators. "Maybe you can tell me about the Nautilus project too?" It came up repeatedly in the years I checked and seemed to take up a large portion of the saved communications I read.

Isaiah hurries to catch up, an easy grin on his face, and I take a moment to stare at him in unabashed appreciation. He's very much a Kosta, though I wonder what it is that makes me so comfortable around him. Something about the way he carries himself, I think. Not as slick and charming as Constantine, not as confident as Nick.

"Nautilus Corp was a small conglomeration of companies," Isaiah says once we're in the elevator. "Constantine and Dom were working together to try and split it up and buy a portion when the deal fell apart. I was working for a competitor at the time, so I don't know all the details of the why."

The doors slide open, and we step out into the building lobby. Marc's name came up enough times in conjunction with the Nautilus project I hoped finding a viable lead would have been that simple. "Maybe they had a better offer. Or decided they didn't want to split up the companies that way."

Isaiah shrugs. "Maybe. Come on. There's a deli a block over that's pretty good."

The deli turns out to be a hole in the wall with exposed brick walls and battered tables scattered over a scratched and scuffed linoleum floor. A long counter runs the length of the space, and a couple of sandwich makers stand behind it, filling orders. It's crowded with other business types getting lunch, some in suits, others dressed more casually like Isaiah. We order our sandwiches, and the bandage on my neck garners some strange looks.

He comments on it when we sit down with our sandwiches. "Didn't see that yesterday." He gestures to my neck. "You had it covered up."

I swallow a bite of sandwich. "There was an incident. I was attacked. He did some damage before I got away."

"An incident?"

"An incident involving a knife and someone who thought it would be a good idea to sneak up behind me. He stole my purse, and the knife dug into the skin a little too far." It's a good lie. I'm glad I thought of it when I was with Denise the other day. "Nick took care of the wound. I'll be fine in a few days." It was decidedly less pink this morning, which bodes well. "Any other failed deals you can tell me about?"

Isaiah doesn't bat an eye at the sudden change of subject. "There's a bunch," he says around a mouthful of sandwich. "It's business. It happens. Is that what Dom has you doing?"

"Mostly." Partly. Failed deals are a good place to start, especially if someone's angry about losing out.

He grins. "Later. Don't want to mix business with pleasure."

What is it with these guys? I lower my lashes, stealing a peek at him, and his grin widens. "You know I'm with Nick, right?"

His grin turns rueful. "Figured as much. Can't blame a guy for hoping otherwise, though."

He asks me about my classes, and I push aside the pang of sadness and tell him about the late night papers and surprise quizzes until all that's left of our lunch is crumpled paper and crumbs.

We walk back to the office and, true to his word, Isaiah rattles off the failed acquisitions with as much detail as he can remember, repeating himself when I beg him to slow down, scrawling notes on my pad. Aside from the Nautilus deal, there were three others that he has quite a bit of information on, two of which were spearheaded by Constantine.

I tap my pen against a half-filled page. "What about the ones that almost didn't go through? Like yesterday's?"

Isaiah winces, and I cringe. Shit. "I'm sorry," I blurt. "That was rude of me." Tact isn't my middle name, but I'm usually better at it than that.

He shakes his head. "No, it's okay. Do you mean in general, or just the ones I've worked on?" I hunch my shoulders up around my ears, and he laughs, the sound snide, tripping a tiny warning bell. "There aren't as many of those. In the early years, Dom handled most of the deals. Didn't trust anyone else to do it properly. Con was usually along for the ride, and after a while he'd handle some, though it's not something he likes doing."

That's a surprise. Constantine's so charming, so slick, I figure deals must be a great way for him to get his rocks off.

Isaiah's still talking. "Marc handled a few over the years. Usually small ones, though it wasn't something he enjoyed." A shadow passes over his face.

Nausea bubbles to life in my stomach, a slow churn eating away at my recently ingested lunch. I swallow against the bile creeping up my throat. "Marc?"

His face goes blank, the shadows sinking deeper into his eyes. "Cousin of ours. We grew up together, more like brothers. Died a little over a year ago." No mention of the police, no mention of how he died.

Sprawled on a cement floor, blood puddling under his head, sightless eyes staring at the wall. Utter peace in his voice when he told me to "just do it." That he wouldn't fight. And he didn't.

I jump up, saliva flooding my mouth. "Where's the bathroom?" My skin's clammy and loose, my legs weak. I am not going to embarrass myself. I *will* make it to the bathroom in time.

Alarmed, Isaiah shoots out of his seat, clasps my elbow, and hurries me down the hall. Swallowing convulsively, I slap a hand over my mouth as he pushes me through the door to the ladies' room, and I race for the nearest open stall, landing hard on my knees in front of the toilet as the first retch wracks my body.

Someone holds my hair away from my face, hands soft on my back, rubbing gentle circles as my lunch forces its way out of my stomach. Empty and shaking, I swipe my fingers under my eyes and sit on my heels, heart beating a sickening tattoo on my ribs.

Memories claw at the walls I've built, sinuous whispers threading their way through the cracks. I'm pretty sure Marc is the only one of his kind, but that doesn't mean there aren't others waiting to rear their heads. Others who didn't deserve the fate I'd meted out.

Isaiah kneels next to me. "You okay for a minute?" I wrinkle my nose and nod once, and he gets to his feet and disappears. A tap splashes on, and he returns with a damp paper towel. I run it over my face and neck, then wipe my mouth. He helps me to my feet and leaves me braced against the sink. "I'm going to get you some water," he says before the door swings shut.

Unwilling to wait for him to return, I flip on the tap again and cup my hands under it. I rinse my mouth and shut off the water. I'm not sure what's worse, puking or crying. Crying, I think as I comb my fingers through my hair and straighten my clothes. Crying usually leaves me with a sense of hopelessness. At least puking only leaves me weak.

The door swings open, and Nick barges in ahead of Isaiah, bottle of water in hand. He twists the top off and shoves it at me, the water cold enough to shock my skin. I take a tentative sip and shudder as the icy liquid hits my tender stomach.

His face a neutral mask, he watches as I drink a quarter of the bottle, waiting between each sip to see if my stomach will expel it or allow it to stay. Finally I cap it and put it on the counter. "I'm okay," I croak. My gaze flits from Nick to Isaiah, who doesn't look at all convinced.

I'm not convinced myself. I don't know that I can go in there and continue scanning files.

"Are you sure? Do you want me to take you home?" Isaiah steps around Nick.

Nick replies while my answer's still forming. "She'll be fine. I'll take her home in a little bit."

All at once, I know I'm not okay. I want a shower, clean clothes, and maybe some tea. I want a book or a movie and a blanket and a few hours to allow my mind to reset. It's the only way I'll get through this without needing a bucket at my feet the entire time. I straighten as much as my protesting stomach will allow and offer Isaiah a trembling smile. "I'll wear him down. Give me a few minutes."

With a hesitant nod and a wary glance at his cousin, Isaiah ducks out of the restroom. I slump against the counter. "I'm done for the day, Nick. I can find another way home, or I can call Denise and see if I can camp out on Charlie's couch for a few hours while you work, but I can't handle any more today."

"He upset you." Instead of moving closer, he leans on the wall and slips his hands into his pockets.

I sigh. Wishful thinking he'd come over here and hold me. "Not exactly. More like my brain got the better of me and instructed my stomach to stage a revolt. He was telling me about what failed deals he could remember, and it looped around to Marc."

For lack of anything better to do, I uncap the water and drink, grimacing when my stomach twists in protest. "I mean it, Nick. Strong Cass has left the building." At least for the rest of the day. Meek Cass is firmly in place, and she's not giving up her spot.

Our standoff stretches for several minutes, Nick blocking the door when a woman cracks it open. Finally he shifts on his feet and jerks his head to the door. "I'll take you home."

A worm of hurt wiggles its way through my chest, whispering he should show more care. I shut it up. I didn't ask for hand-holding and cuddles. I asked for sex, a good, thorough fucking, and I got it.

We stop by the vacant office to back up my work and shut down the computer, and I hand the notepad to Nick for safekeeping. In the elevator, I lean against the wall, trying not to replay the events of the past fifteen minutes, but failing. Turner would have some choice words for my reaction. I press a hand to my stomach as I shuffle after Nick. It doesn't want to settle, and I'm not sure I can handle a long car ride.

The drive to Manhattan Beach doesn't take nearly as long as it has in the past, leaving me to wonder if Nick's more concerned than he's letting on since he's forgoing his usual winding route. More red flags fly when I tell him I'm going to take a sponge bath because I shouldn't have let my wounds get wet last night. He produces some plastic wrap and proceeds to tape it over the gauze.

As a result, my wounds are mostly dry after my shower, though I change the gauze to be safe. After pulling on a pair of yoga pants, a tank, and a zip-up hoodie, I shuffle out to make myself some tea. Then I remember I didn't buy any at the store because I rarely drink it at home, and I bend over the counter, digging for the strength to go out and buy a box. It's a few blocks. Some exercise will do me good.

"Cass?"

"Tea," I mumble without lifting my head. "I want a damn cup of tea, and I don't have any."

"What kind?"

The strength it takes to raise my head is ridiculous. "I don't know. Something tasty. I like hibiscus and chai." Probably not ideal for an upset stomach, but I like the tartness.

He palms the keys sitting on the counter and heads for the door. "Sit. I'll be back in a few."

Sitting. I like sitting. Sitting means I'm on my ass instead of my feet. I make my way to the couch and curl into the corner, staring out through the French doors at the pale blue sky.

True to his word, Nick returns about fifteen minutes later with a paper bag, and I struggle to my feet.

Besides the box of tea bags, he purchased a loaf of potato bread and some chicken noodle soup, as well as a couple bottles of plain seltzer water. He picks up the bread. "Multigrain can be harder on your stomach. Figured you might want some toast."

Then he turns away to fill the kettle.

I fumble the twist tie off the bag and pop a couple of pieces of bread into the toaster. The kettle shrieks about the same time the toast springs up. I carry my mug and plate into the living room, set them on the coffee table, and settle myself on the couch.

I figure Nick will ensconce himself in the next room and do whatever it is he does in there, but he pulls the blinds, takes the plate from my lap and the mug from my hand, and nudges me from my corner, turning on the TV and handing me my snack before pulling me against his chest. He enables the box used to stream Netflix onto the TV and finds the show I'm in the middle of watching.

Comfort. Comfort I didn't ask for. Comfort I don't know how to handle. I finish my toast, body tense, and he sets the empty plate on the table. "Relax," he murmurs.

Heart wary, my body obeys and melts, little by little, assured for now he's not going anywhere.

Chapter 22

I don't have time for this.

I don't know how to handle the mess in my head, all these feelings waiting to burst forth, and Nick's taken to cuddling.

Cuddling.

In the office, he stays on his end of the floor, I stay on mine, and I lock down the riot inside, beating it into submission. It has no place here amongst the mergers and acquisitions and deals gone sour. My stomach jumps every time Marc's name comes up, and Isaiah's concerned I'm still ill because when we have lunch, I barely touch my food.

How can I tell him my stomach's turned traitor, and it's the most innocuous of my punishments?

Constantine's been by as well, adding his insights and pushing a bowl of soup on me. I eat a third of it and stir the rest, hoping he'll think I'm eating, because I can't think of what to say to him, not after the information I found. Seems most of the deals that almost didn't go through were brokered by Constantine, and Nick had to step in last minute to save them. Prime ground for resentment, yet Constantine doesn't show any outward anger toward his cousin. Still, it's not something I can ignore, though I do push it aside.

Nick's careful to stay away the first couple of days. Three days after he took me home early, he locked the door to the empty office, yanked my pants down my legs, and buried his face between my thighs. It marks the start of a change in our relationship, making it clear our age difference is no longer an issue.

Not that I'm complaining. If anything, it's one good thing, his appetite for me. It's insatiable and varied. Torturously slow, rough enough to bruise, fast, soft, but there's one constant.

It's intense.

That, coupled with his newfound hobby of encircling me with his arms and lounging on the couch after a day of documents, documents, and more documents, has me jolting back and forth like the rope in a tug of war. Nick's quiet, confident affection is screwing with my mind. Plain and simple. I'm getting to the point where it's less about the sex and more about sex with Nick.

Sex with Nick is beyond my scope of knowledge. *Sex with Nick* is rapidly approaching the area inhabited by the happy couples of the world. It doesn't help that our evenings involve him distracting me with conversation in an attempt to get more food into me. Sometimes it works. When it doesn't, he gives me his scary face, and I cram a few bites in.

The conversation is the worst part of the whole deal. He tells me about his sisters and the rest of the family. He has story after story of the trouble he and Constantine caused growing up. He'll change it up, throw in a snippet about his college days. They don't sound so different from my own.

If he was a person to me before, a friend of sorts, I don't know what he is to me now. Which makes it so much harder to mention my misgivings about Constantine.

We're in what I've come to think of as our usual spots tonight, dinner over, the kitchen cleaned up and the food put away—he's gotten really good at doing the dishes—slouched onto the couch, my back flush against his chest, a blanket he dug out spread over my legs. He's got one hand tangled in my hair, the other tucked under my tank top, splayed across my belly. We're several episodes into season one of *The West Wing*. Nick's choice, over my protests that I didn't like politics.

The show is so frickin' *good.*

"Cassidy?"

"Hmm?" I crane my neck around. "Yeah?"

The hand in my hair works its way up my scalp. "You didn't answer the question."

I was drifting, engrossed in the show, conscious of his chest rumbling and his hands on my skin. I wasn't paying attention to what he was saying.

I shift so I'm facing him. "Sorry. What did you say?"

"Found anything useful yet?"

It's the same question he asks me every night, and every night I give him the same frustrating answer. "No. I ran a tally of times Marc's name comes up in conjunction with any particular project, and the highest number of instances was the Nautilus project. Either it's a dead end or there's information missing because everything I've read substantiates Isaiah's statement. It simply fell apart. There's no reason that anyone involved would be angry enough to want to eliminate Marc. Or you, for that matter."

My skin tightens, and sweat breaks out along my hairline. I've been steeling myself to do this all week, the urge growing stronger with each hour I spend hunched in front of that fucking computer. I need more information because, so far, all I've got is my gut telling me to take a closer look at Constantine, and I've been afraid to. I don't want to think about what it'll do to Nick if I'm right, and his cousin, his friend, is somehow behind this.

Wanting Nick's complete attention, I grab the remote and shut off the TV, then straddle his lap. "Tell me about Marc," I say quietly.

His gaze searches mine. "What do you want to know?"

I fist my hands in his shirt to anchor myself. I haven't eaten much today, anxiety a spring winding tighter. "Everything. Everything you can think of, everything you assume, what people said about him. Isaiah says they were more like brothers than cousins. One of your sisters was close to him, too, right?"

"George. Georgina," he clarifies. "You think he's the key?"

The room is freezing. I pull the ice inside, coating my stomach, stilling the blood in my veins. I climb off his lap and settle myself cross-legged next to him, stifling a wince as the skin around my leg wound pulls tight. "I think he was ready to die. I'm not sure it matters if we know if it's suicide by assassin or if someone else really ordered the hit. He knew it was coming, and he'd made his peace with it." I have to make my peace with it, otherwise the guilt will swallow me whole.

I snag the blanket and wrap it around my shoulders. "Specifically, I want to know about the last year or so of his life. Did he screw anything up? Stop going out? Anything out of the ordinary, I need to know."

He regards me coolly, the heat between us dwindling to nothing. We're allies here. Not friends, not lovers.

He gets to his feet and walks out of the room. He returns with the notepad full of my scribbles. He drops it in my lap, along with a pen, and retakes his seat. "From what I remember, Marc wrapped up a project about two years before he died. It wasn't an acquisition, more like a reorganization of one of my existing companies. With the personnel shifting, there were grumblings, but that's business. He sat in on a search team to hire a new head of R and D a few months after that. I wasn't involved. Con might have more information, or Terry."

"Terry?" The name's been in the files.

"He worked closely with Marc, and I think they were good friends outside of work."

Nick talks for almost an hour, running down who was most upset by Marc's death. Besides his sister and his cousin, I have a list of ten names, some within the family, some people he worked with.

I tap the pen on the pad. "Of those people, who knew about Josef?"

"Isaiah was the only one high enough in the family to know what Josef was utilized for, but Josef wouldn't have taken orders from him."

"Who could have given them?"

He scuffs a hand over his jaw. "Other than myself, that would be my father, Constantine, and my uncles, unless someone managed to buy Josef's loyalty."

We freeze at the same time as the implications of what he'd just said sink in. I lick dry lips. "How much money would it take to buy him off?"

"Depends. The hit on my life is the first indication I've had there's unrest within the family. If it goes deeper, it might not have been difficult to do."

It comes off like a rationalization, albeit a logical one. I set the pad and pen aside and get to my feet. Instead of narrowing the list of possible suspects, I opened a brand new can of worms. I imagine Nick could use some time alone. I wander into the kitchen and open a cupboard for a glass.

He scares a squeak from me as he comes up from behind and scoops me up to carry me into the bedroom. His hands and mouth everywhere, I meet his fury with one of my own, willing to ignore the elephant in the room for a little while longer.

* * * *

With a viable list of suspects, there's less need for me to go in with Nick every day. I can access information using one of the computers set up in the second bedroom to get what I need. Creating dossiers in a place where a large portion of the staff is related to the CEO either by blood or marriage doesn't strike me as a smart idea.

Nick, however, doesn't want to leave me alone.

"Why? There's no reason for me to come with you. The only person who knows we're here is Constantine. Do you think he's suddenly going to blab?" If he was smart, he wouldn't for a while, and that gave me time to figure out if my suspicions were founded or not. I sit up, sheet pooling around my waist, and start hunting for the sleep tank Nick pulled off me a little bit ago.

His silence is disturbing, especially when it continues. I find the tank and slip it on, then twist around. He's sprawled out, taking up over half the bed, hands under his head, muscled chest on full display.

I check my chin for drool.

He watches me through half-hooded eyes, mouth a slash under his nose. "We have to move."

"Move? Move where? Another safe house?"

The bed creaks as he sits up, swinging his legs over the edge. Naked, he strides to the bathroom, shooting me a glance as I ogle his ass. "People are asking too many questions. We're at my house starting tonight."

I locate my underwear in the sheets, pull it on, and follow him to the bathroom. "Your house is secure." It's not a question; a man like Nick wouldn't live somewhere without safety measures in place.

"Secure like your apartment was secure." He turns on the shower and motions for me to strip.

I lean against the counter instead. "So your house has a security system and a couple of deadbolts. Fabulous."

"I didn't say that. Poor analogy. There are security cameras everywhere, and I spend several hours every few months upgrading the system and moving the cameras around. No gate, reinforced steel doors, bullet-resistant glass, fully fenced back yard. The safest thing about it is the location." He steps into the tub.

"What, it's impossible to get to?"

"It's in Santa Monica. In the middle of the block. Surrounded by houses just like it."

I picture a man like Nick surrounded by snooty, older, rich people and snort. "I'm going to go make coffee."

"Start packing your shit up," he calls after me.

The rest of the day is like all the other days. Nick's off doing whatever it is he does. I stare at the portal icon on my monitor. It's one thing to look into his business dealings and weed out possible suspects. It's another to investigate his family. My fingers tremble as I set them on the keys.

Nick wants this information. Sucking in a breath, I type in the password he gave me and click submit.

The sheer amount of data is daunting, though far easier to search. Nick must have told Constantine what I was up to because he drops by well before Isaiah would show up to take me to lunch and demands I try the new Thai restaurant a few blocks over. He helps me back up the dossier I'm working on and locks the office before hurrying us out of the building.

"Why all the secrecy?" I ask when we're ensconced in a booth at the back of the restaurant.

Constantine lowers his menu enough to level a *seriously?* look at me. "Dom's okay with Isaiah knowing what the hell you're doing?"

I stick my tongue out at him, my stomach a solid lump. All this time spent with him isn't making it easier to eat. "Point taken. He thinks Nick's paying me to go through old files."

"And we'll just let him keep thinking that," he says, going back to his menu.

The afternoon is harder because I've switched to the dossier on Isaiah. He's too new an acquaintance to be a true friend, but he adds another layer of guilt all the same with his friendly grins and ongoing concern over my eating habits. His ties to Marc are too strong to be ignored, though. My attention's split between the computer and the door, nerves fraying as the minutes drag past.

Nick shows up about an hour to quitting time. "You look like shit."

I go to push my hair away from my face and end up brushing at air, having twisted my hair into a tight braid in a fit of nervous energy. "Thanks for that." He's got his jacket on. "We're leaving?"

"Need to do some shopping. There's no food in the house."

I back up the document the way Constantine showed me and shut down. "Somehow I think that's a regular occurrence." I snicker, but sober quickly when he doesn't react. "What?" I follow him out of the room and wait while he locks the office door.

His hesitation is slight, and I might not have noticed if I wasn't watching him so closely. "It's my night for family dinner."

I stop dead in the hallway while he continues toward the elevator. "Your family is coming to dinner?"

"Not the entire family. Parents, sisters, their husbands, and kids. Con and Isaiah and their parents, most likely." He glances over his shoulder. "Coming?"

Hell no. I'm staying right here in this hallway where it's safe. Where I'm not surrounded by Kosta men and women who will likely want to kill me after they learn what I've done.

I fist my hands, wishing for the first time in days I had a knife on me. I'd wave it in front of his face to distract him and escape down the stairs. "I'll call Denise and have dinner with her."

He approaches me like he'd approach a scared puppy, all slow and careful. "Scared?"

Terrified. "Yes," I admit. "They're not likely to be as forgiving as you."

"Too late." He grabs me around the waist and throws me over his shoulder, jerking when my fist lands square in the middle of his back. "Such violence, love."

"Put me down."

He doesn't let go until we're in the garage, and then he pins me to the car with a searing kiss. "You'll be fine," he murmurs. "No one else has to know."

Tell that to my angry stomach. There's no way I'll be able to eat anything tonight.

After a detour by the grocery store that I drag out as long as possible, insisting we needed things we don't actually need, Nick rolls into a quiet neighborhood several blocks from the beach.

It couldn't be farther from what I pictured.

The houses aren't huge, but they're definitely multi-bedroomed, the lots big enough for entertaining yet small enough you could hang over your fence and chat with your neighbor. Nick's house is in the middle of the block, like he said, facing east. The most prominent feature is the front windows, floor to ceiling, the main part of the roof pitched steeply.

All that glass...

I trail him up the flagstone path to the front door and duck under his arm to watch him put in the alarm code. We haul the groceries into the house, and I go back for my bags. "Bedroom?" I ask.

He takes my bag and slings it over his shoulder. "Come on."

His bedroom is huge. Walls the color of the Pacific in a storm, California king-size bed, the furniture some dark wood that makes me want to stroke it to see if it's as smooth as it looks. A set of French doors opens onto a small flagstone patio, leading to a sprawling deck looking over the backyard.

I'm tempted to hide in here. I haven't played *meet the parents* since high school, and I'm strung out enough as it is. This fake relationship is becoming far too real, and I'm not programmed to handle it. One more thing to thank Turner for. My chest squeezes at the thought of my father, how fucked I've become because I spent years begging for him to love me. "How far is the beach?"

"Couple blocks. You're staying for dinner." Once again, he pins me, this time to the bed, halting my struggles with a glare. "Cassidy."

Nausea bubbles in my stomach, and I break out in a cold sweat. "Don't make me do this," I whisper. His parents will ask questions, and I'm tired of lying.

The doorbell rings, and I wince. "Please. I'll stay in here. I'm not hungry anyway."

His hand comes up, and he rubs his thumb over my lips. "You need to eat," he says quietly. "Lia's coming. So's Con. Stick with them. You'll probably have to talk to my parents at some point, but I can tell them you're nervous. It'll excuse you for tonight." He straightens and pulls me to my feet. "Ready to play house?"

Tonight? Only for tonight? Will I have to repeat this performance? Jesus. Someone save me from myself.

Chapter 23

The evening goes sideways almost immediately.

The first people to arrive are George and her family, followed quickly by Shelly, the second oldest daughter, and her husband. After introductions, I retreat to the kitchen and the alcohol, dawdling as I open a bottle of red and poke through drawers, searching for a bottle opener for my beer.

Constantine rushes into the kitchen. "Hey. Have you seen the yard yet? Let's go look at the yard." He rounds the counter and practically shoves me through the kitchen door. It doesn't take a genius to figure out something's up, but since it gets me out of the house and away from all the people in it, I'm okay with putting aside my doubts to hang out with him.

What I can see of the yard is nice. Dusk has rolled in and blanketed the coast, turning the edges of bushes and trees fuzzy. Constantine flips a switch, and the lights surrounding the deck turn on. I lie on one of the lounge chairs and stare up at the sky. No stars. This close to the city with the pollution, the stars get blotted out. "Thanks. I didn't want to be in there."

He chuckles. "Anything to help a damsel in distress."

"If you really wanted to help, you'd find a way to sneak me out of here." And get me someplace where it's marginally warmer. The temperature is falling rapidly, and I'm not wearing a coat.

"Not a fan of family dinners?"

"Not a fan of being surrounded by people who would likely kill me first chance they got." I roll my head to the side, meeting his gaze. "Plus, it's hard to remember who knows what, what lies I've told, what ones I haven't."

"True," he agrees. His gaze slides past me and his eyes widen. His lips turn up in a charming smile. "Tell me a story."

There are more people outside, talking quietly, too soft for me to hear more than a suggestion of words. I twist around to see what he's looking at, but I can't find the source of the voices. Now my curiosity's roused. "You want to tell me what's going on?"

"Story first." He moves his hand in a *get on with it* motion.

Fine. I'll play his way. "Once upon a time, some stuff happened. Then more stuff happened. A unicorn pooped rainbows across the sky, and the world was blown to hell in a fiery ball of fire. The end. *Now* will you tell me what's going on?"

His answer is cut off by Liana stomping onto the deck, leaving the sliding door to the dining room open at her back. "Con! Why did you let your mother bring her?" She drops onto my lounge chair and scrunches her face in sympathy. "Cass, I'm sorry, and I'd like to apologize for my family."

Oookay. "Um, thanks? I think? Why are you apologizing?"

She narrows her eyes and swings her head to Constantine. "You didn't even tell her? Shit." She shifts so her back is to her cousin. "Cecelie's here. Nicky's ex. Aunt Gina thinks they're absolutely perfect together and ignores everyone's protests and keeps trying to push them back together. Cece's not helping by still being hung up on him, even though she's the one who dumped him. She did it over a year ago too."

I hold up a hand to halt the flow of words, my brain scrambling to keep up. "Nick's ex is here? And she's trying to get him to take her back."

"Yup."

"Why is your aunt the one pushing? That's a mom thing." Well, normal moms would. Mine just pretends she's an ostrich.

Constantine shrugs. "My mother is a nosy woman who demands babies. Grandnieces or grandnephews are just as good as grandchildren in her mind. She's not getting it out of me, so when Dom stayed with Cece for, what, how long were they together?" He looks at Lia for confirmation.

"A year." She reaches behind her head and tightens her ponytail. "A year, then Cece broke up with him. Gina's been after them both ever since."

My head hurts. An honest to God headache's brewing, a dull knot of pain forming at the base of my skull. "I need more beer," I announce. Beer will see me through this family dinner debacle.

I stand just as Nick's walking over to the deck, a woman about his age at his side. In the dim lighting I get an impression of lush curves and wavy brown hair, but the closer they get, the better I can see the naked pain on her face.

I make a beeline for the sliding door and safety. That look is on her face because of this stupid charade. That look is there because of me.

In the kitchen, I mumble vague greetings to Shelly and George, dumping my empty bottle in the trash and pulling a fresh one from the fridge. They start asking about my classes, and I decide the kitchen's probably a safer place to stay, so I hide in plain sight, ignoring the sympathetic glances they exchange.

Nick shows up shortly after they start telling me about their kids and slips an arm around my shoulders. It's heavy and wrong, all kinds of wrong, the weight of it uncomfortable. I'd shrug it off except he's using it to steer me out of the kitchen and down the hall to the bedroom.

He shuts the door and wanders over to the bed. I remain standing, hands clamped on my beer bottle. "I'm sorry about that. About Cecelie showing up," he says.

I shrug. "It's not your fault. I'm probably the one who should be apologizing."

He frowns. "Apologize for what?"

I place the beer on the dresser and sit next to him, a careful foot of space between us. "I saw the look on her face, Nick. Unless she's completely delusional, there had to be some real hope that you'd get back together."

His silence grows as heavy as his arm was, and I paste on a smile. "See? You and I, and Constantine, we know there's nothing here. Some good times and amazing sex. But we had to lie to too many of your family members, and now we don't have a choice but to see this through." And I'm hurting someone whose only mistake was realizing she'd made one in the first place. "So I'm sorry." I rub my palms on my thighs and retrieve my beer.

"I'm not."

The bottle slips in my hands and I bobble it, droplets of beer flinging themselves onto my hand. "You're not," I say slowly.

He stands and takes a step toward me. Then another and another, coming to a stop when he's well inside my personal space. "You remember you told me why you had a hard time relating to guys your own age? Same goes, Cass, only it's thanks to you I realized it."

I frown. "I don't understand."

"I don't have to hide from you. I don't have to lie. There may be things I won't tell you, but at least you'll know *why*. The women I've dated before didn't even have that luxury. I was never certain they'd understand."

I tip my head down before he can kiss me, confusion upping the pounding in my head. This is not part of the plan, although if I'm being honest, the plan was screwed once Nick started with his whole cuddling thing.

He cups my face and tilts it up, a small smile on his lips. "You haven't met my parents yet, and I got sidetracked. Come on." Lacing our fingers together, he leads me out of the bedroom and into the main part of the house.

It's a simple thing, hand holding, yet all it does is add to my confusion. The rumbling tangle of emotions comes to a dead halt when he leads me to a couple seated in the living room. "Mom, Dad, this is Cass. Cass, these are my parents, Andreas and Marina."

His mother is gorgeous with brown hair and bright blue eyes, startling in a sea of dark ones. His dad, on the other hand, has my heart lurching in my chest.

It's Turner.

Not my actual father, but he's there in the way Andreas carries himself, in his silence, in the impersonal way he studies me.

Marina holds out her hand, and I go through the motions, smile politely, shake hands, answer her questions, all the while conscious I'm being evaluated and found lacking.

Andreas shakes my hand as well and thankfully allows his wife to do all the talking. My tongue's tied in enough knots as it is.

My discomfort lessens somewhat with the arrival of Isaiah and his parents. "Zeke had to work, and Serena's staying home with a sick kid," he says after greeting his aunt and uncle. He grins and grabs me in a bear hug, jostling my beer. "Dom, I'm stealing your girl." He ushers me out to the deck, and I think of the dossier I compiled earlier today. It can't be him. Isaiah doesn't want my head on a platter.

Constantine and Lia are sitting on the chairs, talking, so I take a seat opposite Lia, sitting sideways on the chaise. "Did you talk to Nicky?" she asks.

"Yeah." I'm not sure what to make of the conversation, and his family dynamics make absolutely no sense. I turn to Constantine. "Dude, what's with your mother?"

He grimaces. "If I knew she'd asked Cecelie to come tonight, I would have told her about you."

"Shit, man, Cece was here?" Isaiah scowls at his cousin as he sits beside me, throwing his arm around my shoulder. "Babe, this is one fire you should not have been thrown into."

My muscles knot up, one by one, tiny fibers locking and holding. Stomach a block of cement, lungs barely functioning, I force a smile. "It's fine."

An older woman steps onto the deck, and Constantine jumps up and hurries over, Isaiah's hand tightening on my shoulder. I lean into him, wishing I could rest my aching head somewhere. Nick's shoulder, maybe. Or bed. A bed would be good, too, along with a dark room. "Aunt Gina?" I murmur.

"Jesus. Is everyone trying to steal Cass from me?" Nick walks around his aunt and ousts Isaiah from his spot, fulfilling my wish for a place to rest my head. "You okay?" The words whisper over my temple, his lips soft.

I huddle closer. One dinner. A few hours. I'm strong enough to make it through an evening with his family. "Could use some aspirin."

"Hey, Lia, could you grab the bottle of Aleve from the bathroom?" Nick's question rumbles through me, the pleasant vibrations easing some of the stiffness. She grumbles something about not being his Sherpa as Isaiah points out he *told* Nick he was stealing me away, and, more to the point, I didn't protest. Nick just maneuvers us so we're sprawled on the lounge chair, me cradled in the vee of his legs, his chest a warm, solid wall at my back.

Dinner isn't as bad as it could have been. Food arrives from a local pasta bar, giant bowls of salad, steaming aluminum containers of pasta, easy food to push around to conceal the fact my stomach's locked up like a safe. I'm seated between Nick and Lia on the couch, away from the meddling Gina and the damning silence of Andreas. Cecelie must have chosen to leave because I haven't seen her.

The family is all over. Some are at the dining room table, a few are in the kitchen, and the rest are in the living room, balancing plates on laps. Conversations overlap and interrupt themselves. Thank God for Lia. Even with Nick's hip pressed to mine, I spend most of dinner talking to her, and the end result is I'm enjoying myself far more than I anticipated when the evening began. With the distraction, I manage a little more than half my meal, and it's not threatening to reappear. Progress.

Lia glances wistfully at my plate. "You've got way better control. How can you not scarf it down?"

I give her a wry smile. "Willpower. Lots and lots of willpower." Or a case of anxiety fast descending into a starvation diet. I rise, plate in hand. "Did I see cake? I have no willpower against cake." My stomach cheers at the thought of cake.

There is cake. Rich chocolate frosting screams deliciousness. I rinse off my plate and stick it in the dishwasher, refill my water glass, and find the silverware drawer. I suppose I ought to be polite and cut up the cake so whoever wants a piece can just wander in and take some.

"Cassidy."

I don't drop the knife, though it's a near miss with his low, calm voice knocking up against my foundations and shaking them hard. Andreas is in the doorway, a glass half-full with amber liquid in his hand. Whiskey, probably. "Mr. Kosta. Would you like some cake?" He's like Turner. Treat him with the same detached deference, and it'll be okay.

His eyes never leave mine. "Would you join me outside for a moment?"

Saying "no thanks" isn't an option. He opens the kitchen door and waits for me to pass through first. The small patio is connected by a path—more flagstones—to the main deck off the dining room, but he remains where he is, the light from the deck not quite reaching us.

He doesn't bother building up to his topic. He jumps right in. "You're the Ghost's daughter."

I no longer want cake. "Yes."

"I've done business with your father on several occasions."

This doesn't surprise me, though it should on some level, given how often organized crime people prefer to handle their own problems. "And?"

Andreas flicks his eyes to me. "And I'm wondering how my son managed to become involved with an assassin."

A man like Andreas Kosta demands the truth, or a part of it, because what does surprise me is he doesn't see through the lies we've told. "I was hired to kill him."

Ice clinks in his glass. "I gathered as much." A deliberate sip, light catching on his wedding ring. "What reason do I have for not killing you in return?"

Sliding into this discussion is like putting on my favorite jeans, it's so familiar. "Two reasons. The first is someone else is already trying, and your concern should be eliminating that person. But the bigger reason is, it's just business. It was a job. It doesn't matter that it was your family."

He takes his time responding, sipping his drink, staring out into the darkened yard. "Someone has attempted to kill you as well."

The bandage should come off soon. I hope. "Yes." Either he knows it was Josef or he doesn't. I'm not about to volunteer the information.

"Someone in my family." The full force of his coolly assessing gaze rests on me, and I want to squirm.

"It's a possibility." It's pretty fucking likely. "I don't have many clues to work with so tracking the person responsible has been hard."

He nods once. "We have used you as well. It's business, though sometimes when it's family, it's difficult to separate the two. We paid you to complete a job, and you succeeded. Rewarding you with your own death is counterintuitive."

Tell me something I don't know.

He dips a hand into his pocket and pulls out a card, hands it to me. "Contact me if there's anything you need."

My nose tingles and burns. As much as I want to believe Turner wouldn't leave me twisting in the wind, I understand my father well enough to know he'd expect me to find my own way out of this disaster. Andreas's offer of help is the hand I wish Turner would extend.

Ice rattling in his empty glass, Andreas leaves me on the patio wondering if an olive branch would go unnoticed.

Chapter 24

Andreas's offer strengthens some of my tethers and frays others. I'm able to eat cake and joke with Constantine, make plans for lunch with Lia the next day, and engage in polite conversation with Aunt Gina without wanting to stab her in the eye with my fork.

Nick shuts the door after the last relative stumbles out and gives me a look. It's a *bedroom now and get naked* look. I'm a fan of this look; it's one he's used before. But tonight I need some distance. Too many objects poking through my armor: his ex, his meddling aunt, his dad, the constant lies about who I am and why I'm here and what we're doing. I need the distraction of sex but none of the connection.

We race down the hall, anticipation simmering under my skin. Our mouths come together as the bedroom door clicks home. Tongues slipping and sliding, my hands desperate for any part of him I can touch, he lifts me and tumbles me onto the bed.

I want fast. I want heat and sweat. I want mindless whimpers and bodies grappling over messy sheets. I don't care if I have an orgasm or not. Although knowing Nick, he'll work me over until I have one.

Clothing's yanked and ripped away until there's nothing but skin. His, mine, rubbing together, his cock trapped against my belly as his tongue invades my mouth. I'm a squirming, incoherent mess. I am *this close* to insanity, the temporary madness of his body on mine a heady rush.

Then he stops.

He eases his way down, his lips soft and sweet and warm at my throat, along my shoulders, on the tops of my breasts. I suck in a breath, fisting my hands in the blankets as he flutters his tongue along my rib cage. It's so weird, the gentleness, and terrifying the way it sends a signal straight to my core, fuck me fuck me *fuck me now*. It ramps up when he dips his fingers in between my legs, my hips undulating to meet his lazy thrusts.

I need a distraction from the embarrassing wetness coating my inner thighs, something to throw off his slow, steady rhythm. Closing my hand around his dick, I copy one of his moves and suck his tongue into my mouth, pumping him, taunting him. He pushes himself into my hand. "Spread your legs, love," he says, voice hoarse.

Nope. I have other ideas. Other naughty ideas. I roll away from him and get on my hands and knees, sending a heated look over my shoulder.

Nothing says fucking like doggy style.

He curses and fumbles for a condom. Hands on my hips, he plunges forward, his hard length splitting me open. I brace myself on my forearms and snap my hips back against him, the harsh sound of flesh slapping flesh giving me what I wanted.

They're lonely sounds, the stuttered breaths, the bitten off moans, because they're loosed into a void. He's my living, breathing sex toy, and each drag of his cock through swollen tissues increases the emptiness.

Then he hauls me upright, molding us together, one hand cupping my breast, the other banded around my waist. The only friction on my clit is from my own hand.

This isn't happening. My cells aren't crying out with glee at the change. The tempo and tone of this has morphed into what I couldn't handle tonight. Close, close sex, the intimacy of it staggering. It shouldn't be, not this position, not how impersonal it is. No face to face contact. But my hips rock in counterpoint to his. The security, the *surety* of his body on mine, his mouth teasing my earlobe, smashes the distance from good old-fashioned fucking fun to more. This is *Nick* making me feel like this, *Nick* holding me to him as if he'll catch me when I fall, *Nick* tipping my head back and kissing me as if he needs it more than he needs air. And all the while he's thrusting into me steady, deep strokes designed to make us both insensate.

The low, heavy thrum of the gathering tension gains strength, my body vibrating with the need for release. My legs can't take much more of the strain. "Nick." Help me help me help me. I can't reach it. I can't get there on my own. "*Please.*"

"Hold on," he mutters. The arm around my waist loosens as I cup the back of his neck, and he strokes his hand down, sliding his thumb over the aching bundle of nerves. The world flashes bright, blinding white, and I dig my fingers into his skin, seeking purchase.

"Again," I gasp. Again again again *again*. He does, thumb taunting, a scream building in my lungs. I've never screamed before.

But then, I've never felt an orgasm as massive as the one bearing down on me now.

It decimates. Levels me, shatters everything I know about sex and pleasure and reforms it into this...this *thing* that devolves into that scream. He goes rigid, his hands holding tight enough to bruise, and we fall forward, Nick twisting at the last minute so we land on our sides.

I am so totally, thoroughly, and utterly screwed. This is not just sex anymore. This is absolutely Sex With Nick, sex that Means Something, and I can't imagine what that is.

Apparently it means I whine when he leaves the bed to get rid of the condom. He returns a moment later and lays down in front of me, expression wary. "What the fuck was that?"

Blunt words. True words. A question I don't have an answer for, and neither does he. "I was hoping you'd know." Any other guy, any other situation, I'd say I'm well into the *I seriously like you and not just in the I want to get in your pants all the frickin' time* point in a relationship.

How long have I known him? Two weeks? Less than that. It's not love. It's more than lust. This is A Relationship. It has the power to be big and important, and I feel like those words deserve capital letters.

His grin doesn't reach his eyes. "If I did, I wouldn't have asked." He lifts a hand, then hesitates, uncertainty clear on his face. "Come here."

I scoot forward, not stopping until my nose is smooshed against his chest. "You have a cuddle fetish?"

"No. But I think I'm developing a Cass fetish. It's more pronounced when you're naked."

I'd laugh, but I think I'm developing a Nick fetish to match his me fetish. "Your timing sucks."

"No doubt. Don't really care." He laces his fingers through my hair and tugs gently, tipping my head back. "Figure we'll just make it up as we go along."

Yeah, I'm definitely in the *I seriously like you* phase. At least I don't have to pass him a note to know he feels the same way. "I can do that." Improvisation is my friend. "Is there more cake?"

His laugh spins through me, slinking into the dark places and warming them. "If there's not, I'll have another one delivered."

Oh, goody. I do like me some cake.

* * * *

Cake tastes even better after amazing sex.

I dunk a bite of cake in the melting vanilla ice cream I'd scooped on top and pop it into my mouth. "Umf. Good."

He sits up and leans forward. "Gimme."

I shield the cake with my body. "Mine. Get your own."

He reaches around and sticks his finger in the ice cream before dabbing it on my lips. He licks it off, giving me a lazy smile. "Yours is better."

When he puts it that way, it doesn't take much to convince me to share. We polish off the piece, and then he goes and gets another, adding chocolate syrup this time. I groan. "Jesus. You're trying to kill me."

"Nah. I leave that to my other family members."

He did not just say that.

"Too soon to joke?"

I snatch the cake plate from him. "Tact much?"

He has the decency to look sheepish. "Sorry. Age doesn't always equal maturity."

"No shit," I mumble around a mouthful of cake. I swallow and lick my lips. "Your dad offered to help."

"Did he? Or did he tell you to call him if you needed anything?" Stealing the plate back, he scoops up cake. "There's a difference where my father's concerned. He'll step in once you've run into so many brick walls your face is unrecognizable."

"Oh." The vague warm fuzzy I'd gotten over his offer cools significantly. Stupid of me to think he was any different from Turner. I tip over onto my back. "I'm tired of this. Someone wants me dead. Someone wants you dead. It would be much simpler if they'd just come out, announce their intentions, and then shoot. Or something."

"Where's the fun in that?"

I lift my head and stick my tongue out at him. "Don't tell me you don't wish something like that would happen. Don't you want your life to go back to normal?"

He must have set the plate down somewhere because his hands are gliding up my legs. "Depends. Is it the old normal or the new normal?"

"What's the difference?"

My blood heats as he works his way up, the gentle touch reminiscent of his earlier caresses. "Old normal was work, take out someone's kneecaps, more work, and work again. New normal?" His fingers find their way into the leg of the boxers I pulled on. "New normal's pretty much the same except I keep getting distracted by a very pretty assassin." Heat flares across my cheeks, and he grins. "Cute. I like it when you blush."

"Shut up." I squirm, trying to make contact with his wandering hands, blowing out a frustrated breath when he withdraws. He settles himself between my legs, bracing himself on his forearms. "So I guess that means I don't need to have you check yes or no?"

"Yes or no?" He dips his head to nuzzle my temple. Sigh. The many, many sides of Dominic Kosta. The sweet, languid side might turn me into a puddle someday.

"You must have gotten those notes in school. The ones that said 'Do you like me? Check yes or no.'" Turning my head, I press my mouth to the first piece of skin I find, a spot just in front of his ear.

"I remember those notes. Maybe I should pass you one." One hand sneaks under the hem of my tank. "Mine would say 'Do you want me to fuck you? Check yes or yes.'"

"Hmmm. I don't know. You sure I don't have any other options?" I curve my leg around his hip, rubbing against his erection, groaning when he nibbles on my earlobe.

"Sure. There's also 'Yes please and thank you.'"

I laugh, loving the smile he's pressing into my neck. "Oh, that one. Definitely that one."

He raises his head and smooths the hair away from my face, all teasing gone from his expression. "We could do it, though. Word spreads through the organization pretty quick. You want to put your face out there, take a chance someone will come straight at you, I'll make it happen. You'll never have a second alone until the threat is gone, but you want it, I'll do it."

If only it were that simple. I give him a half smile. "Wouldn't work. The whole point is to get me alone. Next time I'll be more prepared. And I'll try not to kill the guy before I get some answers." I kiss away his frown. "Distract me," I murmur. "Yes please and thank you."

"So demanding." He captures my lower lip between his teeth, an enticing preview of coming events.

I don't think of anything but him for the rest of the night.

Chapter 25

Normally, bullet points are fantastic. They lay out information in a clear, concise manner, leaving little room for error or interpretation.

The bullet points staring me in the face right now are not fantastic. These are the points I have to bring to Nick, and he's not going to be pleased.

My gut is right. It says Constantine is behind all this, that he's hiding his desire to oust his cousin from the top spot behind an affable and charming façade.

In the past four years, Constantine was the lead on fifteen different deals, split between Nick's legitimate holdings and the family's ever expanding empire. Of those fifteen, Marc played a crucial role in five and dropped the ball, much like they were worried Isaiah would do, forcing Nick and Constantine into taking over to close the deal.

And of those fifteen, four fell through, four were saved by Constantine, and the remainder were saved by Nick. *After* Constantine was brought on board.

It's not nearly enough to prove anything. There's only so much I can determine by looking at files. What I need are impressions. I need people who will talk to me. I have to figure out what questions to ask because I'm almost certain Constantine is in the trenches here, whispering in a few well-placed ears, planting the seeds of dissatisfaction.

I'd be unhappy. From what it looks like, Nick had to step in over Constantine's protests to save the deals. And I can't forget Constantine is one of the few who could give Josef orders and expect him to follow through.

The list taunts me. I have to show this to Nick and convince him he needs to take a closer look at the cousin who's more like a brother to him. There's always the possibility I'll be wrong, and that could damage whatever's building between Nick and me.

Good. I'm not cut out to handle feelings, anyway.

Liar.

Tucking my hair behind my ears, I stand, smooth down my skirt, and pick up my notepad, resisting the urge to tug at the hem of my shirt. I'll get the bad thing out of the way so I can move on to the fun thing: lunch with Lia.

Nick grins when he sees me in his doorway. The expression fades when I don't return it. I shut the door behind me and lock it for good measure. Being interrupted during this conversation would not be a good idea.

This is going to suck so hard.

"So what've you found?" His tone is casual, relaxed, and you'd think he's talking about a movie he enjoyed or the weather.

"Um," I hedge. I draw in a breath, blow it out. Remind myself my gut's never led me wrong before, and it's not going to now.

"I think I may have figured out who's behind this, but I can't go much further with the information I can access." His gaze sharpens, and I try to reach the cold, dark space inside me and fail. Fuck it. I can do this without the detachment. "It's someone in the family. Someone who has high clearance, or whatever you want to call it. Someone who has seven valid reasons to resent you."

I hand over the list. "These are the deals, both legitimate and within the family, that were headed by Constantine over the last four years. As you can see, he's got a reason to resent you from those alone based on the money they brought in. He's placed high enough people will listen to any mutterings he passes along about needing a change in leadership. He's one of the few who is authorized to give kill orders to Josef. That's a pretty strong case to look closer.

"I'm not saying I'm positive," I add, withholding my wince at his carefully blank face. "Just that he's got an awful lot of reasons to want you out of your position, and not a lot of reasons to keep you in it. The only thing I can't understand is why he wants me gone too. Unless he had his doubts from the beginning that I'd follow through and sent the men after you to ensure the job was done, and I just got caught in the crossfire."

Nick stares at my list, his shoulders rigid with tension. I study the blinds, his bookshelves, the potted tree in the corner. Anything to avoid looking at him. The longer the silence stretches, the more fearful I become because his expression has only grown emptier. Colder. This is the man I knew he was all along—deadly and not to be messed with.

Finally he sets the list down. "You believe he tried to have us both killed," he says slowly.

"I believe he wanted you dead. I'm still not sure how I fit into all of this."

"Your argument, from a logical standpoint, makes sense, but lacks evidence." He gets up, walks to the window, and yanks open the blinds with a violent tug. It's the only outward sign he's unhappy. "You're certain."

I shake my head. "Not certain. But my gut's never been wrong." My exhalation is shaky. "My gut told me not to kill Marc," I whisper. "He shouldn't have died. I ignored it. Only time I have, and it's come back to bite me on the ass."

He simply grunts, and his gaze drifts to his desktop and the offending list. I let myself out, sure I've just knocked our forward progress back about fifteen steps. Nothing like calling into question the trustworthiness and loyalty of someone who's held both for possibly decades.

The underground parking garage is deserted as I make my way to Nick's car. Footsteps echoing off the cement floors, it takes me a minute to figure out I'm not alone, and I stop short of the car, scanning the garage. Isaiah appears from around a corner, and I smile. "Hey."

"Hey, Cass." He comes up and wraps me in one of his bear hugs. "How's your project coming along?"

I shrug. "It's going. Where are you off to?"

His smile drops, leaving behind the cold lines of a seasoned warrior. "You'll find out in a minute."

The shock of the Taser screams up my spine.

* * * *

Feeling's returned to my legs, though it doesn't do me any good. They're currently bound together and secured to a pipe. Same with my arms. The rope chafes my wrists, and for one hysterical moment I wish for Nick's fuzzy fuchsia handcuffs. My shoes are missing, and my feet are freezing.

We're in some sort of small machine room. The hum of the large metal box Isaiah's sitting on is loud enough he has to raise his voice somewhat for me to hear him. That is, I'm pretty sure he's talking. I'm more interested in the large knife in his hands.

Light glints off the blade as he turns it around, a wicked, thin piece of steel too wide to be a stiletto. Focusing on that is better than wallowing in the fear licking its way through my body.

A knife like that means business. A knife like that means I won't be leaving this room alive. The only question is if he'll slit my throat or if he'll go for someplace slower. Stomach maybe, or my wrists.

I keep my mouth shut. I already know why I'm here: Marc. My instincts failed me. My instincts said dig into Constantine's life. I underestimated the depth of Isaiah's grief. I wonder what else I've underestimated about him.

"Why?" He stops flipping the knife, dark eyes alive and agonized in an otherwise perfect mask of bland.

He's not going to like this answer. "It was a job."

"Who hired you?" He crouches in front of me, knife at the ready.

The metal box ceases its hum, the quiet in the small room deafening. "I don't know."

The knife swings down in a flash of steel, slicing along my left shin. A quick, searing pain races outward from the cut, dulling to a slight ache as blood chugs from the wound. It's not deep, though it'll leave a scar. One more for my collection.

"Wrong answer."

Fearful, screaming Cass is crowding out cold, unaffected Cass. I shove her away. My pride's about all I have left here, bound as I am. I wiggle my wrists behind my back, the rope burning into my skin with each twist. The man knows his knots. By the time I loosen these enough to free myself, I'll be well on my way to dead. Isaiah's clearly not worried about being found, which tells me either the security cameras are disabled or no one's watching them. "Would it matter if I knew? It was business, Isaiah."

He really should have taped my mouth shut. He carves another line, this time in my right thigh, though he's careful to stay away from the femoral artery. Can't have me bleeding out before I answer his questions.

What the hell. He wants an answer; I'll give him the one that's been bumping around in my head for days. "You know what I think? I think he called it in himself."

Another cut, tearing through the delicate skin at the arch of my foot. Gritting my teeth against the pain, because *fuck* that one hurts, I push on. "He didn't fight me. He could have. He was bigger, stronger. He knew I was coming for him." The pain in Isaiah's eyes leeches out onto his face. "You think I'm right, don't you? Suicide by assassin. He was unhappy, but he didn't think anyone would understand." The psychology of suicide is something I've avoided, though I guess in this instance it's similar to Catholic guilt. Can't die by your own hand or you won't get through the pearly gates. Can't die by your own hand because the family won't believe it and will go looking for vengeance where none is needed. "He hired me to do what he couldn't do for himself."

God, what that must be like. Finding out after the fact that one of your loved ones would rather die than seek help. Does he blame himself?

Blame himself for not seeing Marc's desperation to get out from under the thick cloud bearing down on him?

"You're lying."

I grit my teeth as he drags the blade along my ribs, tearing through my shirt. "What reason do I have to do that?"

We play this game for a few minutes, Isaiah asking for the truth, me telling him I don't know. He adds another new scar to my flesh, but for the most part, he digs his fingers into the wounds he's already caused, the blood flowing anew.

"Why Nick?" I gasp out. "Why does he need to die too?"

Isaiah pauses with the knife inches from my chest. "Do you have any idea what it's like? Being seen as the screw-up? I wouldn't do it nearly as much if Nick could just be patient once in a while."

His reason makes sense in a twisted, sick sort of way. If I can keep him talking, maybe I can get my hands free. "Have you tried talking to him about it?"

He shifts the knife. "Enough. We're done," he growls.

Fear's a white-hot flash, burning through my veins as I twist my wrists helplessly, trying to free myself. Throat, wrists, or stomach? He opts for the stomach. There's no escaping the burning pain as he plunges the knife in, twisting it for good measure. It's what I'd do, cause the most internal damage so on the off chance someone found the body in time, there was little hope of saving the victim.

Blood pours from my belly, soaking my lap, tears streaming down my face as a muddled red haze fills my brain. I should have tried harder to free myself. I shouldn't have trusted him in the first place. So many things I could have done, and now it's too late.

He cuts the rope tying me to the pipe. The room's starting to cool, the blood starting to slow. I'm sleepy. Slipping one arm under my knees and the other behind my shoulders, he picks me up.

He's carrying me somewhere. "'Saiah? Wha' you doin'?"

"Shhh."

Seconds or minutes later, I'm lying on the ground. The cement's as soft as a feather pillow. I'm colder. Frozen. Everything is numb, and I'm exhausted. There's a welcoming pool of black looming closer, and I'd crawl toward it if I could, but I can't even move a finger.

Keeping my eyes open is impossible. The black shows me an end to the pain and the cold, seducing me with promises I know it can uphold. I can sleep forever if I want. And I do. I want it more than anything.

"Cass! *Cassidy*!"

No no no *no*, don't do this. Don't pull me away from my beautiful oblivion.

"Cassidy. Stay with me."

I know that voice.

"Give me your jacket."

Something's pressed against my stomach, and the pain ratchets back up, my eyes flying open at the impact. Garbled sounds like protests tumble from my mouth.

"Looks like she's lost a lot of blood."

I know that voice too. It's different from the other voice. Why won't they both leave me alone? The black's receding, taking its warmth with it, cold insinuating itself into my bones. My jaw tenses against my chattering teeth, but my eyelids still feel like there are one-ton weights on them.

"Come on, love, open your eyes for me."

Love. Nick. Nick and Constantine. I slit my eyes open, meeting Nick's frantic gaze. *Sorry.* I can't get the word out. Sorry he had to be the one to find me. Sorry I didn't try harder to fight. Sorry I didn't see it was Isaiah the whole time.

If I had the strength for it, I'd tell him he shouldn't waste his vengeance on me. I'm a blip on his radar. Now that I'm gone, he'll need to watch his back.

"Hey." His quiet voice is still unnaturally loud. "We've got paramedics on the way. Stay with me."

Can't. Can't do this anymore. I'll drag myself to the black if I have to. It's the only thing that will make this better. The cold's unbearable, and the muddled red haze in my mind is thicker, more opaque.

There's a high-pitched wail whining closer. It doesn't matter. The black's decided to accept me after all. It shoulders aside the cold and cloaks me with its warmth, encouraging me to shut my eyes. Shut my ears. Just shut down.

"Cass, *no!*"

Chapter 26

Empty.

It's like I imagined. The absence of all things. No sound, no scent, no touch. There's no light at the end of some tunnel. No warmth. It's a void, one I'm suspended in.

"Clear!"

Death isn't peaceful. It's not painful. It's not anything. It just is. It's a place to rest for eternity. I guess that makes it peaceful. My heart, my blood, my brain—all finally have a chance to just *be*. There's no guilt or anxiety or regret. No happiness or love. I don't miss it.

"Charging three hundred."

"Where's the blood? Someone call the blood bank. Stat!"

"I can't...come on, you little fucker...there! Found the bleeder!"

If you're wondering if there's a heaven, the answer's no. There's no hell, either, which is sort of where I expected to end up. I'm being absorbed, atom by atom, into this yawning, unending cavern of black.

"Clear!"

"OR Two is ready."

"Go!"

* * * *

I am cement. I'm a cement block. I'm at the bottom of the ocean.

This is definitely hell.

Something furry curled up and died in my mouth. My throat is as scorched as the Mojave. Fire scores my belly, spreading its gleeful tendrils through the cement, breaking it into pieces. I'm rising through fog, away from the cool deep, the fire eating away at the wisps.

"Cass?"

Moving hurts. Breathing hurts. My eyelids are glued shut.

Firm lips brush my temple. "Sleep, love. It'll keep."

Pushing the words past my lips takes forever. "Hurts." Hurts to speak. Hurts to think. The red behind my eyelids resembles blood.

"Here." Cold presses against my lips, parting them, sliding onto my tongue. Ice. It melts and seeps through my mouth, slinking into the crevices and clearing away the fur. It unlocks my jaw, and my lips part, seeking more.

A few more ice chips, and I open my eyes, blinking slowly. Everything's slightly fuzzy and out of focus. "Hurts," I whisper.

There's a short beep, and I manage to roll my head to one side. Nick's in a chair next to the bed, several days' worth of stubble covering his jaw, his hair a lazy mess, eyes a little red and bloodshot. But he's smiling, a gorgeous lifting of lips that wipes away the fatigue. "Welcome back," he says softly. "A nurse will be here in a minute. She might be able to increase the pain medication."

Medication. I like the sound of this.

"You look like shit," I croak.

His smile turns wry. "Thanks. You look worse." I stick my tongue out him, and he chuckles. The sound fades as his smile drops. "Wasn't sure I'd get to see you again."

"I'll never deprive you of your cuddle fetish object."

He laughs, a rusty, unused sound as a pink scrub-clad nurse squeaks in. "You're awake! How are you feeling?"

Nick jumps in before I can answer. "Can you increase her pain medication?"

The nurse busies herself checking my IV lines and the readouts on the various monitors. "The doctor will be in momentarily. He'll be able to give the authorization."

A few more random checks, and she leaves, the squeak of her shoes drowned by the squawking of an intercom in the hallway.

"I met your mother," he says out of the blue. I stare at him blankly. My mother? I guess that would make sense that she'd be by. I might have cut her out of my life, but she hadn't cut me out of hers. "She's been by every evening. Your dad was here the first night. Haven't seen him since."

Typical Turner. "Who else?"

"Constantine. Liana. Denise and her boyfriend. Charlie?" I nod. "The guy who walked you to drama class. Scott?"

"Scott came by? Wow." The list of names brings the one I've avoided so far to the surface. "Nick? What happened with Isaiah?"

Whatever good humor he has flees, his face shutting down. "He's dropped off the radar. No one can find him."

The memory crashes over me: the Taser, the ropes, the random cuts, the horrific pain as he twisted the knife. Being carried and laid out on the floor of the garage. My stomach throbs. "Why did he do it? Carry me out into the middle of the garage? He could have just left me."

He takes my hand, lacing our fingers together, tight and neat. They fit together scarily well. "He wanted you to be found. And I think he wanted *me* to find you. The security cameras caught everything. You didn't see it coming. Tasered you right in the back."

"I know." My tone's as dry as toast. "I was there."

He squeezes my hand. "He placed you in full view," he says quietly. "Motherfucker knew what he was doing. Con says the guy normally manning the security desk takes a break around the same time every day. I think Isaiah got lucky, saw you walking toward my car, and headed you off. Not so much a crime of opportunity since he was prepared, but if it hadn't happened that day, it would have another. Some place else where I might not have been so lucky."

I arch a brow. "You got lucky?"

"I got lucky." He doesn't sound all that happy about it, just grim. "You died on me a couple times that day. Once in the ER, once on the operating table. You're really fucking lucky to be alive, Cassidy, but you're really fucking lucky because *I* was lucky. Con and I were on our way out to meet Isaiah. He'd called me, saying he was grabbing lunch, and since you weren't around, maybe I ought to join him. Con tagged along because he wanted to talk to the security guard about the possibility of extra security. We both saw Isaiah carrying you through the garage."

He leans over the railing, cradling my hand in both of his. "He was staring right up at the camera. A set up. You probably should have been dead by then, but he wasn't going to leave you wherever he'd taken you. You were meant to be found, and found quickly."

Pain flares, tearing a gasp from my abused throat. Nick strokes my hand until it relaxes. "We can talk more when you're better."

The *why* batters me. I understand why Isaiah tried to kill me. Why Nick, though? Isaiah's explanation made sense. I know what it's like to be viewed as a failure and a screw-up. But does his hatred of Nick really run deep enough to want him dead?

And how could I have been so wrong about Constantine?

The doctor strides in, stethoscope sticking out of his pocket, the green scrubs not doing his complexion any favors. "Ms. Turner. I'm Dr. Smith." His smile is perfunctory. "You want the short version or the long version?"

"Short, please." I'd really like to go back to sleep.

"You lost a lot of blood and suffered a great deal of internal damage. Since you're awake, we'll mark that as a sign of improvement. You'll be staying in our fine establishment for a while." He picks up my chart and flips through it. "What's your pain level, scale of one to ten?"

"Nine."

He glances up, then makes a notation on the chart. "We can bump you up a bit. Not too much, but should be enough to help you sleep." He fiddles with one of the machines next to the bed and then hands me a remote attached by a covered wire. "Pressing the button will give you a boost. It's not a constant flow, and it'll only allow you a hit twice an hour." I press the button. I'm rewarded with a soothing warmth spreading through my limbs. Dr. Smith grins. "Maybe now you can convince your boyfriend to go home and sleep."

Boyfriend? Confused and overwhelmed with exhaustion, I glance over at Nick. In my fatigued state, he looks even worse than he did before. "Go home," I mumble. "Sleep."

He plants a kiss on my forehead. "In a while."

The next few days blur together, spent in a fog of pain and sleep. When I'm awake and coherent enough for conversation, Nick's there. He's commandeered the other bed in the room over the hospital's protests. If someone, a security guard, a nurse, Dr. Smith, tries to kick him out of it, he glares at them.

He doesn't trust anyone else to keep me safe. Not even Constantine, which leads to a shouting match. They stop when my pillow hits Nick in the face. "Nick, go home. Constantine will stay with me until you get back."

He stalks to the bed, pillow in hand, the gentleness of his touch at odds with the anger on his face as he helps me sit up and places the pillow under my head. "Cass—"

"Nope. Not hearing it. Go home. Get some real sleep. Reacquaint yourself with your house. You come back here looking like a bum, I'll kick you out again." His fear isn't unreasonable, but his constant presence is…weird. Very, very weird. Completely out of place for someone he barely knows.

But a part of me, a big, selfish part loves it, thinks it's sweet, uses it to spin new dreams of a future, complete with the two-point-five kids, picket fence, and a dog.

After more grumbles, he gives in, threatening Constantine with bodily harm if anything happens to me. His cousin flips him the bird and settles into the hard plastic seat next to the bed and picks up the TV remote.

He clicks through the channels, too fast for me to see what's on each one before he's on to the next. "Is he always like that? Uber protective?"

"You mean with the women he dates? Not really. Cecelie's the only one I've seen him do anything close to that, but since she was pretty much in the dark about the family business, there wasn't much call for it." He shoots me a sidelong glance. "He feels responsible for what happened to you. Thinks if he'd insisted on going with you, nothing would have happened."

Responsible. That explains it. Guilt's what's keeping him here, not his feelings for me. The guilt's much more realistic. It sucks the breath from my lungs and refuses to give it back. I pack my sweetly fuzzy dreams into a box and nail it shut, heart shuddering with the final hammer blow. "What's going to happen now?"

If Constantine's surprised by the question, he doesn't show it. "Dom thinks Isaiah's the one who hired you to take him out, though he's still unsure as to why." Our thoughts align there; getting stabbed banished my misgivings about Constantine, placing blame firmly on Isaiah. "Once we confirm, we'll start at the bottom. Isaiah didn't get as far as he did without help, without people loyal to him. We'll weed them out. It might be time to trim the fat, anyway."

From the little Nick's told me about his family, they've got all their fingers in all the pies. What Constantine's describing sounds like cutting off some of those fingers. "So things might get a little... unstable," I say slowly.

"That's probably the most accurate way of describing it."

"Nick will need to focus on work." Not me. Not me and my safety.

Constantine turns away from the TV. "What are you thinking, Cassidy?" The question is quiet with the barest hint of inflection. Like he knows what I'm going to say.

I pluck at the blanket covering my lower body. "I'm thinking it's time to call my dad."

* * * *

Turner's expression is impassive, as usual. "You're certain about this."

"It's the right thing to do." I hold his gaze, that steady, unflinching, X-ray stare. He knows I'm right, which is the reason I asked for his help in the first place. Believe me, if there was a different way to accomplish this, I would have gone that route.

The plan is to get me away from Los Angeles. I need a place to recover in peace. Since Isaiah didn't accomplish what he'd set out to do, there's a strong chance he'll come after me again. I'll tell Nick where I am once I'm gone so he won't worry. He needs to concentrate on staying alive.

The plan isn't an entirely selfless act on my part. Knowing why Nick's spent so much time, first waiting for me to wake up, then refusing to leave, has dulled any shine his devotion had. Simply put, it hurts, far more than I'm comfortable with, and I want distance. I want to hide away and lick my wounds. If I try hard enough, they'll be nothing more than bittersweet memories.

It'll give me time to stop playing what-if. What if Isaiah had never gotten his hands on me? Would we have continued how we were?

Turner glances at the clock on the wall. "He'll be here soon. I'll talk to the doctor. Plan to leave tomorrow night. I'll have your mother pack a bag for you."

Swallowing against the lump in my throat, I nod once, then snuggle deeper under the thin hospital blankets. It's for the best. It's the safest option for both of us.

The right thing to do sucks balls.

Epilogue

The water's incredibly clear, a bright turquoise you don't see off the coast of California. Sugar-white sand absorbs the sun's heat and burns the bottom of my feet, so I've learned not to take my sandals off. I'm getting stronger. I'm no longer out of breath by the time I reach my tiny hut.

A little over a month into my stay in Phuket, and the doctors pronounced earlier today I could go home. The surgeries on my scars, the one on my stomach, the random ones on my arms and legs, are healing well. They'll be much fainter when it's all said and done.

Yup, everything's just swell.

I'm so fucking lonely here, cut off from everyone. I've spoken with Denise twice a week since I arrived, and even Scott a couple times. I was desperate enough for human contact I even called my mother.

The rift in our relationship isn't anywhere near being closed, but it's getting there. Bridge building takes a hell of a lot longer than burning.

No contact with Lia or Constantine. Definitely no contact with Nick.

I thought a month apart would have caused my feelings to fade. It hasn't. If anything, they've been replaced. I left to keep him safe, but I made sure he knew where I was. So yeah, part of me hoped he'd be in touch somehow. E-mail, a phone call, hell, a text message would have worked.

The rift in my heart is harder to heal than my scars, and my ongoing game of *if only* has taken on a new facet—if only I'd kept my hands to myself.

Lonely as I am, I'm not ready to go home yet. I need to resume my classes, find a new place to live, get on with the business of being Cass Turner, college student. I need to find an actual part-time job, preferably one that doesn't involve bloodshed.

The steps creak under my weight as I climb them to the front door. I dig through my bag for my key. The rough edge scrapes my fingertips as I pull it out. I unlock the door and step inside, the dim interior noticeably cooler. It might be November, but this close to the equator, the heat never really lets up around here.

"Your note left a lot to be desired."

I squeak and drop my bag. Nick's sitting at my kitchen table, sprawled in a chair. I will my heart to calm as my eyes adjust to the shadows. "You were going to be busy with your family. Giving you specific information seemed pointless since you wouldn't need it." Rather than sit across from him, I curl up on the shabby, small two-seater couch in the living area.

"Would have been nice if you'd let me be the judge of that." He huffs out a breath and crosses his legs at the ankle. "It was a smart move, though," he admits. "Didn't mean I wasn't still thinking about you."

In a guilty way or a non-guilty way? "Me, too." Definitely in a non-guilty way. I missed him like a piece of me was gone.

"Your dad picked this place?"

The abrupt change of subject was a little startling. "Um. Yeah. Thailand ranks at the top for most gender reassignment surgeries, so their plastic surgeons are excellent. They worked on a couple of my scars."

He stands, crosses the short distance to the couch, and sits on the other cushion. He raises a hand and traces the faint ridge of the wound on my arm. "That's pretty fucking good." He lowers his hand and glances at my stomach, covered by the thin cotton of my tank top. "Can I…?"

The heat of his touch on my skin already caused my mind to blink out. His hand on my stomach might render me incapable of speech. "It's still pretty visible. The damage was more extensive, so they weren't able to cover as much." I cover my stomach with my hands, unwilling to pull up my shirt to let him see.

A faint line appears between his brows. "Your father has some very definite opinions on where you should stay when you return to the States."

I figured he would. I shrug. "I'll probably stay with my parents until I can find a place. There are plenty of roommate listings on Craigslist, and there's probably a campus bulletin board or something I can check."

The line grows deeper. "Isaiah hasn't been found yet."

Now it's my turn to frown. "I thought…since you were here…"

"That everything was back to normal?" He shakes his head. "The weed-out didn't go so well. Media's calling it a crime wave. We're pulling back, reevaluating. But no, it's nowhere close to being over."

He takes my hand and threads his fingers through mine. "Cass, I came here to get you. It's time to go home. Your father and I talked, and we agreed the safest place for you would be with me."

Great. More guilt, more responsibility. I tug my hand free, get to my feet, and walk to the kitchen area for a bottle of water. "I'm so glad you and Turner are okay with making important decisions for me. Because I'm totally not capable of doing it myself." I uncap the water bottle and drink half, hoping to drown the anger surging to life. It doesn't work. "I'd rather stay here, thank you very much. I can afford it." Maybe. I haven't accessed the off-shore account Turner had set up for me years ago in a few months. I'm not sure how much money is actually in there, but it should be enough to buy me several months' worth of lodging here.

He rakes a hand through his hair. "Fuck, Cass—"

"No, we've tried that already. It was fun. Let's do something else. I know! How about we remember that Cassidy is an adult, just like you, and as such, has opinions and thoughts and feelings and really appreciates it when people acknowledge that? I'll stay here if it's not safe to go home, Nick. Hardly anyone knows where I am." I drain the rest of the bottle and toss it into a nearby bin.

"Cassidy." He gets to his feet and stalks over. "I *want* you to come home."

I edge away. "Look, I get that you feel responsible for what happened to me. I'm trying to make this easier. I stay here, you don't have any responsibility to me."

He clamps his hands around my biceps. "Where the hell did you get that idea?"

"Does it matter? I may not know you very well, but I know you feel guilty about what happened. I brought it on myself. It's not your job to protect me."

"No, it's not," he says slowly. "You managed to take out Josef on your own. You get scarily cold when you're in danger. You can handle yourself. But I don't feel responsible for what happened to you, not the way you're obviously thinking. I care about you. I want to protect the people I care about."

"That's…great. Fucking fantastic. If you 'care about me,' then why didn't you call, you asshole?"

He bares his teeth in a vicious smile. "Phone works both ways, love."

I throw the bottle cap at him, hitting him on the forehead. "Nuh-uh. You are *not* pushing this off on me. I told you where I was so you wouldn't worry. You knew how to reach me. I wasn't about to endanger you further by contacting you first. So this is on your shoulders, bud. Not mine." I cross my arms over my chest and give him a bland stare.

He growls. He actually *growls*.

"Still not an answer, Dominic." I turn away and grab another bottle of water. "So you're here. You care about me, and you've made the decision I'll be returning to your house where you can watch out for me. Gee, that sounds like such an exciting time. When do we leave?"

Plucking the bottle from my hands, he scoops me up and carts me to the couch. He imprisons me in his arms when I try to squirm away. "Stop being a brat," he mutters. "I feel guilty as fuck for this, Cass. You can take care of yourself, no doubt about that, but you never would have gotten into this if it hadn't been for my family."

Disappointment pierces the anger, doubt on its heels. "Is this the part where you tell me it's been great, but we shouldn't sleep together anymore? For my own safety?"

He jerks his head up. "Where the hell did you get that idea?" His eyes narrow. "I thought we'd been over this already. The night before you got knifed, I thought we agreed we were giving this a shot. Or did they surgically remove that memory when they patched you up?"

And here's where my immaturity rears its ugly head. "I remember," I whisper. "But in the hospital, you wouldn't leave, and it made no sense. We barely knew each other. We *still* barely know each other."

He cups my face, thumbs sweeping over my cheeks. "Think about it. If you died, we wouldn't have a chance to get to know each other better. That fuckin' pisses me off."

I grin. "Can't have that."

His thumb finds my lower lip and rubs it. "You got to me. I'm not ready to let you go. We can slow this down. Sleep in separate rooms. When it's all over, I'll help you find a place to live. Whatever you want, I'll give it to you. The timing's shitty, but I want this."

It's a good thing I'm already sitting down because his words make me all melty. It's scary how badly I want this to work. How badly I want this man, and no doubt, Nick is definitely a *man*. One who's seen some of the darkest parts of me and isn't turned off by them.

I cannot screw this up. I need to figure out how deep I want to go. Until then, keep it light. Fun. Or as fun as it gets when you're recovering from a traumatic injury. "Nick. Nick Nick Nick. Could you just shut up for a minute and kiss me already? I mean, I haven't seen you in a month and—"

He uses his mouth to stop the flood of words, and I couldn't have asked for a better gag.

Meet the Author

When she's not plotting ways to sneak her latest shoe purchase past her partner, Amanda K. Byrne writes sexy, snarky romance and urban fantasy. She likes her heroines smart and unafraid to make mistakes, and her heroes strong enough to take them on. Amanda lives in the beautiful Pacific Northwest, and no, it really doesn't rain that much. Visit her website at Amandakbyrne.com, find her on:

Facebook at www.facebook.com/authoramandakbyrne

Goodreads at www.goodreads.com/Byrneafterreading

Twitter @amandakbyrne

Coming October 2016—the second book in the Game of Shadows series!

Game of Vengeance

An eye for an eye, blood for blood.

UCLA student Cass Turner was hoping to move on from the family business—but when the business is professional assassination, that's easier said than done. And sleeping with the man she was supposed to kill only complicates things. Her relationship with Nick Kosta, a lieutenant in LA's largest crime family, was supposed to be no-strings-attached fun. But if the two of them want to stay alive, they'll have to keep each other close.

Nick's traitorous cousin, Isaiah, is out for blood, so Cass can't afford any distractions as they try to hunt him down. Yet she can't help puzzling over Nick's motives—does he really share her deepening feelings or does he just feel responsible for her? And if their relationship is for real, will they even have a future? Because with their enemies several steps ahead of them, one false move could bring disaster for everyone Cass holds dear... and in this game of cat and mouse, no one will leave unscathed.

Chapter 1

"No."

I huff out a breath. "What else am I supposed to do? Sit at home, twiddling my thumbs?"

"Nah. You'd be sitting on the couch in my office twiddling your thumbs." Nick's trailing his fingers over the scar on my stomach as if he's trying to reassure himself it won't split apart at the slightest provocation.

"You can't force me to come into work with you every morning. Unless you're planning on handcuffing me and tossing me in the trunk of your car." I try to scoot away from his touch and almost fall off the bed, biting back a sigh when he tightens his hold.

I liked my little beach hut when it was just me, and I could walk around in my underwear because it was too damn hot to wear any clothing. For the last three days, I've liked it even better, but two full-grown adults crammed into a double bed isn't exactly my idea of a good time. There's not a lot of action happening in said bed, though I have to admit I've slept a lot better tucked against his side. My libido's taking a vacation while I recover, and Nick hasn't so much as hinted at sex.

"You remember the handcuffs?" he asks, a lazy smile on his face. It's distracting, that smile, causing my brain to misfire even as I want to smack him for it.

I shoot him a death stare. "Do I remember the handcuffs?" He cuffed me to the door of his car with a set of fuchsia fuzzy handcuffs a few days after we'd met. It's pretty hard to forget those things. "You're not seriously saying you'd use them?" I pull his hand off my waist. "I can't keep the rest of my life on hold, Nick. I want to go back to class."

He slips his hand free and glides it over the curve of my hip. "It's only for a little while longer."

A little while longer could easily turn into *not just yet*, and the next thing I know, I'm a college dropout, forced to either work a dead-end job or continue killing people for money. I struggle to keep my annoyance in check. He's worried. I can work with worried. I roll off the bed and pad across the room to the miniscule kitchen for a bottle of water. "You can't know that. I'm not made of glass, and I can't live in a bubble."

He gets to his feet and stalks toward me, brows lowered as he glares. He nicks the bottle from my hand and drains it. "You died. Twice. I don't want to find out if the, and, during the day, full of students. The student body is *huge*.

"It'dtake some mad skills and serious *cojones* to pull something off there. I'm more likely to get jumped in the parking garage again than on campus."

He threads his fingers through my hair, rubbing the muscles of my neck until I want to purr with contentment. "You're not helping, love."

My heart sputters at the endearment. I went a month without hearing him say it. A month where I hadn't heard *anything* from him, and as the days bled into weeks, the doubts started creeping in. He's ten years and a world of experience older. I wouldn't blame him for not wanting to be tied to someone as young as me.

Yet every day since he's been here, he's proving it's not just heat and blind lust between us. The things we went through together and the forced proximity have thrown us directly onto the *I really like you and not just in the I want to fuck you senseless* track, and I'd be foolish to think the connection we forged isn't strong enough to withstand a few weeks apart.

It's not love. But it's getting closer every day, and it's scaring the poo out of me.

"C'mon. You've seen the campus. You'll have a copy of my schedule. You can have someone pick me up instead of letting me drive myself." I tip my head back. I hate the glimmer of fear in his dark eyes, hate that it makes me question his motivations, because it's the one doubt I can't lay to rest. A part of me is convinced this protective bent he's got is simply because someone in his family tried to kill me.

Not because he cares about me.

Whenever I stumble down that rabbit hole, though, I claw my way back out, determined to give him the benefit of the doubt. *He came for me*. He could have ushered me onto a plane as soon as he arrived or moved us to a hotel where we could have separate rooms. Instead, he stayed. I lost a lot of strength and stamina confined to bed for two weeks in the hospital, then off and on over the past month, recovering from plastic surgery. So all we've really done is wander at a snail's pace through Phuket, trying to get the other to eat the fried grasshoppers from the various food carts. And that's only when we're not staying out of the heat of the day in my hut.

Honestly, those are my favorite times. The times when we're just sitting here, talking. The times that mimic the evenings in his condo in Manhattan Beach, where he distracted me from my guilt enough to eat.

It might have come out eventually that Nick's favorite food is an In and Out burger, but because we're here, with little else to do, I learned it earlier. Like I learned his favorite color is green, his favorite movie is *Stand and Deliver* tied with *Billy Madison*, and that he and Constantine grew up like brothers, much like Marc and Isaiah.

He presses his thumb into my lower lip, then lets it slip down to my chin. "How many classes?"

I can't stop the giddy joy rising in my chest and smile. A normal life. I get to go back to a normal life. Or as normal as I get. "Four. If they have the last courses I need to graduate during the summer term, I'll be done by September." Then I have to worry about getting a job, what to do with the rest of my life, and my lack of work history. Somehow I don't think putting "assassin" on my resume will score me any interviews.

His hand drifts farther, brushing over my neck and along the faint scar left by Josef, a member of the family who tried to kill me on Isaiah's orders. The doubts stir from their slumber at Nick's constant touch tonight. They should make me happy. I *am* happy. I step back and tell those doubts to shut up.

He studies me a minute more, the light on the little porch buzzing when another fly gets trapped. It's so damn loud, that buzzing, filling the silence. "Fine," he says. "I get a copy of your schedule?"

The worry line between his brows makes my heart sputter just as badly as when he calls me "love," only in an entirely different way. "Yes. A copy of the schedule, and anything else you think I need to stay safe. *Except* a babysitter. I've still got Josef's knife." Somewhere. It's probably buried in a bag at Nick's.

"I'm getting you your own. Something that fits your hand better." He picks up my hand, holding it palm out, using his thumb to trace the creases.

My excitement dims a smidge. Carrying my own weapon is a permanent sort of thing, one that speaks of Nick's faith that I can handle myself and the scrapes I get into. It's also part of the life I'm trying to leave behind, if only Isaiah would pop up from whatever rock he's hiding under.

And I wonder, not for the first time, if staying with Nick means I can't shed that identity. If it'll dodge my steps like an unfriendly ghost.

Nick's phone rattles angrily across the table. He kisses my palm, drops my hand, and reaches around me to pick it up. "Kosta."

Knowing the call could take anywhere from a couple of minutes to an hour or more, I grab another bottle of water and wander out onto the porch.

The sticky heat of the night drops over me like a wet blanket, smothering in its weight. The humidity around here is insane, giving the air a tangible quality, like I can squeeze it between my fingers and watch it ooze out like syrup. The hut is at the end of a row of other huts just like it, some with their porch lights on, some dark. This close to the beach, there isn't much of a bug problem, and I lean on the railing, staring out over the black water.

Funny how the ocean is the same no matter which one you're looking at. People earn their living on it. Swim in it, play in it. The color is different. So's the temperature, and the creatures swimming through it.

It's the same because it's always, always changing, breaking apart and reforming, holding on to most of the old stuff that keeps it recognizable as a salty body of water, letting in enough of the new that scientists either scream with delight over previously undiscovered species or moan about the fate of the planet as its levels rise.

It's also not mine.

My ocean is the one near the Santa Monica pier. The place I'd go after a job, a kind of meditation that allowed me to slip back and forth between Cass the College Student. and Cass the Assassin. I miss my ocean. I miss Los Angeles, I miss my friends, and I miss my mother.

I miss Turner something fierce.

The door opens behind me, and Nick steps onto the porch. He props his elbows on the railing. Our bare shoulders touch, the only body parts that do, and out here in the messy heat it's almost too much. "Good news? Bad news? Indifferent news?"

"Har." He shifts to wrap his arm around my waist, pulling me to his chest, ignoring my half-hearted protests that it's too hot to cuddle. "That was Con. LAPD raided one of the escort agencies, and the manager's being brought up on charges. Con's concerned he'll talk."

"You let a man run that service?" In the movies, it's always women who run those businesses.

"Hedid a good job of it until he got greedy and started selling drugs out of the office. Been charged with possession with intent to distribute.

Fucker had a couple kilos worth of cocaine waiting to be doled out. Tough as the drug laws are, he'll be going away for a long time."

Well, shit. "What are you going to do?"

His chest rumbles at my back as he growls in frustration. "Let him use our attorneys. Pretty much the only way we might have a chance of him keeping his mouth shut."

Which means if he doesn't, his fate will likely be very different. I turn around and place my hands on his chest, needing some space. I can't stumble around in the dark any more. I've already done two jobs for his organization. With Isaiah in hiding, the chances of me taking another life are pretty high. I need to know what Nick does with the people who betray him. "What happens if he doesn't? What if they offer him a deal? If he was stupid enough or desperate enough to run drugs while engaging in other barely legal activities, his loyalty might snap."

He dips his head, his gaze locked on mine. "I think you can guess what happens." His voice is quiet, the words final and brutal, the last swing of the gavel. "The organization demands loyalty. You reach a certain point where to be trusted with the scope of what we do, who we are, means if you break the oath, you pay the price. Whatever the price might be. It's always high, and it's never what you expect. Right now, he's probably thinking if he talks, we'll come for him. We might. It might be his brother. It might be his wife."

My stomach clenches in a violent, shuddering knot, my mouth dry as I stare at him. No. No *way*. Innocent people. He uses them like...like... tools. "His *wife*? You go after women? Do you murder children, too?" *Say no. Please say no.*

In the low light, the shadows on his face take his blank expression and twists it into something sinister. "We do what needs to be done, Cassidy. Sometimes that means using whatever leverage we've got. Sometimes that's women and children, though those are last resort measures."

I back away, out of his arms, skin prickling as the truth hits home. I knew Nick was as deadly as me. Without seeing it in action, I guess I didn't really believed it.

I sure as fuck do now.

www.ingramcontent.com/pod-product-compliance
Lightning Source LLC
Chambersburg PA
CBHW050738250626
47155CB00005B/1820